SEA OF TRUTH

First published in the United States of America in 2008
by Rizzoli Ex Libris, an imprint of
Rizzoli International Publications, Inc.
300 Park Avenue South
New York, NY 10010
www.rizzoliusa.com

© 2008 Rizzoli Ex Libris
Cover photo © Mike and Doug Starn/Artists Rights Society, New York
Courtesy the artists

2008 2009 2010 2011 / 10 9 8 7 6 5 4 3 2 1

Translated by Aaron Maines
Designed by Margaret Trejo
Cover design by Gabriele Wilson

Printed in the United States

ISBN-13: 978-0-8478-3157-9

Library of Congress Catalog Control Number: 2008927572

SEA OF TRUTH

ANDREA DE CARLO

THE MORNING OF NOVEMBER 24

On the morning of November 24 there were at least fifteen inches of snow on the ground, and my brother called to tell me our father was dead.

When I had woken up and opened the window shutters, I had stopped to look at the unchanging white covering the trees and fields and woods and distant houses all the way to the horizon where rippling hills blended into the clear gray sky. I had listened to the silence, inhaling the icy air down to the bottom of my lungs, exhaling vapor. A few snowflakes had landed on my forehead and chest and hands, the cold passing over my bare skin. It snows too often here for you to feel the magical sensation snow brought you as a child, and yet I am always fascinated by the way sounds are muffled and distances stretch away, the dry wood and brambles and the stones and holes and crevices disappearing underneath the white surface, creating the illusion of a perfectly homogenous landscape. I knew that my surprise at the transformation wouldn't last for long, and that soon all kinds of practical complications would arise, but for the first few minutes I had let myself be enchanted while I got dressed in layer after layer of cotton and wool.

I had boiled water for tea in the kitchen and made some oatmeal. I had done a few push-ups and squat thrusts to warm up. As I was eating, I had leafed through an essay on oceanic currents that I needed for a book I was writing about surviving in the open water after a shipwreck. Then I had gone to check the phone; it was perfectly silent. I had been expecting this because the lines run through the woods for a couple of miles, and a thunderstorm or a strong wind or snow can be enough to cut the line. Each time it happens it takes days for someone to come fix it, and then only when I'm patient enough to pester the service people more than once a day. But being isolated didn't bother me: it made me feel safe from the world's urgent issues, distancing them to the point where they were almost incomprehensible.

I had taken my cell phone out of the pocket of the heavy jacket near the entrance: I had forgotten to charge it and the battery symbol was blinking on its minuscule screen. There was also a symbol for "missed calls," but before I could check to see who I'd missed, the phone rang: a little pseudo-Caribbean tune I'd selected from various options through a process of elimination. I had slipped on my tall rubber boots and gone out into the snow in front of the house, toward the tree where the signal is strongest. I had sunk in deep with every step. It was like walking on another planet.

My brother Fabio was more agitated than usual: he said, "Lorenzo, I've been trying to call you since last night on both the cell and your home phone."

"The home phone is down because of the snow, and the cell doesn't work inside," I answered, using the vaguely singsong tone of somebody who is repeating information already widely available.

"Dad is dead," he said.

"What?" I said, with a mental image of our father in the living room of his house, turning toward me to say something. The snow was up to my knees. The laurels were bent over under a mass of snow that threatened to break them.

"Yes," said my brother.

"When?" Just one of the many partially formed questions shooting through my head.

"Around ten." He was in a hurry, as always: issues almost as important as this one were waiting for him beyond our phone conversation.

"How did it happen?" Even though I'd never thought our father could literally live forever, he'd been a part of my mental landscape since I was born, part of every period and phase: reorganizing my world without him wasn't easy.

"Heart attack," said my brother.

"Where?"

"At home, in his study. Luz called the ambulance right away, but by the time they arrived there was nothing left they could do. They didn't even take him to the hospital."

"Ah," I said. I picked up a long stick from under the portico and started whacking the bent laurel branches. The snowy mass dropped off in floury blocks, the branches swung back and forth. I started striking them harder: a few branches freed themselves and leapt back up toward the sky, tossing snow in my face and hair, into the neck of my sweater.

"What are you doing?" asked my brother. "What's all that noise?"

"Nothing. It's the snow."

"When do you think you can get here?" he asked, impatience nipping at his flanks and heels.

"Right away. Now." Independent of his tone, I felt guilty I wasn't already there, and yet I couldn't resist giving the laurel branches a couple more liberatory whacks. Miniature avalanches slid over the dark green leaves amid powdery clouds, then plunged into the soft white layer covering the ground.

"Hurry up," said my brother. "I can't do everything myself."

"I'm going, I'm going. Just the time it takes to travel a hundred-and-sixty-five miles, and I'm there."

I wanted to add something about the probable road conditions, but my cell phone ran out of juice and shut off. I went back inside to brush my teeth and throw a few things into a backpack. Other images of my father were running through my mind. They weren't recent, because some two months had passed since the last time we'd seen each other: in each image he looked at me with an unresolved expression, somewhere between curiosity and perplexity. I ran back outside, locked the front door and went sliding down the hill toward level ground.

I could just barely make out the pickup underneath the blanket of snow covering it. I started freeing it with furious sweeps of a shovel. I felt embroiled in the material, and at the same time I couldn't help thinking that it was pointless to hurry. This is one of the collateral effects of living outside the world, with no clocks and precarious phone connections, but it was greatly increased by what had happened. I had a clear feeling of the uselessness of intentions and programs, schedules, calendars, appointments, waiting.

As soon as it seemed like I'd cleared off enough, I got behind the wheel and turned the truck on. The wipers cleared blocks of snow off the windshield. The seat was cold. The glass fogged up immediately; my knees shook and my teeth chattered while the primitive diesel motor warmed up.

I drove without being able to see very far down the road, and around the first curve the way was blocked by a mass of snow-covered trees that had fallen across the road. I got out and tried to move them, but it was useless. I had to turn around and walk slowly back up the hill and get the chainsaw out of the tool shed. Naturally its small tank was empty, so I had to sit down and blend oil and gas, then pour the mix in through a funnel, my hands rigid with cold and anxiety. I yanked on the cord to start the chainsaw, but for some reason its little single-cylinder motor wouldn't start. I yanked and yanked, tried shutting and reopening the air intake: nothing. I threw the chainsaw into the snow and it disappeared. I got a handsaw from the tool shed and went back down toward the trees, stumbling and sliding more wildly than the first time.

I sawed through branch after branch, and then the trunk in sections, tossing every piece aside one at a time. The snow got into my boots and eyes and ears, soaking my fingers through the frayed, threadbare leather gloves. I drove myself so hard that within just a few minutes my cotton shirt and the first sweater were soaked with sweat, but I didn't have the time or desire to take a break, not even to take my jacket off. I sawed and my arm muscles hurt, my eyes grew teary with fatigue. Every so often I took a few steps back to survey my progress, and it didn't seem like I was any closer to opening a way through. But I kept going, completely absorbed in the systematic act of demolition, until at a certain point I realized that the road was cleared. I jumped into the pickup, soaked with melted snow and sweat as I was. I turned on the engine and drove down the little road, trusting my memory more than my vision.

It wasn't easy to drive the three hundred yards to the main road. I was pushing a rising wall of snow ahead of my hood, and I could only guess at the edges of the road. I had to keep jerking on the wheel to avoid winding up upside down among the trees.

When I finally bounced out onto the snowplowed road, I felt a quick sense of relief, immediately overwhelmed by growing anxiety.

Crossing the Apennines was tougher than I thought. The road was covered with snow that crunched and built up under the wheels and formed compact walls on either side. There were old people wielding shovels in front of the blocked access roads to their houses, little stone villages where the clocks were turned back at least a hundred years, thick chimney smoke, big trucks stopped on the side of the road or in service station parking lots, all colors annulled. It might even have been evocative, if I hadn't been in such a hurry to get to Rome. Occasionally a new image of my father crossed my mind: seen from various angles and stopped halfway through a gesture, between one expression and another.

At a certain point amid winding mountain passes between Gubbio and Perugia the wipers iced up and I had to drive with my head out the window in order to see the road. I kept the stick shift in third, diesel engine growling, heat vents blowing. During the more difficult sections I instinctively moved my shoulders and hips as if to help the pickup stay the course and move forward.

After Perugia the snowfall thinned, retreating progressively from the landscape until, at the border with Lazio, there was no trace of it left. There was a pale blue sky instead, the fields and buildings on either side of the highway drenched with yellowish western sunlight. The reasons for my delay had melted around me, leaving me clinging to the steering wheel transmitting the vibration of the wheels, my gaze constantly dropping down to the speedometer, which hovered around my top speed of seventy-five miles an hour.

When I Got to Rome

When I got to Rome I felt the same old sense of bewilderment I always felt when confronted with the city enveloped in its privileged good weather. Everybody was walking around in light coats and jackets, without so much as a care for the brutal winter raging just two hours away. I looked at the people in their cars and along the sidewalks with a mix of incredulity and annoyance; I wanted to roll down my window and shout something, honk the horn to communicate alarm.

My parents' former house was located in one of the first areas of Rome that you hit coming in from the north, a residential outpost of balconies and high-rises that must have suggested the possibility for an unexpectedly modern development in the city during the 1970s. Almost on the banks of the Tiber River, which can run swift there at times, on the outskirts of a neighborhood inhabited by horribly spoiled mama's boys and forty-something couples with cold looks, rich notary publics and lawyers and admirals' widows, and the male and female Filipinos who serve them and accompany their children or walk their dogs. My parents had moved there when I was twelve and my brother was ten, motivated by reasons that were practical in the abstract (more green, more air, more space compared to the downtown street where we'd lived before), without considering in the least the repercussions that this place might have on their children. And they continued to live there as if neither the building nor the neighborhood nor, ultimately, the city had much to do with them, renting because my mom had always opposed any kind of permanent acquisition.

I thought about this as I went up in the elevator, looking at the intercom's little copper grille. When I was a young boy I discovered that it could produce sounds if you pinched it with your fingernails. An elevator in which I had probably spent entire days, if somebody added up all my rides up and down, in the mirror of which I had checked my reflection an infinite number of times, back when my life was still unformed. The way I could stand, my look from straight on and in profile, haircuts, pants and shoe styles, expressions experimented with well before I could put them to actual use. I had been inside there sleepy and hungry, bored, in love; with bicycles, schoolbooks, schoolmates, my first girlfriends, with luggage when I left, with a woman to present to my parents, with flowers for my mother, with subjects that would become controversial conversations at the lunch table. I had even gotten stuck in there a couple of times when the elevator broke, suspended between the sixth and seventh floors, almost certain I'd never make it out alive.

On the eighth floor the door to the entrance was open; there was the murmur of low voices, careful movement. I said "Hello?"

and walked into the entryway with my wet, dirty boots. My father's hats and canes were hanging there. In the big living room illuminated by many windows I found my brother and his wife Nicoletta, Luz (the Ecuadorian caretaker), Nadine Lemarc, my father's assistant and ex-lover, his colleague and longtime friend Dante Marcadori, the doorman Gianni, and two or three other people I didn't know. They were talking among themselves, but they stopped as soon as they saw me, moving aside and paying a great deal of attention to where they put their feet. Within this strange emptiness, my brother came over to hug me, but his expression and gestures seemed at least partly for show; they didn't correspond in the least to the tone he'd had on the telephone a few hours ago. Immediately after that Nicoletta embraced me, whispering a few words between my ear and neck, then retreating in a cloud of vanilla perfume. The others all took turns hugging me.

Once the embraces were over we took turns facing one another, our hands at our sides and our gazes held just below our eyelids. There were more small lateral steps on the marble pavement.

Fabio half-whispered to me, "Do you want to see him?" He was already making his way toward the corridor.

Our father, or better yet his composed and carefully dressed body, lay on the bed in the room that had been his ever since our mother's death. My brother pointed to the door; I told him to stay too, but he slipped away quickly all the same. I had no idea what to do, so I knelt down and touched our father's forehead: it was cold and smooth. He looked relatively serene, apart from the fact that I couldn't remember ever having seen him asleep or with his eyes closed. He had always relied upon the intensity of his gaze, as well as on the timbre of his voice: he had this way of moving across a room, keeping his fiery eyes on you in order to accent the pressure of his words. He had been demanding, impatient, totally concentrated on whatever he was doing, quick to distinguish his interlocutor's potential interest or boredom. He was not an easy father, neither while I was growing up nor after, until I managed to find my own path entirely independent of him. We had only had a few authentic conversations, and I had even fewer memories of things we'd done together, aside from a few strenuous mountain walks and two or three fishing expeditions. As a child, I had often perceived the jealousy he felt of me and my brother for the fact that we'd drawn away part of our mother's attention; and as an adolescent I had been aware of the irritation he felt for my physical and mental uncertainties. But besides that his life had taken place almost entirely outside the family, between the hospital and university and his studio and assistants and students. He had always had a reservoir of young disciples who proved much more gratifying than his two sons: much more willing to love him, with far fewer requests for attention. He probably couldn't tolerate the idea that we could take him for granted since he was our father, and this produced in him a slight disinterest in us. Thinking about it now, it doesn't seem like this was all bad, given our respective characters.

I sat down in a chair, staying there for a while to look at him. It wasn't a particularly painful situation; it seemed like I was facing nothing more than a bodily shell, abandoned after eighty-three years of intense use. I had the same sensation when I'd faced my mother two years earlier, and a dog I'd been very fond of a year before that. I remember that while I was looking closely at the dead dog I had felt his spirit clearly, with all the vital and emotional manifestations it could produce. He had simply gone elsewhere, leaving his old form there on the grass. And yet my ability to detach was anything but complete, because I was intermittently struck by the idea of just how definitive the absence of movement was in a body that had been so very mobile; that had in fact based a great deal of its ability to communicate on that mobility. I thought about the terrestrial elements that had passed through my father's earthly body over the course of his life: the air he'd breathed; the foods he'd eaten, distinguishing their different tastes each time; the hot and cold liquids that he'd drunk up until the day before. I thought about the clothes he'd worn, the different consistencies of their fabrics, their animal or vegetable origins, the importance he'd given their color and cut. I thought about his clothing hanging in his closet or folded in his dresser, of their sudden, total uselessness.

As I was thinking about these things, my brother Fabio came back into the room. He stood looking silently at our father for a couple of minutes then said in a rush, "I've got a meeting with the cultural commission in a half hour. This is a tough time. I can't skip it."

"Sure," I said. Rather than irritate me, his way of portraying himself as the key exponent of the Democratic Myrtle Party, one of the center-left Italian parties that had taken on the name of a plant in recent years, made me look upon him almost tenderly. His had been a progressive transformation, from a research doctor "dabbling in politics," to full-time politician, to increasingly important politician. By now he'd reached the second line, just behind the front line where the party secretary and president stood; all it would take was for one of them to be nominated minister at the next elections and he would come fully into the spotlight. As a result, in just a few years he'd acquired a new way of moving and speaking, looking, dressing, calling, reading, thinking. He lived in a state of permanent alert, never able to stand still in one place for more than a few seconds for fear that something fundamentally important was taking place somewhere else. He could concentrate on a given subject with all the intensity he was capable of, and then suddenly tear his eyes and attention away and direct them elsewhere: all of a sudden he wasn't listening to you anymore; he was checking his watch, taking his cell phone out of his pocket with the urgency of someone who has to receive or communicate vital news. He gave me the impression of someone who wants at all costs to return to a party he's been called away from for inconsistent reasons, and who knows that in the meantime the party has been moved to a new location and therefore has to keep himself perfectly up-to-date if he wants to make it back. The fact that the party was boring and repetitive and they played bad music probably allowed him to view his inexhaustible anxiety as a commitment to the good of the Country, devoid of any trace of self-satisfaction or other egoistic motives.

I accompanied him back into the living room, where his wife Nicoletta was caressing Nadine's shoulder as she wept behind her slim, pink glasses. Dante Marcadori was explaining to the other visitors the precise dynamic of a myocardial heart attack. They stopped as soon as they saw Fabio and me; we stood immersed in a new silence for a few minutes, with gazes and hands that didn't know where to rest.

My brother said, "You'll have to please excuse me, but I'm afraid I have to go. Please forgive me." Even this statement came in a tone of voice and using expressions designed to communicate displeasure and respect for the rules and commitment and a deep human sympathy for each individual present. It was another effect of his transformation into politician, the need to create wide-ranging good impressions, fulfill every expectation. He embraced everyone, thanking them, saying goodbye as he was heading toward the exit where one of his assistants awaited. It seemed like an exhausting way of doing things, and yet this permanent state of alert dragged him through exhaustion just like it dragged him through everything else, chasing after his continuously moving, musicless party.

I stayed in the living room with the others for about an hour. I listened to their quiet, celebrative considerations, the comments dictated by profound affection and long familiarity, the evocations of episodes that had already been talked about many times before, as well as others that were less familiar. Nadine clarified dates and places and peoples' names, consulting Nicoletta in order to define organizational details. Nicoletta answered the phone calls that Luz passed to her, oscillating between her role as good, distraught daughter-in-law and that of a journalist who maintains her operational lucidity even under the most painful circumstances. She gave me the obituary official's comments to read along with the press release she'd written together with my brother, both of which had already been released. Soft and precise as always, unstoppable. There was an evident competition between her and Nadine, but it was equally clear that they had divided their roles in a manner acceptable to each, confirmed by the glances and caresses that they exchanged from time to time.

I didn't feel like I had much to do except be there, so I walked around the living room looking at the fish prints and paintings hanging on the walls of the room, the porcelain and glass and carved wooden fish on the shelves. I thought about how happy my father had been with his collection, gathered over the course of voyages around the world, and enriched by gifts from friends and lovers and admirers; of how absurd and inexplicable it seemed now. It had never been a comfortable living room, because of my mother and her refusal of well-to-do forms, despite that it was in an entirely well-to-do building in an even more well-to-do neighborhood. There was an assortment of unaccompanied sofas and armchairs, too low or high or rigid or slippery, which my father had gotten used to while never ceasing to repeat that he would have loved to live in a more comfortable house. I thought about how the subterranean debate between my parents on the comfortableness of life had seemed as permanent to me as their personalities and the nature of their relationship. But now it had dissolved along with them, disappearing into nothingness: my family had self-destructed in the space of three years, incredibly quickly. A heartbeat ago there had been two eighty-something parents in surprising physical and mental form, and a heartbeat later a mother suddenly become extremely fragile, a heartbeat after that a mother who was dead, a heartbeat after that a father alone and overcome, but who recovered with the courage of a lion as if he could keep going for who knows how long, and a heartbeat after that a father dead; the end.

I wandered around the living room in which each piece of furniture and lamp and object was a trace left behind by their gestures, their tastes and travels and manias, where I had listened to them discuss the world and seen them moving around and reading books and newspapers and playing records from different perspectives ranging from child to adolescent and adult. I thought about how in a short time the space would be emptied by one or more moving companies, cleaned and painted white, sterilized so that another couple or family could perform its play of permanence for a time.

A few other friends arrived for a mournful visit, and Dante Marcadori and Gianni the doorman left.

Nicoletta looked at her watch and said, "I have to run home. Tommaso will be home from school. I have to go buy something for dinner."

"Go ahead," Nadine replied, acting like someone who has the situation in hand.

Nicoletta touched my shoulder saying, "What are you going to do, Lorenzo? Are you coming with me? You're going to stay at our place, aren't you?"

I took a look around, unsure what my dutiful son duties were under these circumstances. Nadine said, "Go, go ahead. There's nothing else to do here, at least not until tomorrow morning."

There was a new ritual exchange of hugs and kisses, then I followed Nicoletta into that elevator in which I had spent entire days of my life.

IT WAS GETTING DARK OUTSIDE

It was getting dark outside. The western sky was crisscrossed with purplish stripes, running over the great city, which vibrated and buzzed with millions of motors spread all over its roads. The air was certainly not as gelid as it had been back in the Apennines, but it was much more humid.

Nicoletta looked at me and said, "Do you mind if we pick up a couple of things and then go to the house?" She pointed to the other side of the river. She was nervous, standing in her low-heeled, good-girl's shoes.

I followed her across a widening of the road that wasn't exactly a piazza, and across the street crammed with violent traffic, along the footbridge over the Tiber. On our right, the streetlamps of the much larger bridge that led out of Rome were coming on one after the other like gigantic matches. On our left, the infinite number of lights in homes and windows and moving cars. I went over to look at the river running underneath us, its waters dark and threatening. In truth, all of Rome seemed threatening. It was as if living for a long time by the sea and then in isolation in the countryside had little by little deprived me of the immune defenses that had made it possible for me to grow and live and work and establish friendships and love for most of my life. It wasn't a new feeling, but at that moment it struck me more powerfully than it had before, slowing my steps as if my boots were full of lead.

"Well, that's life," said Nicoletta.

"In the sense that it ends?" I asked.

"Yes."

"Do you still like being here?" I asked.

"Where?" She was walking quickly, checking her cell phone from time to time the same way my brother did.

"In Rome." I made a vague, panoramic gesture. We were halfway across the bridge, near the lights multiplying in flashes and ribbons along the street and in the piazza just on the other side of the river.

"Why?" she said, looking at me with a rather diffident expression. She was much more Roman than my brother or I, since our family came from Città di Castello, and hers had lived in Rome for ages. Despite the fact that we had grown up in the same places and attended the same schools, and our accents were quite similar, she had a patrimony of mental and behavioral nuances that is simply impossible to acquire in a single generation. I'm talking about the automatic echoes of a place, the words behind words, the names behind names; of knowing even before hearing, of being before you even get there.

"Nothing," I said. We had already passed the spot where I had kissed a girl for hours when I was sixteen. I thought how it had seemed like I was the only mobile element in a fixed landscape that included the city and the balconied building on the other side of the bridge, and my parents' apartment and my parents and their role-playing games and my relationships with my brother. Somebody raced past on a scooter, leaving behind him a wave of noise that he dragged along toward the traffic over on the main street.

Nicoletta said, "Your father will leave an enormous void behind him. In the world of science, in culture, in Rome, in our family. There aren't a lot of men like him, not in this damn country."

I nodded yes, even though they struck me as generic words, pronounced in the tone of voice appropriate for a press statement.

I followed her across the main street and along the crowded sidewalks of the piazza, into a large bakery full of carefully dressed people who seemed to have known the employees for a long time. Nicoletta selected some walnut ravioli from among the diverse options on display, bread, little focaccias, pastries. She pointed with her finger and told the man what she wanted, in that half-confidential, half-arrogant manner almost all the customers were using. In turn, the man behind the counter followed the orders with a mix of indifference and servility, saying "Anything else, Miss Telmari?"

"No, that's it, Franco," said Nicoletta. "No, no, wait. Give me a couple of those, too!" She pointed once again, dressed in her half conservative, half casual style, apparently distracted but actually all too aware of every detail. I looked at her white, regular teeth, her hazel-colored eyes highlighted by a faint touch of eyeliner and an almost imperceptible dusting of blush, her hair cut medium length and variegated with chestnut streaks. I was irritated by her fake simplicity, and at the same time struck by just how solid and free of doubt she was. I understood how reassuring she must be for my brother.

We went to a few other shops; each time that we came out the sky was darker than before, the streetlights and shop windows and car headlights becoming more intense. We walked side by side, holding the shopping bags. Every once in a while Nicoletta put her arm around me. It felt like I was part of a simulation of a bourgeois Roman couple, exactly the thing I'd always run away from in a succession of fights and breakups and abandoning houses and jobs, escaping toward distant shores. And yet at this moment I felt an indescribable desire for stability, almost as intense as the need for discoveries and surprises and continuous change that had driven me for so many years. I thought of the girls and women with whom I could have had what my brother had with Nicoletta: the offers of organization and dividing roles that I had vaguely considered and then refused as if my survival depended on it.

Once the shopping was finished we walked back across the bridge and got into my pickup, heading for my brother's house. Nicoletta seemed shocked by the amount of earth and stones and leaves and little branches in the cab. She even said, "How do you live in this?" Her contained way of smiling wasn't caused simply by the death of my father: it was her style, one of the measures she'd taken to deal with the world. She made three or four calls on her cell phone in the time it took us to get to the house; she gave and received information in diverse shades of sincerity. Out of the corner of my right eye I registered her nervous, precise movements, the way she opened and closed her purse or adjusted her hair with one hand.

Their house was on the last floor of an early twentieth-century building in the Prati neighborhood: an apartment with long corridors that wound around a vaguely Middle Eastern-looking courtyard in which several palm trees grew. Just outside the elevator Harry and Emily, the Filipino servants, arrived to take the shopping bags off our hands. Nicoletta gave them a few orders, then asked about her son Tommaso. He was in the living room, lounging on a sofa in front of a big plasma TV broadcasting images of a soccer game.

"Say hello to your uncle, meathead," said Nicoletta, giving him an affectionate cuff.

"S'up," he said, barely intelligibly and without looking up.

"What a rude son," said Nicoletta with a hint of self-satisfaction. She went to check the answering machine. She returned a couple of minutes later with a few little bite-size pizzas we'd bought and gave them to him, asking him how classes went.

Tommaso mumbled "Yeah, alright," took a bite of the mini pizza, and adjusted his position on the couch in such a way as to make it clear that he was only interested in the game. I was continuously struck by his total lack of interest or even curiosity in me, or for anyone or anything that wasn't connected with soccer. I wondered if his mind was equipped exclusively with mechanical connections, or if he had another dimension he hid very, very carefully.

Nicoletta led me down a corridor, opening the door to the room where I'd slept on other occasions. She explained that she'd already had the bed made up, and pointed to the clean towels set on a chair.

I thanked her, and put my backpack down on the floor.

She asked, "Is that all the luggage you have?"

I nodded yes.

She shook her head, just barely, and said, "You're a true vagabond sailor," with one of her half-smiles.

I started to walk toward the window and we ran into each other due to an uncertainty in my movement. She put one hand on my side, laid her forehead on my shoulder and said, "I'm incredibly sorry about your father."

I pressed lightly on her back with one hand, a little uncomfortable with the body heat and legibility of different anatomical parts in this shared mourning between brother and sister-in-law. I tried to think as little as possible about her breast and stomach and thighs pressing against me. I registered her breathing and interior trembling, looking down at the chestnut tones in her hair, smelling her vanilla perfume.

An instant later Tommaso appeared at the door to the room, saying, "Where the hell are my new sports socks? I need them for the game at school tomorrow!" He had no reaction to seeing his mother and me embracing, which was further proof of his total absence of interest in non-soccer events.

Nicoletta immediately detached herself from me and said, "I have no idea. Ask Harry." She had a surprising ability to pass from one state into another without an intermediate phase, because looking at her now I could see no sign of commotion or any other thing that might have gotten the better of her just a moment earlier. She went out into the hallway with an entirely neutral backward glance at me, and started calling Harry.

I closed the door and went to look out the window into the Middle Eastern courtyard. I did a series of squat thrusts and push-ups, then got into the shower. As always when I came to the city, I was struck by the almost unreal sensation of the seemingly endless flow of hot water ready to come gushing out with a simple twist of the handle. I wondered if my choice to live in the countryside in relatively primitive conditions really made me freer, or if it didn't trap me in a thick net of acts necessary to stay alive from day to day. I wondered about the sense of any life choice, whether instinctive or meditated, improvised by chance or set in place with great attention, when the destiny of every single life was to end from one instant to the next, as had happened with my father. I looked through the opaque glass of the shower and wondered about the meaning of Nicoletta's sudden embrace: I asked myself if behind the smooth, unassailable surface of her social behavior there weren't more sincere aspirations, uncertainties, boredom, simple lack of sense. I wasn't in a very positive mood, which was probably understandable, but I wasn't really depressed either; I moved slowly around in the echo of a brusque change of scene.

I GOT DRESSED AGAIN AND
DRANK A GLASS OF RED WINE

I got dressed again and drank a glass of red wine in the kitchen where Harry and Emily were moving around preparing dinner; then my brother Fabio came back home.

He was coming down the hallway, talking with someone on his cell phone. I heard him say "Yes, of course. Yes, of course. The important thing is that they know that if they keep this up they're going to get hurt. But when somebody's got two point four percent, where the fuck can he hope to go?" He ended the conversation just as he reached the kitchen; he seemed stunned to see me, and said "Hey!" and put away the cell phone.

"Hi," I said, holding the wine glass in one hand. Behind me, Harry and Emily said "Good evening."

He said, "Wait," but neither to me nor to them: he was talking to one of his flunkies who had followed him down the corridor. The flunkey and I exchanged a look of reciprocal diffidence while my brother headed for some other point in the apartment. He came back a few moments later with some envelopes and said, "To him personally, okay? I'll see you tomorrow at seven." The flunkey took the envelopes, said "Okay, okay," and took off quickly down the corridor as if he too had a mobile party to get to.

Fabio took the glass of spring water with a slice of lemon that Harry offered him, and motioned for me to follow him into the living room. He took a long sip, then said, "A damn difficult day, all things considered." But he didn't seem particularly exhausted, in his well-tailored, dark blue suit: he seemed ready for other family emergencies and other commission meetings and other interviews and phone calls, other crucial information to be given and gathered.

I thought that working in politics, as much as it was a largely abstract and verbal activity, required a psychophysical training halfway between running marathons and playing professional poker. I could understand how Fabio might do well in that field, because he lacked neither perseverance nor determination. He had been that way even as a child, when in the public gardens or at the beach he stayed just a little behind me and studied the other children from a distance in order to understand who might be with him and who against before so much as making contact with them. Having an older brother gave him a margin in which to get ready and work out strategies, without being forced to throw himself straight into the thick of things the way I'd had to do.

His son Tommaso was still stretched out on the sofa in front of the gigantic screen. Fabio said, "Hey, how's it going?", his gaze directed at the screen instead of at his son.

The son mumbled half a hello, more or less the way he'd done with me.

Fabio said, "You'll really have to excuse us, but we have to watch the news." He picked up the remote and changed the channel, moving from satellite TV to the state television's main channel, which was broadcasting images of the wave of snow that had struck central Italy so hard that communications between the north and south were all but interrupted.

Tommaso said, "Gimme that back!" in a surprisingly distinguishable tone of voice, leaping up and grabbing the remote out of his father's hand.

"Are you crazy?" said Fabio, with an inflection that was too slow and strained to actually be effective.

Tommaso pressed the buttons to get back to the satellite soccer game, then flopped back down to watch it.

Fabio snapped: "Give that here. Your father has to watch something much more important!"

Father and son fought over the remote: the father had height to his advantage, the son had elasticity. I was struck by the fact that there was no real physical struggle in their fight: both had the same mental determination in their eyes, the same way of contracting their eyebrows and clenching their jaws and moving their hands and arms angrily, but emptily. My nephew kicked too, his big feet clad in untied technological sneakers; at one point he caught my brother in the head.

Fabio brought a hand to his forehead and retreated, saying "Do you realize what you just did to your father?"

Tommaso let the remote fall on the sofa, an expression of infinite boredom on his face.

Fabio picked up the remote, but now he was too upset to find the right channel; he said, "Your grandfather's dead, and you couldn't give a fuck! Nothing!"

Nicoletta arrived. She'd put on an outfit with pants and a jacket, in keeping with her grown-up good-girl style. She said,

"What's going on here?!"

"He wouldn't let me watch the news!" shouted Fabio.

"And he wouldn't let me watch the game!" shouted Tommaso.

"Oh, stop acting like children, both of you!" said Nicoletta, her hand on Fabio's arm. "We'll just watch the news in our room."

"That's ridiculous!" said Fabio. "It's the principle, that's what I can't accept! Your son has become an unbearable bully! He's turned into some boorish scoundrel from the southern curve of the stadium!"

"He's your son too, right?" said Nicoletta. "Isn't he?"

"You're the one who spoils him!" said Fabio. "You always give in to him! Even when there's just been a terrible death in the family and there's every reason to expect some different behavior!"

Nicoletta put one finger to her lips, as if to say it wasn't right to talk about such things in front of the boy.

Fabio said, "You see? You see?" But he'd already given up the fight for the gigantic screen: he gave the remote to Nicoletta, who gave it back to Tommaso, who went right back to the soccer game.

Nicoletta headed out of the living room; Fabio checked his watch and followed her, gesturing to me to follow them.

In their room we watched some more images of natural catastrophes on a big, normal television, then it was time for politics. Fabio gestured for us to be quiet. He became rigid. A sort of frenetic flurry of politician's declarations began, first from one side, then from the other, one speaker per party, each surrounded by a thicket of microphones held out by journalists overcome with anxiety, as if the speaker's words might have repercussions on the destiny of the whole world. In most cases, the audio was just a rapid, meticulous synthesis given by a studio voiceover, but two or three politicians were left their own voices. At a certain point Fabio appeared, his gaze fixed straight on the camera. In a tone of firm calmness he repeated the Democratic Myrtle Party's position with respect to the issue at hand. Behind him and to either side stood half a dozen characters who stared off into space and shook their heads in approval of his words, or perhaps just for the enchantment produced by the TV cameras.

I asked, "Who are those people?"

"Who?" said Fabio, entirely too absorbed by his own televised image to receive any other signal.

A moment later the frenetic flurry of declarations from all the Italian political representatives ended. Piazza San Pietro appeared on the screen, filled with groups of immobile faithful, and immediately after that the pope. With his strong German accent, he systematically attacked couples living together outside the bonds of holy matrimony and the demands of homosexuals and the criminal presumption of those who in any way attempted to hinder the multiplication of new lives as God desired.

Fabio looked at Nicoletta and asked, "How was I?"

"Good," she said, "good." She took a few photographs off a dresser and passed them to me: the pair of them smiling, behind the helm of a sailboat, upon a wintry sea.

"Where were you?" I asked.

"The Argentario," said Nicoletta. "They were shot by Erminio Kovanich, for *Navigare*. They're giving us five pages in the January issue."

"Don't you think I was staring too straight into the camera?" asked Fabio, still turned toward the screen.

"No," said Nicoletta. "It's better to stare into the camera than to turn your head from side to side like a robot." There was a certain mechanical reactivity in her words, as if she were drawing upon an archive of reassuring precedents to placate any doubt or insecurity in her husband without having to really think about it.

Fabio, on the other hand, had already started receiving comments on his brief appearance in the form of a flurry of text messages and calls on his cell phone. He answered while pacing up and down the room, then went out into the hallway saying, "Thanks. Yes. Oh, you know. Same to you, same to you."

Nicoletta gave me a sideways glance that wasn't easy to interpret, then came halfway around the room as if to head me toward the door. I went ahead of her and left the room first. She overtook me in the hallway, perhaps to make up for before, and said, "I'm going to go see about dinner for Tommaso. If he doesn't eat something soon he'll never go to bed."

I stopped in the living room, finishing my glass of red wine and watching my nephew watch the soccer game on the gigantic screen as if soccer demanded every single little particle of his attention, without leaving so much as a single one free. Alienation caused by my father's death and the trip and the change in weather filtered into my thoughts and muscles and nerves, lending images and sounds an almost hallucinatory quality.

MY FATHER HAD WRITTEN THAT
HE DIDN'T WANT A FUNERAL

My father had written that he didn't want a funeral, so all we had to do was organize the transfer to the cemetery and inform anyone who wanted to come pay their last respects before he was cremated. Rather than get into my brother's blue car together with Nicoletta, who was wearing a black and gray suit, I preferred to ride in the funeral car with Luz, the Ecuadorian maid. It seemed like the most intense way to experience the event. Luz was silent, drying her tears every once in a while. The driver worked his way rather brusquely through the traffic; I looked outside the dark windows, registering the reactions of other drivers and passersby. Some pretended to have no reaction, others moved their hands in religious gestures or to ward off bad luck; a woman with glasses almost fell off the sidewalk when we drove past in front of her.

A boy on a moped coming down from a side street hit the brakes suddenly, spun around on one foot and went back the way he'd come. It was a strange way of crossing the city, like a mobile note of bewilderment in the interweaving flux of man and machine.

When we reached the cemetery a small crowd of my father's friends and acquaintances and colleagues already stood there waiting, displaying expressions that ranged from deep sadness to contained, fashionable cordiality. Fabio, Nicoletta, and I received hugs and handshakes from people I remembered from when I was a boy, or whom I had met only briefly, or whom I'd seen in newspapers or magazines, or whom I didn't recognize at all. Their words spread across a range of different tones as well: brief revelations of intensely personal pain, clumsy or generic phrases, a few formulaic sayings so stereotypical they seemed ridiculous.

I looked at my brother and his wife in order to see how I was supposed to respond to these outpourings, but their ways were too well orchestrated and standardized for me to imitate without becoming embarrassed. Regardless of how they actually felt, it seemed to me that they would have behaved the same way on opening night at a theater, or a garden show, or a demonstration for peace or to fight world hunger: I saw the same professional attitude in their sorrowful smiles, the same way of sliding their eyes to meet their next guest.

There was even a state television crew, probably here more for my brother than for my father: they shot the coffin as the cart it was on crossed through the small crowd. Then several men set the coffin down on a platform near a window. Everyone gathered around, leaving perhaps a three-yard margin, their looks and bodily gestures waiting, expectant. Fabio and Nicoletta were still intent on gathering and distributing gestures and whispered words, so at a certain point I found myself alone next to the coffin, separated from the line of friends and colleagues and acquaintances.

I wondered how many of those present limited their thoughts to the wooden surface, how many of them went all the way inside to consider the coffin's contents. I thought about how my father had continuously readapted and perfected his public and private roles throughout the various phases of his life, until he'd finally taken on the apparently definitive role of great wise man of medicine, still gifted with strength and dynamism and irony, still capable of conquering others. I thought of how over the years he had accumulated personal experiences, scientific knowledge, reading, voyages, encounters, spoken and written languages, acknowledgements, conversations, sensations, and how all of this was now perfectly erased. I thought about the structural complexity of the human body, its surprising resistance, its ability to modify itself over time; the sudden interruption of all its functions, leaving behind a conglomeration of inert cells headed for rapid dissolution.

Then I became very aware of the looks converging on me, standing there alongside the coffin, and I wondered if as the eldest son I was expected to give some kind of speech. My thoughts pushed me toward pure contemplation and reflection. I couldn't think of any collection of commemorative sentences. Furthermore, I didn't feel the least bit comfortable, standing there wearing my only black jacket (which Nicoletta had dismissed as "totally unpresentable" and made Harry iron it), a sweater impregnated with wood smoke, earth-stained jeans, and dull, worn American boots with square toes. I knew that my father would have known how to face this situation without so much as thinking about it, putting his charismatic qualities into play for an audience that was already on his side, producing a speech capable of moving everyone, making them smile, sending them home satisfied.

But my father's spirit was gone, and his body was in the coffin to my left, and the expectant looks in front of me didn't waver, so at a certain point I struggled mightily, stepped forward and cleared my throat. I said, "As far as I know, my father wasn't religious, in fact I think he was a pretty convinced atheist. So from his point of view this whole affair was over two days ago. From my point of view, the essence that lived in him is now traveling toward some other form, in some other dimension. It has probably already arrived, seeing as how outside this type of life our parameters for time and space don't mean anything anymore. In any case, thanks for having come."

I certainly wasn't expecting applause, but I didn't even get nods of approval or just simple smiles, not even from my father's assistant and ex-lover Nadine, or from his best friend Dante Marcadori. The wall of stares facing me was remote, veiled with perplexity. It seemed like most of those present didn't understand who I was, why I was talking, or even what I was talking about. I turned around. My brother and Nicoletta were standing right behind me, both cringing with embarrassment. Fabio stepped in front of me, took a little piece of paper out of his pocket and started reading in his well-tested tone of voice and with an extra dose of pathos: "Dear friends, today I am—we are—here to pay our last respects to Teo Telmari, a man of science, but also and above all else, a *man*. The father, friend, master; a reliable point of reference to whom we repeatedly turned in our moments of uncertainty or confusion . . ."

I slipped away through the little crowd, headed toward the white light of the exit door. I wasn't particularly disconcerted by the conventionality of my brother's words or tone of voice. Ever since he'd entered politics I'd gotten used to considering him a sort of actor who would start performing as soon as he had an audience, using prepared phrases as the instruments of his profession. More than anything else, I felt stupid for not having realized he'd have a speech ready, for having exposed myself so clumsily. Immediately after that I thought that it didn't matter: it was enough to look at where we were and everything returned to the right proportions.

Outside I breathed in the open air, looking at the rolling grass upon which thousands of white and gray tombstones were aligned. Along the entrance road a few men wearing gray uniforms were removing the flower wreaths from another funeral car that had arrived in the meantime, dismantling them with brutal efficiency, tossing roses and leaves and ribbons into piles to be picked up by other men. On a little cement bridge, someone's relatives or acquaintances were talking among themselves. My brother's driver was smoking and talking on his cell phone. Three or four pigeons were pecking at seeds along the cracked asphalt. Leaning against a little wall some twenty yards away there was a girl with honey-red curls and a long jacket with colorful designs on it. She smiled at me.

I smiled too. Immediately after that I turned around because I wasn't entirely sure that her smile was meant for me. But there was no one behind me, and when I turned back to look at her she was walking toward me.

She said, "Hello," and half-raised one hand.

"Hello," I said, my heart beating just a little bit faster.

"You're Teo Telmari's son, aren't you?" she asked. She had a clear face with high cheekbones, blue eyes, shapely lips and a short, upturned nose.

"One of two, yes."

She was so visibly a foreigner that I wanted to ask her where she was from, but she made a gesture suggesting we move away, with a strange mix of timidity and decision.

We walked along without looking at one another, stopping alongside the little wall she'd been leaning on before. On our left there was a little lake, flanked by burial niches with flowers and little candles. I could see a few big fish swimming under the surface of the stagnant water.

The girl with honey-red hair looked me straight in the eye and said, "Did you hear any mention of Ndionge?"

"Who?" My thoughts were imprecise, unfocused.

"Ndionge," she said. "Cardinal Ndionge." Her features corresponded to her accent. I realized that she could only come from one of the northern European countries.

"No. Who's he? And who are you?"

"Mette Dalgaard," she said. "I'm from Stopwatch."

"From what?" I asked, not understanding.

"Stopwatch. Have you heard of it?"

"No." I felt very uninformed.

Her mouth folded into a little smile and she said, "I need to talk to you. It's about something very important."

"Shoot." I followed the movement of her eyes and lips from a short distance, in part diffident, part curious and part attracted.

She looked over my shoulder, seeming suddenly hindered by hesitation. She said, "But not here. Not now."

I turned around and saw the small crowd of my father's friends and colleagues and acquaintances swarming outside the big cement building. Nicoletta was waving me over. I made an equivalent gesture in response, then turned back around. But the honey-red haired girl was three or four yards away and looking into the distance. She was leaving in a hurry. I said, "Hey!", but I was already too late: a moment later she was already across a distant green, a moment after that she had disappeared behind a little group of trees.

Nicoletta came over to me just as I was about to run toward the main gate. She said, "How come you left like that?"

"I needed some air," I said, looking toward the little group of trees.

"You found some nice company," she said.

"She was a foreigner. She wanted to know something."

"Ah," said Nicoletta with a barely perceptible flash in her eyes.

I was full of frustrating impulses for rapid movement, unsatisfied curiosity, a sense of oppression at seeing the darkly dressed people who were about to catch up with us. I asked, "Is everything over?"

"Yes. Your brother made a brief, but really beautiful speech. Very moving." She took a tissue out of her little purse, and blew her nose. "Yours was beautiful too. A little surreal, perhaps."

"Thanks." My legs were electric. I pressed my hands down into the bottoms of my jacket pockets.

Immediately after that there were other hands to shake and conclusive phrases to exchange, hugs and fabric-rubbings, chafing of cheeks, cheeks, cheeks.

MY BROTHER AND I HAD
BREAKFAST TOGETHER

My brother and I had breakfast together in his very well organized kitchen while Harry threw away a surprising quantity of plastic wrappers and cans and dirty cups and plates my nephew Tommaso had left behind before he went to school. Nicoletta passed by in the hallway, her hair held back by a terrycloth band and her face white with cream. She was holding a cell phone in one hand; she said, "You go ahead and eat, I've got things to do." Emily brought the coffee and milk to the table, along with the pancakes my brother couldn't do without ever since he'd gone to the United States for a master's.

We poured the maple syrup, eating the first forkful. It was too hot. We both blew on our plates in a very similar manner. We laughed, looking at each other. Fabio said, "Damn it, Lorenzo. We're orphans."

"Yeah," I said, surprised I hadn't realized our condition had a name.

"All on our own, no? Left to our own resources and that's it."

"Yes." I wanted to add that in any case I'd always be there for him like I hoped he'd always be there for me, but I lost time formulating a sentence that wouldn't sound stereotypical, and in the meantime he'd started reading.

All the main Italian newspapers were there on the table, plus a little pile of fresh press agency dispatches. A small television on the counter was turned on, broadcasting a political commentary show. Fabio held his mug of caffe latte in his right hand and flipped through the newspapers with his left, moving his gaze rapidly over the pages, occasionally casting a glance at the television screen. It didn't seem like he intended to continue our conversation, so I flipped through a newspaper too. Inside there was a piece on our father in which they celebrated his global stature as an epidemiologist and his ceaseless efforts to study AIDS and other global communicable diseases. They listed the international groups he oversaw and the awards he'd been given; acronyms and abbreviations that seemed like purely invented sounds to me, that made no more sense now that he wasn't the one pronouncing them emphatically in our living room, in front of our mother, who was accustomed to his work obsessions, and we two boys, both distracted by diverse thoughts.

My brother passed me the pages in which there were similar pieces with similar titles, photographs of similar phases in our father's life. Fabio and his political role were cited in almost all of them, Nicoletta and her TV show on health made it into two or three. I was cited in only one, as "the eldest son who abandoned teaching history to pursue his passion for the sea."

Fabio was concentrated on the political pages, one newspaper after another. He had an impatient and very specialized way of running his eyes through the lines, searching for his and other key names: he would only stop for the amount of time necessary to assimilate the relevant information and immediately move on, taking a sip of coffee or a bite of pancake, flipping more pages, tossing the newspaper aside. It was a sort of fever that kept him in an agitated state: the constant thought of that mobile party to keep an eye on, so that he would be able to get to it at the right moment.

"Is this what you do every morning?" I asked him.

"What?" His eyes kept running through the lines of newsprint.

"The newspapers, the news agencies, and all that?"

"What do you think?" he asked. "In this line of work, my dear man, if you don't row hard enough the current drags you away in a hurry. Two minutes later you're a dot at the end of the river. Nobody sees you anymore."

I thought it was a shame he'd used the metaphor from my favorite ending of a novel in order to explain his politician's itch to stay abreast of events, but I reasoned that all things considered, it was appropriate.

"And how's it going, the rowing?" I asked.

"Pretty good," he answered. His lips were half closed because he was responding to a text message that had come on his cell phone. "Don't you read the papers?"

"Rarely." I looked at the newspapers on the breakfast table, now drained of the relevant information they'd contained.

"How are things going with you?" asked Fabio, raising his eyes toward the little television, on which an undersecretary was very carefully playing his role.

"Pretty well. I'm writing a book on shipwreck survivors."

"What kind of shipwrecks?" he asked, diffident. Another message arrived on his cell phone; he read it, barely shaking his head.

"In the ocean. There are eight different stories, from the 1800s through today." I took a kiwi out of the fruit basket and cut it in half so that I could eat it with a spoon. Nicoletta passed by in the hallway again; she came back, came into the kitchen and poured herself some coffee.

"What about your work?" asked my brother as he quickly punched the buttons on his cell to respond to the new message. "What are you doing out there on that desolate mountain?"

"They're hills," I said, more to Nicoletta since he wasn't looking at me and she was. "And writing a book is work too. At least for the moment."

"What about Ancona?" asked Nicoletta. "What about the travel agency and the sailing school?"

"It's the saddest seaside city in all of Italy," I said. "The agency still belongs to Simona and Alberto. They bought out my share. I don't think I've got much flair for commercial ventures."

My brother's cell phone started ringing John Coltrane's *In a Soulful Mood*. He answered saying "About time. It's nine o'clock," and made a few jokes I didn't understand with whomever was on the other end. He got up and put his jacket on, grabbed the press agency papers and kissed his wife's head. He said to me "We'll see each other later. You're going to stay a few days, right?"

"I don't know," I said, suddenly desiring to leave right away.

He disappeared down the hallway. I could hear the sounds of his good leather soles tapping on the wood parquet.

Nicoletta looked at me steadily, her head slightly inclined. "What do you mean you 'don't know'?" The band of terry-cloth across her forehead made her look even more girlish, like she was playing with the potentially seductive effect of her expressions.

"It depends on what there is to do here. As soon as I'm done I have to go back to my book. I'm maybe a third of the way through the first draft." I cut another kiwi in half, plunging my spoon into the semitransparent green pulp.

"What do you mean, 'what there is to do'? Sometimes you seem like you've dropped down from the moon, Lorenzo," she exclaimed. "We have to read your father's will, verify his bank accounts, deposits, and investments. We have to divvy up what he's left you and Fabio, including the furniture and paintings and other valuable objects, decide about his publications, pay Luz, close accounts, organize the move, empty the apartment because as absurd as it may seem, it was rented."

"But I don't want to," I said. I felt a growing sense of entrapment. "You and Fabio can have everything. I don't need anything."

"Oh, cut it out. Don't act like a child. You'll see a little money comes in handy, especially now that you don't have a job anymore."

"I *have* a job," I said, embarrassed by her attitude.

"Of course. A book about shipwrecks. I'm sure it will be a goldmine. Like that other one you wrote about medieval pirates."

"It was the Vikings."

"Yes, yes. The Vikings. Nice. But I don't think it ended up a number one international bestseller, did it?"

"No," I said. "But still I hope it wasn't *nice*. It was a serious piece of work."

She bowed her head, an expression of exasperation on her face. She said, "Oh, what a drag you are! 'Nice' was just the word that came to mind. It was stupendous, okay? A milestone in the exploration of the Viking spirit. Happy?"

"Stop acting like an idiot," I said. These were our roles, the girlish woman who was ultra-aware of the rules of life, and the man-child who tries to keep himself separate at all costs. That's the way it had been since the beginning, in our visits together interrupted by long empty periods and sudden alienation.

She jumped up and said, "Here I am chatting away, and I have to be on TV in zero minutes!"

"Where?" I asked, lagging behind her when it came to change of spirit.

"On 'Fine, Thanks, and You?' They invited me to come on a month ago. I can't possibly miss it."

"Have fun," I said.

She looked at me. "Why don't you come along?" she asked. "Then we can go to your father's house together and take a look at things?"

I didn't want to, but I didn't want to sit around their house or wander around the city alone either. I said yes. She immediately called the television studio to tell them not to send a car for her, that she'd get there on her own.

I put on my jacket, then waited for her for almost half an hour between the living room and terrace and entryway before she was ready to leave.

WE CROSSED THE CITY, HEADING NORTH

We crossed the city, heading north in Nicoletta's super-mini car with a canvas convertible roof. She was a nervous driver in traffic: zigzagging among the other cars, running through yellow lights, cutting curves with sharp turns of the steering wheel. Every once in a while she answered calls on her cell phone from work or friends, checking her face in the rearview mirror, looking for something in the bucket purse behind her, sticking a CD into the stereo to play a song for me, taking it out, stretching to get another one from the dashboard or from the floor between my legs. I registered all these movements with a certain tension, my right hand gripping the door handle.

"What, don't you trust me?" she asked at a certain point.

"Oh, of course," I said, my feet pressed against the floor, anticipating some violent braking.

"No you don't. Typical man when there's a woman behind the wheel! You know I've never had an accident in my life! I even took a race driving course, a serious one!"

"I can tell." I tried to relax, but the simultaneous omni-directionality of her gestures was stressing me out. In order to distract myself I looked at the mechanical and human life outside the car window: the wheels and sides in intermittent movement, the faces of other drivers, the shop windows, the different ways of walking along the sidewalks, the aggregations and exchanged looks at intersections. Each detail gave me a sensation of extreme familiarity and extreme distance, the shock of severed roots, relief for not having set roots down. I wondered what it was like for Nicoletta and Fabio to feel undeniably part of this place, possessors of a role, in control of all the codes and maps, each road and personal path having been experimented with and acquired in such a way that they could move from one point to another and from one gesture to another and one word to another without hesitation or surprise.

We made it to the TV station in half the time it would have taken me, amid the fabric of warehouses and train stations and hills of calcareous tuff and highway on-ramps and desolate fields that lay on the city's western edge. Nicoletta pointed to the metallic sculpture that looked like a horse agonizingly reined in by a steel cable, located in front of low cement buildings that seemed like a military or prison facility. She smiled. She drove along a small street and down a dip, coming to a stop in front of a traffic bar. A uniformed guard said hello to her, then insisted on taking my identification before slowly climbing back into his small bulletproof booth and finally bringing back a laminated ID with my name and the word *Guest* written underneath. Nicoletta drove a few dozen yards further, parking in a space reserved for employees. She gave herself one last look in the rearview mirror, fixing her hair: tension for the public appearance was clearly growing inside her.

A thin studio assistant was waiting for us in the atrium; she led us to an elevator, then along a corridor on the second floor. She pointed to the *On the air* sign that was turned on over a door that seemed like the entrance to a vault or a butcher's refrigerator, with a lever instead of a doorknob, and whispered, "In there."

"I know, I know," said Nicoletta. She spoke in the annoyed tone of voice of someone who had produced her medical shows in that room up until last June. A director's assistant with terrible skin appeared from another door and came over to introduce himself. Nicoletta made a gesture toward me without looking at me and said, "My brother-in-law, Lorenzo Telmari."

The director's assistant shook my hand unenergetically and asked, "Do you want to come in during this commercial break, or wait for the next one?"

"I don't know," I said, in reality thinking that I'd much rather wait outside.

"He'll wait for the next one," said Nicoletta for me.

I continued to follow her and the assistant down the corridor, into a little mirrored room where a make-up artist made Nicoletta sit down in a chair. Nicoletta said, "Not a lot, okay?"

"Just a littlelittlelittle bit," said the make-up artist. "Just a teeny-tiny, teeny-weeny touch-up." Then she picked up a brush and started dusting her face with compact powder, while Nicoletta closed her eyes and the director's assistant read her the list of questions.

Given that it seemed to me like a rather private situation, I took another walk down the corridors. I saw people pushing two carts with plates of pasta and chicken and fish that looked artificial, dishes of celery and carrots that may have been colored and plastic-coated. Another assistant came along pushing a guy wearing a hospital shirt or butcher's apron, and a large girl with extremely high heels and her bellybutton showing. He handed them off to one of his colleagues, who in turn led them away. Further down the corridor there were offices at the doors of which functionaries or journalists appeared, drinking coffee or talking among themselves or on cell phones or staring vacantly. There was a feeling of permanent drift, shot through from time to time with lightning bolts of verbal and motor frenzy, cell phone rings, sudden accusations, excited steps and short dashes that were followed by a new semi-immobility.

When I went back to the dressing room, Nicoletta and the make-up artist were no longer there. As I was looking around the thin assistant came running in and said, "Hurry, hurry, they're about to close!" She grabbed my sleeve and dragged me along the corridor and through the soundproof door and past long black panels and among winding cables into the blinding light and garish colors of the studio. She sat me down in the little seating area where a dozen-odd members of the audience were seated, then immediately ran away.

The scene portrayed a fake living room with fake windows through which we could see mountains and the sea, the Coliseum, the leaning tower of Pisa, the Venice lagoon. The two hosts were just finishing having their make-up touched up, exchanging jokes and comments with technicians and assistants. They seemed stunned by a condition of secondary limelight and permanent subjection, their faces disillusioned underneath a layer of base make-up, their hair puffed up with hairspray and blow dryers. On cue a voice shouted, "Silence in the studio!" and they settled back into their fake living room armchairs. The male host made a joke about the time, and the female host responded, "And our next guest is a journalist, a wife, and a mother: Nicoletta Fornasetti!"

Bouncy music played, signaling the arrival of a guest. Nicoletta came in through the fake door with a smile that seemed perfectly natural. She sat down in the free armchair, fixed her hair, and laughed at a gallant compliment from the male host.

I sat among the audience, watching her and listening, the heat of the lights rendered almost unbearable by my country clothing. I was struck by her apparent calm compared to the tension she'd displayed just before going on; the way she played the well-bred, well-married girl in such a way that she could highlight frivolous aspects or wise insights according to the different questions.

The director ran a shot of her as a little girl in her father's arms. He had been the director of a natural history museum. Then a shot of her as an adolescent on a scooter in front of her high school, another of her in her twenties, wearing a bathing suit and surrounded by friends, another of her wearing motorcycle gear with my brother Fabio during a trip in Africa, one of her with my nephew Tommaso on their apartment terrace, one of her and Fabio and Tommaso being given an audience with the pope at the Vatican.

Nicoletta seemed surprised by these images, as if she hadn't been the person who very carefully selected them and sent them to the show's producers. She exclaimed, "Ohmygoodness!" and "Mamma mia!" and "Noooo!" and "Ah!" she looked at the two hosts, adjusted her hair, smiled, nodded with self-parodying or nostalgic or moved or deferent expressions, depending on the image. The two cameras alternated close-ups with full body shots from different angles, zooming in on her hands or eyes or feet according to instructions from the director.

The hosts spoke of Nicoletta the journalist and Nicoletta my brother's wife and Nicoletta the mother of my nephew, and of how these three roles were integrated with miraculous equilibrium, never stealing room from each other. At a certain point, the female host said, "Be honest, what's the secret to being an all-around woman, Nicoletta? Can you share it with mere mortals like us?"

Nicoletta smiled again with an expression of extreme modesty and simplicity. She said, "Time, time, time. The only secret is managing to find time for everyone and everything."

A studio assistant gave the signal for applause. The meager audience's weak clapping was mixed in real time with fuller, more convincing recorded applause. Then the host pointed a finger at one of the two cameras, and with an expression of fake resignation said, "Commercial." Nicoletta got up out of the armchair and shook hands with both of them. Then she left quickly behind a studio assistant.

I left too, taking advantage of the fact that the studio door was still open. I waited for Nicoletta for almost twenty minutes between the corridor and the elevators, amid passing guests and assistants and functionaries. I thought about the previous morning: the little crowd of my father's friends and acquaintances awaiting some conclusive words, the flower wreaths that were dismantled as soon as they'd reached their destination, the girl with honey-red hair and her strange questions, her way of disappearing without telling me anything. I found the idea of having to stay in Rome for days in order to resolve inheritance issues distressing, and yet I didn't really want to go back to my stone home in the snow, to reconstruct stories of overloaded lifeboats and ocean currents on the table by the lit fireplace.

In the end Nicoletta showed up, the thin assistant following her. "I'm sorry," she said, "but they drive me nuts every time with the contracts you have to sign and bowing and scraping and chitchat."

"I'm sure," I said.

She turned nervously toward the assistant and said, "Thanks, we can head down on our own."

We didn't speak in the elevator. Nicoletta fiddled with her rust-colored jacket. We went out the glass door and headed toward where we'd left the car. The sidewalks and streets that ran between the different buildings were full of news hosts and hostesses, financial and sports journalists who were all chatting or smoking cigarettes. Nicoletta exchanged a few words with some of them without stopping, blowing kisses with one hand.

As soon as we were beyond them, she said, "If you think that I've got some professional advantage at work because of Fabio, you're dead wrong."

"Why should I think that?" I asked, even though of course I did.

"If anything it's exactly the opposite."

I turned back to look at the people she had just said hello to: they were watching us too.

"You have no idea," said Nicoletta. "I had to stop doing the health program because of the war of attrition they waged on me because of Fabio. They kept changing schedules at the last minute, bringing in pointless union squabbles, making demands in the hallways, all kinds of sob stories. You have no idea."

"Why did they do that?"

"Why?" she asked, her voice sharp. "Because there isn't a single chief or general director or host or film director or announcer or actor or assistant or technician or gofer in here who isn't aligned with some political party."

I thought I should keep my mouth shut. But I said, "Well, you're part of the Democratic Myrtle party, aren't you?"

"I'm not part of anyone's party," she retorted. "And you can't just say 'party' and that's it. Here we're talking about party *currents*. Even saying 'part of' is too broad. We're talking about *going to bed with*, going to *lunch and dinner*, going to see the game on *Sunday morning*."

I nodded yes, but I still thought that her position wasn't much different, for all it was ennobled by the bonds of matrimony and a higher level of knowledge about the world.

She opened her car doors with a little remote and said, "That's Italy, Lorenzo. Group warfare continues. Clan against clan, family against family. Here supporting a relative or burying a neighbor means a lot more than producing something good. Is it any surprise that our television programs suck?"

"I'm not surprised," I said.

We headed back into the city. Nicoletta got two or three calls on her cell phone and made as many. In order to pass the time I skimmed through the car's owner's manual.

Then we were driving along the Tiber, waiting at the stoplight where we had to turn toward my parents' old home, and she looked me in the eye and said, "Look, I'm not a crybaby, Lorenzo. Not at all. I have a great job, a fantastic family; I live in the most beautiful city in the world. What do I have to complain about?"

"Sure," I said, a little embarrassed by the way she was depicting herself.

She changed expressions once again, squeezing my arm and saying, "You know just how terrible the loss of your father was for me, don't you?"

I nodded yes, then turned to look at Gianni the doorman standing on the steps to the building entrance.

WE WANDERED AROUND MY FATHER'S FORMER LIVING ROOM

We wandered around my father's former living room where Luz was finishing washing the windows with silent movements. Nicoletta was still in the grip of her contradictory tensions: she answered a work call on her cell, rifled through a few condolence letters and telegrams lying on the table, adjusted several bunches of flowers that had been sent by individuals or organizations.

I looked at the paintings on the walls: in reality I didn't want any in the division that my brother and I were supposed to undertake. It seemed like they'd already played their part in my life. I looked at the books on the bookshelves, our mother's poetry collections, the nineteenth-century Russian novels and twentieth-century American novels, the edition of the *Encyclopedia Britannica* Fabio and I had as kids. I thought about all the occasions in which some member of our family had leafed through one of those fake red leather volumes in order to corroborate some point of conversation: the illusion of definitive clarity that it gave each time. I thought about the attention my mother and father had paid to the indefinable quantity of pages enclosed between the covers on those shelves; the sensations and images and ideas they'd put in circulation, the time spent in extreme slowness and ultimately compressed into one instant after another until it became entirely imperceptible.

I went into my father's studio next to the living room, looking at his desk by the window, his backless Swedish chair, his fountain pen, a pair of glasses, envelopes with exotic stamps, various colored papers, a glass full of pencils, a yellow highlighter, a sheaf of papers in a letter holder, a package of new envelopes. I thought that in reality I knew almost nothing about his personal or public lives, just something about his family life, up to the point where there was still family. I thought for perhaps the first time that I could measure my life in decades, and that each life contains a very limited number of decades.

Nicoletta knocked on the open door. She stood there with a hesitant expression, as if to mitigate the potential violation of intimacy. She said, "Am I disturbing you? Do you want me to leave you alone?"

"No, no," I said, slightly uncomfortable. "I was just looking." I made a gesture that included the desk and other furniture, the glass-cased bookshelves along the walls.

I opened one of the glass doors to get a better look at the books: they were all scientific publications, some very recent and others very old, in Italian and English and French and Spanish, ordered relatively precisely by argument. I took a brown-colored volume out, its corners faded and worn. It was entitled *The Spread of Yellow Fever in Southern Africa*, written in small golden letters. The colophon included "Rome, 1942." I wondered if my father had bought it as soon as it was published back when he was a student, or if he'd picked it up years later in some bookshop out of pure curiosity. I took out a few more books. Nicoletta did the same. I thought about my father leafing slowly through them, integrating the data they contained with what he'd already gathered through research and experience.

I asked Nicoletta, "Where do you think all the knowledge you have goes, once you cease to exist? Does it just disappear into nothingness?"

She was looking at an illustrated book that dealt with hygienic conditions in London during the Elizabethan era. She raised her eyes and slowly shook her head.

I said, "If you abandon your old body in order to take on a different form in another dimension, do all the things you've intuited and understood and learned suddenly become completely irrelevant? Are feelings and sensations the only part of your past life that keep any meaning?"

She seemed upset or moved. "I would really like to know," she said. Then she put the book back and came closer to me.

I kept leafing through the book I was holding, even though I was aware of her breathing close to my right ear. "For example, what about when a great pianist or violinist dies? Or a master chair maker? Where does all that technical knowledge go, all those things he transmitted through his fingers with such unstoppable certainty?"

"No idea," said Nicoletta, her breath warm on my neck.

"Where do the miraculous fruits of natural talent go? Or those of a meticulous, tiresome effort of acquiring and accumulation?"

"Who knows," she said.

I turned to look her in the face, and she looked me in the eye, then at my lips and suddenly she came against me and kissed me on the mouth, pushing me backward with the strangest sudden determination. It took me a couple of seconds to figure out what was going on, and in the meantime her pressure was becoming more insistent and her tongue more invasive. Her hands were everywhere. I dropped the book and said, "Wait."

She said, "Oooh Lorenzo," in a husky tone of voice, our foreheads colliding.

I said, "Nicoletta," backing up without managing to gain any distance.

She kept grasping and pushing and kissing me. She pressed a hand around my groin, breathing heavily.

I tried to detach myself, but I was having trouble thinking clearly. It was a strange sort of fight, with her coming toward me and me continually backing up. There were no explanations, or at least none that could be communicated now, above the lines of our roles and the years we'd know each other. But I wasn't attracted, and not even remotely turned on. It wasn't because of the place or the moment, but simply because of the total absence of some background of gestures or words or thoughts that might have ever suggested this possibility between the two of us. The only sexual interest I could have ever felt for her had been purely hypothetical and automatic, the kind a man feels for a fraction of a second with any woman he meets. I had always looked at her as my brother's wife; neither particularly attractive nor spontaneous, nor socially or intellectually or emotionally free.

She took one of my hands and pushed it underneath her shirt, pressing against me even more insistently. I backed up again, bumping into the desk. She climbed on top of me. I wound up with my back and head among my father's papers and other objects, almost overcome by Nicoletta's weight and body heat and the feel of her left breast and her shirt and her movements and breathing and the taste of mint chewing gum in her mouth. Then I put both hands on her chest and pushed her backward, applying delicate but increasing force.

She resisted, but little by little she released her grip and her breathing slowed and her mouth stopped pressing and pulled back. She let herself be pushed away. She stared at me from a yard and a half away, the expression on her face almost that of a wounded child. She straightened up and adjusted her jacket and sweater and shirt. She seemed just about to tell me something definitive before turning around and walking away. Instead, she turned and laid her forehead against a shelf that hosted several of the fish from my father's collection. Then she began sobbing.

I got up, overcome with tenderness and instant feelings of guilt. I touched her arm and said, "Nicoletta?"

"Leave me alone!" she said, jerking away. She went out into the hallway, opened a few doors, then went into what used to be my room when I was a boy.

I followed her in there, among the odd furniture that had collected there during my mother's last attempt at converting the space.

"Get out of here!" said Nicoletta between sobs, trembling and red in the face. "Since you find me so disgusting!"

"That's not true," I said in a vain attempt at a steady voice. "It's not true."

Nicoletta knocked into an old coffee table, going to stand by the window. She said, "I've never been so humiliated in my life! Not even by your brother!"

I tried to disentangle the thoughts and feelings I'd had in the other room from those I was having in this one. I said, "I didn't want to humiliate you at all. Not at all."

"Well, you did! You did a damn good job of it!"

"But I didn't want to."

"I was stupid, letting myself get enchanted by your fucking act as sensitive man who lives outside the world and can understand and appreciate things in a woman that other men don't even see!"

I tried to take her arm again. "Take a deep breath," I said.

She didn't take any deep breaths. She shouted, "You're birds of a feather, you and Fabio! Two egocentric bastards who think they've got everyone at their feet!"

"That's not true at all," I said, because not only did I see nothing of myself in her description; I didn't see my brother that way, either.

"That's the way it is!" she said in an even more bitter tone. "You want me to write you a list of all the women your brother has had some kind of affair with? Huh?"

"What women?" I said, slowed by incredulity.

"The ones he fucks!" she said through tears. "There's Giulia, his dear assistant. Very intelligent, an extraordinary girl. Rossana, the wife of his great friend Zighelli. That damn slut Marcella Carbonai who, thanks to him, is going to star in a new TV movie about Santa Theresa. Paola Sottomauro who came on vacation with us in Spain last summer, along with her wonderful little husband who'd throw himself into a fire for Fabio. Natalia Girga, who now has an exclusive on late-night political commentary, with her damn ant face and unacceptable accent! And those are just the ones I know about!"

"Are we talking about the same Fabio?" I asked. I remembered my brother being almost paralyzed with shyness around girls when we were still kids and then young adults. In reality, I remembered him that way up until he got together with Nicoletta.

"Yes, the same fucking Fabio Telmari!" shouted Nicoletta, her lips trembling. "Your honorable, false and bastard little brother who discovered that in politics he could scoop up all the girls and gals and ladies in Italy without so much as lifting a little finger!"

"Are you sure?"

"Yes I'm sure! I have *proof*!"

"How do you mean?"

"I mean that last spring I came back to the house and Tommaso says, 'Dad wrote me a ridiculous text message.' He showed it to me, and Fabio had written 'My dear *biscottina* (little cookie), you drove me absolutely crazy yesterday!"

"To Tommaso?"

"To Tommaso. A boy who quite correctly asked me if his father had lost his mind. Then, when Fabio came home I said to him 'You know, you were in such a hurry that you sent a message for one of your lovers to your son's cell phone' and he said, 'Let me see,' and read it and with a perfect poker face and said to me, 'No, that was meant for Tommaso. I meant to write biscottin*o*.' And I said to him, 'Oh yeah? And what is 'you drove me absolutely crazy' supposed to mean?' And he says, 'Because he never does his homework.' That false, lying son of a bitch! Do you get it?"

"No."

"Oh, yes you do!" she said. "And he's never called his son 'dear *biscottino*' in his life, that asshole! And when does he ever send him text messages in the middle of the morning? And I was so stupid, I let myself be convinced, swallowing his bullshit!"

"Maybe it was the truth," I said.

"The fuck it was! And in fact in July he got a text message on his cell phone at midnight while he was taking a shower and I looked at it without even thinking about it, and it said something like 'A goodnight kiss from your hot, wet little kitten.'!"

"For Fabio?"

"No, for my grandmother! Of course it was for Fabio! It was his cell phone. And don't act so shocked!"

"What did you do?"

"As soon as he got out of the shower I said, 'Here, read this. What's the message?' and he just glanced at it and shrugged his shoulders. He said it was a joke from a friend of his. Still with that same fucking smug certainty of a professional liar, do you understand? Seeing as it's his job, to bullshit everybody all day long!

Everybody! And I said 'Alright, fine. So let's just call your friend right now and we'll all have a good laugh, all three of us, okay?'"

"And Fabio?"

"Of course he refused. I don't remember what excuses he made up. He tried to rip the cell phone out of my hand. So I looked at his 'messages sent' file, and there were the names of *five* women, one after the other! And to save time your honorable little brother had sent the same fucking message to all five, in a *row*! Something like, 'My thoughts are running up your leg' or some lame pseudo-erotic bullshit like that!"

"In a row?" I asked.

"Yes, one after the other, in a row! In the end he managed to tear the cell phone out of my hand, and he removed the SIM card, threw it into the toilet and flushed! Can you believe that? Can you believe it?"

"Then what did he do? I mean with the cell phone?"

She stared at me as if she didn't understand. She said, "He must have bought a new SIM card the next morning. What the fuck kind of question is that, Lorenzo?"

"I don't know. I was just wondering."

"In any case, now he's got *three* cell phones, that little brother of yours. One for work, one for the family and another one for his lovers. And you can bet your ass he makes damn sure he doesn't leave that one lying around."

"I'm sorry," I said. I could only muster a partially formed image of my brother as serial seducer.

"I'm a lot sorrier," said Nicoletta. "I guarantee it."

I shut up, not knowing whether I should also feel guilty about having prevented her from at least partial vengeance with a little in-house sexual vendetta.

Nicoletta took out a tissue from a jacket pocket and blew her nose. She said "Bastards," but it wasn't clear if she meant Fabio and me or the male gender on the whole.

I said, "But where does he find the time? Isn't he busy enough with all the stuff he has to do as a politician?"

"He finds time. He finds it. The same way he finds time to go on TV and the radio and inaugurations and association meetings and openings and all the rest. That's political work too."

"Yes, but where does he take all these women? He can't exactly wander freely around cafés and gardens in Rome, can he?"

"What cafés and gardens?" said Nicoletta, now back in control of herself, although her minimalist make-up had melted in the tears, and the tip of her nose was red. "One of his dear buddies lends him a pied-à-terre, or the owner of some hotel he got a license for keeps a suite set aside for him."

My cheeks were burning a little from the earlier chafing and excitement. I was still having trouble getting a grasp on the situation in real terms. I said, "But how does he get there? Does he put on sunglasses and a fake beard and hope that nobody recognizes him and calls the press?"

"Oh yeah, because the journalists in this country are *so* dangerous," said Nicoletta, the muscles in her face contracting nervously. "Take it from a journalist. Ninety-nine percent are comparable mostly to waiters, with all due respect to the waiter profession."

"You think?"

"Yes I do, signor naiveté. Find me one willing to risk his job and corporate privileges just to go muck around in a politician's private life. Everybody's all curled up in ministry hallways and party headquarters, waiting with their tongues hanging out until they can snap up some declaration that's nothing but empty words."

"Jesus."

"Or, if they really have to leave the headquarters, they go lay siege on the house of some murder victim, desperate to ask the family if they've pardoned the assassins."

"You paint a nice picture," I said.

But she didn't want to get too far from her earlier theme. She said, "Just consider the fact that almost all Italian politicians, even the lowest order, have at least one lover, including the most conservative, bigoted officials. And their sex traffic makes other crimes pale in comparison. They could write the book on it."

"Why don't you write about it?" I asked.

"*Me?*" she exclaimed, as if I'd presented the most absurd suggestion in the world. "How do you think that would jibe with the fact that I'm Fabio's wife? And besides, my field is *scientific disclosure*, not investigative journalism."

I looked at a few photos of Fabio and me on display on the shelf: the two of us on two Shetland ponies at the zoo; Fabio in a wet-suit holding an octopus; me in my aikido suit; Fabio the politician at the Campidoglio; me at the helm of my old boat, the one I'd spent so much time and effort to fix up, and which I'd sold a while ago.

Nicoletta looked up at the ceiling as if to readjust her lachry-mose abilities, but then a moment later folded back over and started sobbing even worse than before, one hand held up in front of her eyes.

"Come on, Nicoletta," I said. "Please."

"Fuck come on!" she said. "That asshole of a man! After I've thrown away years of my life supporting and encouraging him! When he acted the poor, honest, and ingenuous new elect, tossed into an environment too dirty and difficult for him!"

"We all make mistakes," I said, even though I realized just how generic a phrase it was.

"I'm the one who made a mistake, believing him! Staying behind him, proud as an idiot when he started moving up the ladder inside his party! Giving him advice on how to talk and move during the interviews! Reassuring him all the time, every time he had a nervous breakdown and came crawling back to the house to cry at my feet! Being all understanding on the evenings when he said he was too tired to have sex, poor little boy!"

I searched for the right facial expression for the situation, but I couldn't find one. I simply nodded my head yes.

Nicoletta said, "All those times I asked him to spend time with his son and he responded that he didn't have time! That he didn't have time, can you believe that?!"

"Yes," I said. I thought of my nephew, sitting with his elbows on the table and his head lowered over his plate, walled up in a non-receptive attitude.

She seemed helplessly overcome by the reasons for her unhappiness, but suddenly at a certain point she blew her nose, glanced at her watch and said, "I have to go to the newspaper."

The rapidity of this transition left me completely disconcerted. I asked "Don't you want to grab a bite to eat together?" just to have something to say.

She ran the back of her hand across her eyes and said, "Thanks, but I don't have enough time."

"Are you sure?"

"Of course I'm sure," she said sharply. "Let me get cleaned up, I don't want to look like a zombie." She left my room and went into the bathroom at the end of the hallway.

I went into the kitchen to drink something, but there was a strong burning smell in the air.

Luz was coughing amid acrid smoke. She took a red-hot pot out of the oven, set it on in the sink and turned on the cold water, producing a puff and a whiter cloud that was accompanied by furious sizzling.

"I forgot the rice," she said.

"I understand," I said, thinking that in all likelihood Nicoletta and I had distracted her, with our voices and perhaps even by pushing all that furniture around.

A moment later Nicoletta stuck her head into the kitchen and said, "Is the house going up in flames?"

Luz and I explained what had happened while we opened windows and doors to try and get some fresh air in the room.

She was perfectly refreshed: she displayed one of her untouchable woman-girl (and wife and mother and lucid, balanced, ultra-organized professional) smiles. She came into the living room while we opened windows there as well, gathering the condolence telegrams she would have to answer together with Fabio. She settled a few practical matters with Luz, kissed me on the cheek with aseptic civility, and walked out, leaving the door wide open.

I went out onto the balcony for some fresh air. I watched the Tiber run between its two asphalt rivers of traffic, the outskirts of the city extending beyond the banks and into the hills in the yellow light.

Luz came out as well, coughing. "I forgot about it," she repeated.

"It happens," I said again.

She looked at me, with her dark eyes. Her presence calmed me, and made think back to when I was a boy, even though she'd only started working there five years ago.

I thought that she'd probably known my father better than I had. I wanted to ask her something about him, but I couldn't bring myself to. Instead I said, "What do you think you'll do, when we've finished emptying the apartment and all of that?"

She nodded at the horizon and said, "I'll go home. Then I'll come back to Italy. But first I'll go home."

I was just about to ask her something about her village in Ecuador, but she turned toward the living room, her face suddenly tense, and said, "Who's there?"

I looked too, but I didn't see anyone.

"Luz raced back into the apartment with great speed and determination, and I heard her yell, "*Que pasa aqui? Madre de Dios, cabrón maldito!*" Then I heard the sound of glass or porcelain breaking.

I ran inside and found her standing amidst the shards of a vase and flowers spread around in a big puddle of water. She pointed to the open door and shouted, "A thief! A thief!"

I ran out into the stairwell just in time to see a guy with a thick head of curly hair run quickly down the stairs. I shouted, "Hey! Stop!" and ran after him, my feet flying more and more quickly, step after step after step down the stairs, my hand sliding down the railing, a glance at each curve. I had run down those stairs more times than I could count over the years, when I was late for school or when I couldn't wait to get to a date with a girl, when I couldn't wait to get back to my life after another noncommunicative meal with my parents. I knew the height of the steps and the railing by memory; the combined play of propulsion and gravity and centrifugal force. The knowledge gave me a lateral push at the end of each flight, jumping two or three steps at a time.

But despite all this, the guy with curly hair was going down at the same speed as I was, keeping me from reducing the flight-and-a-half advantage he'd held from the beginning. I heard the sound of his feet hitting the floor together, the sound of him running across the ground floor. I got there maybe three seconds after he did, sprinting across the green carpet that ran along the entryway, beyond the window where Gianni the doorman was looking out, and beyond the glass door, down the steps to the road in three leaps. Once on the street I caught my first full glimpse of the guy with curly hair: he was wearing a brown-striped velvet jacket, his strong legs in mustard-colored jeans, and with techno-running shoes that had undoubtedly given him an advantage over my leather boots on the way down.

I went after him as quickly as I could, sustained by the formless, instinctive anger of territorial defense and incomprehension and frustration for not being able to catch up with him: I drove my feet as hard as I could, beating the air with my arms. I reduced the distance between us to perhaps a yard, the frenzy to grab his jacket so strong in my hands that I could almost feel the fabric between my fingers, but suddenly he dodged right and jumped onto a moving scooter, climbing on behind someone wearing a colored coat and a white helmet with honey-red hair sticking out from underneath. It was Mette, the girl who had come asking strange questions at the cemetery the morning before.

I was so surprised that I stopped up short. The scooter accelerated out onto the big street that flanked the river, running a red light and weaving into the traffic in a very risky way, then disappearing into the vast flow of traffic. I stood there on the edge of the sidewalk, my heart racing. I had to bend over with my hands on my knees just to catch my breath.

I TRIED TO CALL MY BROTHER

I tried to call my brother from my parents' old apartment, but his cell phone number was constantly busy. I called Nicoletta, although I didn't really feel like it. Her cell phone gave a recorded message that said it couldn't be reached right now. The answering machine picked up at their house number; I left a message for them to call me.

I told Luz to keep trying them. She said she would and watched me while she picked up the flower vase shards, her face worried.

I went back down the stairs, more slowly than before. I walked alongside the tram tracks, uncertain where to go or what to do. I tried to call up my mental images of Mette, the girl with honey-red hair, in order to remember her expression when she came over to talk to me at the cemetery. I tried to recover my acoustic memories of her tone of voice, but it wasn't easy; it had been too brief and strange an encounter to be deciphered so easily. I couldn't even remember the name of the cardinal she'd spoken of, although I seemed to remember he had an African name. The only thing I was sure of was that the interest she and her friend had in my family was neither generic nor in passing. I tried applying my mental detachment technique, pulling my perspective back miles above the earth's surface in order to take the importance out of what had happened. It didn't work: my blood continued to race with a strange blend of curiosity and alarm that were all out of proportion with the importance or length of the events.

I made more attempts to call Fabio and Nicoletta. Nothing. I ran through the names and numbers memorized on my cell phone, coming to a stop at Nadine Lemarc. Without thinking about it too much I pressed the button and called her.

She answered after a couple of rings, saying "Yes?" in a dry voice.

"I'm Lorenzo Telmari," I said. "I need to talk to you." Even though we'd known each other for a dozen years, ours had always been a distant familiarity, made that much more difficult by Fabio's dislike of her.

"About what?" she asked, diffident.

"It's better if we talk face to face," I said, even though I wouldn't have been able to say why.

"I'm working. I'm busy all week." Her French accent was barely discernible beneath her Roman dialect.

"Five minutes. Tell me where you are, I'll come to you."

She might have blown out some cigarette smoke, and there was resistance in her silence. She said, "Couldn't you at least tell me what it's about?"

An image of the honey-red-haired girl and her curly-haired friend escaping on the scooter passed through my head. "No," I said.

"I really can't, Lorenzo," said Nadine. "I'm working."

"Five minutes," I said, stubbornly sticking out the little battle of positions.

"I can't."

"Tell me where we can meet."

She stayed silent for two or three seconds, then finally told me where.

It took me half an hour to get back up the hill, out of the thinning traffic in the residential area toward the increasingly convulsed and insistent flow around the offices and stores. Practically every street was connected with some personal memory: a scooter accident, a date, a fight, a party, an encounter, a time I stood waiting, a boring walk, a glance caught on the fly and then lost forever. I walked at medium speed, noting just a few details of the scenario. Other details I'd noted in various moments of the same scenario kept surfacing in my mind. At a certain point, I imagined various different simultaneous me's during different periods of my life, each thinking different thoughts. It wasn't an innocent landscape; it had too much stratification.

By the time I reached Via Veneto I felt hunted, with an intense physical and mental desire for open spaces and silence. I passed by shop windows displaying shoes and watches for tourists, by bars and restaurants for tourists, past the newsstand for tourists with all its international newspapers and maps of the city in countless languages. I waited at the corner where I was supposed to meet Nadine. I watched the Americans and Japanese going in and out of their hotels, the waiting taxis and the moving buses, the lawyers and notary publics and bankers and clerks returning home from work in twos and threes or small groups, the waiters casting skeptical eyes from copper doorways.

Nadine arrived ten minutes late, just as I was starting to wonder if she hadn't just pretended to agree to see me in order to get rid of me. I saw her waving to me from the other side of the road, tall and nervous in a vaguely male-cut iron-gray coat that was a little too big for her.

We exchanged kisses hello with minimal contact, asking each other "How's it going?" with just a shade less mourning than the day before.

I didn't ask her where she'd come from or why she'd asked us to meet there, though it struck me as strange that she was working here. I asked her where she wanted to go. "Anywhere," she said. "I don't have very much time."

We went into one of the bars that had been the haunt of movie stars and paparazzi and nightlife experts more than forty years ago, and which now lived on a blend of tourists and office employees. I pointed to a table, but she went straight to the bar. She ordered a coffee. I ordered a fresh-squeezed orange juice, although by this time of day I was hungry. She watched the waiters moving around; I watched her in the reflection of the large mirror in front of us: her slim, long nose, her gray eyes behind narrow glasses, her thin lips and blond, decisively cut hair. The waiter put a coffee and orange juice down in front of us. Nadine put sweetener in hers, and without looking at me said, "Tell me everything."

I didn't really know where to begin. I took a long sip of the juice, coughing because it went down the wrong tube. I said, "The fact is that I was never told very much about my father's activities."

"That was your choice, wasn't it?" she said, immediately on the defensive. "It seems to me that you were the one who insisted on doing something completely different."

"That's true," I said, trying to assume a nonthreatening tone and posture. "I meant that I know hardly anything about what he did."

"If you and Fabio are wondering whether your father left me secret bank accounts in Switzerland or diamond tiaras, he didn't. And I'll pay my rent next month with my own money, don't you worry."

"That's not at all what I mean," I said, shaken by her interpretation and her tone. "How can you think that?"

"Yeah, I wonder how?" She seemed completely overcome by a cold fury, but she raised one hand to hide her eyes from me, and I saw tremors run through her thin body.

"Hey . . . Nadine?" I said, not daring to touch her since I could see one of the waiters staring at us openly from beside the coffee machine.

She sniffed and looked up at the ceiling. "I know that you and your brother hate me," she said, "but I never wanted to destroy your family. You father was the one who wanted us to be together. He was dead set on it, I'll guarantee that."

"I don't know what Fabio thinks, but I don't hate you at all," I said, casting a hostile eye at the waiter so that he would stop watching us. "We were all adults. As far as I'm concerned, your affair with my dad was nobody's business but yours."

I think Nadine made a superhuman effort to keep from crying. "You're wrong!" she said. "It was your mother's business too! And yours and your brother's! And everybody who knew Teo, the whole international scientific community!"

"I'm sorry," I said. I had never imagined talking about this with her when I had been so insistent about seeing her.

"But no matter what you think, it was a very beautiful, important love affair! And I've got nothing to be ashamed of! Nothing!"

"Of course you don't." I wondered if I'd ever make it to the topic I was interested in, or if I'd remain crushed beneath the emotional ashes my father had left in his wake.

"If you and your brother think it's easy being the secret woman of a man like Teo Telmari, you're wrong. It's not! Not even a little bit!" she said. Her voice broke, and two or three regulars and another waiter turned around to look.

I extended a hand very carefully toward her right shoulder.

She moved, took a breath and said, "Eight years of being the one who has to give deep, unconditional love and advice and attention and one-hundred-percent dedication, and as soon as required has to become invisible and keep her mouth shut and behave until further instructed!"

"It must have been difficult."

"It was *atrocious!*" she said, loud enough that even a couple of American tourists turned to look. "Do you and that brother of yours have any idea what it means to give your life to a man, and to know right from the beginning that he can only give you scraps of his in return because he'll never leave his mommy-wife, the woman he's completely dependent upon?"

"I can only imagine," I said in a tone of voice and with a look that I hoped might calm her down.

"I don't think you can! A man who plays the strong, reassuring patriarch to the whole world, an indestructible point of reference, and then turns into a child who can't even tie his own shoes when he's with his mommy-wife! In a perverse, irresolvable web of dependency and emotional and mental blackmail! And meanwhile, I'm the one who sticks her nose in it trying to destroy somebody else's marital bliss! The 'virus,' to use your brother's thoughtful nickname!"

"Look," I said, "my brother and I have very different opinions on a lot of things, including this."

She wasn't listening to me. "Eight whole years!" she said, "without once, and I mean not even one time, taking a vacation or a trip that wasn't for work. Not even one normal, ordinary, entire *Sunday* together! He always had to be back by eleven-thirty at night!"

I scratched my head. I couldn't figure out a way out of this.

"And then when the mommy-wife dies, and he finally gets over the pain and we finally have an opportunity to live our little scrap of life together, it's 'thanks so much,' a thousand kisses and he dumps you because he needs someone even younger and more adoring like the dear Giovannina Zambion! Seeing as how with all that deep love and comprehension and extraordinary balance you've become a sort of mommy too! So with your heart broken you try to figure it all out and think you can at least console yourself with a higher level of communication with him and then what happens? Then what does he do? He dies!"

A guy with a shaved head holding a ball of fried rice had stretched toward us to try and hear more clearly: I made a cutting gesture with one hand and he unwillingly turned away again.

Nadine continued, "Do you and your brother have any idea how much I'm going to miss your father now? Do you have the faintest damn clue?" She extended her trembling fingers to pick up her little cup of espresso and, in a quasi-heroic effort at self-control, raised it to her lips.

I nodded yes, lacking any more significant words. Then, in order to force a way out of this train of thought, I asked, "I called you to ask if you'd ever heard talk of a certain Cardinal Ndiembe? Or maybe Ndiambe, or something like that? I can't remember the name exactly . . ."

She stared at me with the strangest expression on her face: the cup of coffee slipped from her fingers, struck the edge of the bar and smashed to pieces on the floor.

The breaking cup also broke the quasi-immobility of the people who had been standing around and watching: a woman gave a little yelp of fear, the Americans slid into the back of an adjoining room, the shaved head swallowed the last piece of fried rice, a waiter moved away from the coffee machine. The other waiter came over with a little broom and dustpan and said, "Don't worry, leave it." He started cleaning up.

Nadine headed straight for the cash register. She paid before I could, then walked out.

I ran behind her, catching up to her on the sidewalk. It was much more crowded than before. "Wait," I said.

She continued to walk as if she could neither hear me nor see me, crossing the road and heading toward where the taxis were parked. I kept following her, but was so disconcerted I didn't know what to say. She got into a taxi and closed the door behind her. I gestured to her through the window; she stared straight ahead, and the taxi took off.

MY NEPHEW WAS IN HIS ROOM FULL
OF EQUIPMENT FOR HAVING FUN

My nephew was in his room full of equipment for having fun and studying and working out, sitting crosswise on a rotating chair, fiddling with an electronic console that allowed him to participate in a game of virtual soccer. I didn't say hello because I didn't feel like receiving one of his indistinguishable utterances in response. I just nodded. He didn't take his gaze off the screen. His thumbs pressed the buttons, his head and feet moving as if he were in a trance.

I pointed to the computer on his desk near the bed, in between the gigantic stereo speakers and just beyond an enormous electric running machine. "I'm going to take a look at something," I said. He didn't answer, continuing his clickety-click-click and the unstoppable oscillation of his head and feet.

I sat down at the keyboard of his computer: it was five generations younger than mine, ten times more powerful, and boasting a connection twenty times faster. I opened a search engine, typed "Stopwatch" in the query box, then hit return. Almost immediately a webpage appeared filled with the word "stopwatch." At the bottom it read *1 of 10 out of some 4,270,000 results.*

I clicked on a pair of websites and read the descriptions of five or six others: they were software producers who created programs that measured download or execution times. The "sponsored links" section included the website of a Shanghai company that produced real stopwatches, which according to the text enjoyed a *high reputation in China and abroad.* The next page gave similar results: virtual stopwatches, real stopwatches, stopwatches cited in sports pages. Then, at the beginning of the third page, I found an address with *Watching the World's Balance* written underneath it.

I clicked on the link. An image of a red stopwatch super-imposed on the planet earth appeared, with *Stopwatch* written above it in typewriter script. Immediately below there was a two-columned counter displaying white numbers on a black back-ground: *Current Population* was written alongside the first column, and *Calendar Population* was written alongside the second. The first column totaled 6,565,293,114, but the numbers on the right were constantly running, increasing by three per second, second after second. Below that, a short paragraph explained that the data was a logarithmic approximation, calculating both deaths and births. I watched the numbers grow for half a minute, and in the meantime the world's population had reached 6,565,293,204 people.

The second column of the counter displayed numbers corresponding to other dates that could be changed according to day, month, and year. I tried seeing how many people inhabited the earth on November 26th, 1970: 3,963,417,989 people. I looked to see how many there would be on November 26th, 2025: 8,773,536,495 people. I went to November 26th, 2035: 10,137,051,338 people. I typed in other dates, at once enchanted and horrified by numbers that continued to run, like those on the gas meter of a gigantic house whose owners had left, forgetting to close billions of valves.

I clicked on the stopwatch image: that led me into a succession of pages filled with graphs and texts on the growing human population, the exhaustion of prime resources, the extinction of animal and vegetable species, melting polar ice caps and desertification, the spread of AIDS, malnutrition and hunger, access to water and education. I ran my eyes across the pages, stopping at points that caught my attention with alternating feelings of distance and closeness. When I was a skipper I had collaborated with an environmental organization that was gathering data on poisoning in the oceans, and during other periods I had contributed some money and my signature to campaigns to fight hunger, defend old-growth forests, abolish hunting, help sub-Saharan populations and inhabitants of South American jungles. I was worried about the destruction of the ozone layer and the increasing greenhouse effect. I could feel the effects of the changing climate just as well as the next person, I suffered because of the destruction of landscapes and the degeneration of interpersonal relationships. It was increasingly hard for me to believe that we could block or even affect our species' devastating and suicidal tendencies. I had the feeling that the damage had become irreversible; the point of no return had already been surpassed. Reading Stopwatch's webpages and seeing the human-being counter run on and on without stopping confirmed my sense that there was nothing that could be done now. I didn't feel cynical or resigned; I just felt appropriately prepared for the worst.

There was also a "contacts" section on the website that boasted a short list of email and postal addresses. Under "Italy" there was an address in Rome. I copied it down on a piece of paper, using the golden marker that Tommaso had used to write a few comments alongside the photos of soccer players on a poster hanging on the wall. Then I closed the website and stood up.

My nephew had finished his virtual game and was now yawning and bouncing his legs on the backrest of his rotating, office manager's chair.

"You bored?" I asked him.

"Mmmph," he said.

"How's school going?"

"Eaah."

"Don't you have any favorite subjects?"

"Nah."

"Any girls you like?"

"Nah."

There was a poster of a science fiction movie on the wall behind him, as well as another of wrestling. I said, "Do you want to see an interesting martial arts move?"

"Whuh?" he said.

"Get up for a minute. Come over here."

"Umph."

"Come on. You can do it. Just for a couple of minutes."

Finally he got up, as if he were battling some terrible resistance, and came over into the middle of the room.

I said, "Try to punch me."

"Ahw-nah," said Tommaso.

I couldn't believe his total and utter refusal to leave the cocoon of soccer and school and home and boredom and video games and gadgets and accessories and emotional difficulties and guaranteed attention and significant absences in which he was enveloped.

"Come on!" I shouted. "Move, you sack of potatoes! Larva! Chicken shit!"

Finally my nephew punched me. And he did so with the strength of a big, powerful thirteen year old fed a high-protein, hyper-caloric diet; a boy who worked out daily on the soccer field. I dodged his hand, grabbing his wrist and turning to one side, dragging him in after the wave of his own punch, pulling his arm toward me and pushing on his right scapula. He flew over, his full body weight crashing onto the parquet floor.

He looked up at me from down there, dazed and surprised. He massaged his shoulder. Then I saw a sort of slow smile take over his lips, the liquid light of attention filling his eyes. He said, "How'd you do that? Can you show me again?"

Dinner was almost entirely dominated by Fabio's discussion of the internal power struggles in the Democratic Myrtle party, as well as those between the Democratic Myrtle party and the other parties that formed the current government. Given his tone of voice and looks and the emphasis he put into pronouncing the names of his rivals or allies there was no doubt that for Fabio, Italian politics equaled the universe, every secretary and president and commission chief and leader gifted with the gravitational force of a spinning planet. I was struck by how his vision was totally devoid of openings, or even mere cracks through which he might glimpse the lights and colors and dust of a normal life. I was struck by the naturalness with which he spoke of pincer movements and consortiums and shifting pressures and extending influences, commanding control by newspapers and television channels and state agencies and state-controlled organizations from those on his side or the others'. It was the nature of the game he played, and he was a professional player on a national league team, aware of all the rules and techniques he could use, facing a championship to play and win. The alternative worlds we'd spoken of as boys were as far outside this logic as sex before a game; his ultra-detailed descriptions of tactics and strategies were devoid of so much as a trace.

Nicoletta registered the names and roles, occasionally asking him for more detail, though even this was done with well-oiled automatism. She sat up straight in her chair, the muscles of her face held in a tense nonexpression. She looked at her husband rarely and at me not at all, chiding her son to sit up straight, complaining to Harry and Emily that the broccoli wasn't cooked enough and there was too much salt on the sea bass. And yet she didn't seem like an entirely different woman than the one who had unexpectedly embraced me and kissed me and then revealed her ferocious unhappiness in my parents' previous home: her cold and hot parts were contiguous, probably compensating and justifying one another in turn.

My nephew Tommaso ate with his head hung low, one elbow planted on the table, his thoughts light years away from his father's talk and his mother's behavior. As soon as his raspberry cream cake was finished in a series of rapid spoonfuls, he stood up without saying a word and went into his room, chased along by useless urgings from his mother.

Then Nicoletta got up as well, answered her cell phone, gave new instructions to Harry and Emily, and informed her husband that she was going to the movies with Tiziana Ramorini. She disappeared down the hallway, reappearing with her coat on and her purse in one hand. "Bye-bye," she said, and left.

Fabio and I moved into the living room. He asked me, "How's it going?" without expecting any real response. He sat down on the sofa and then got back up again, made and received calls on his cell phone, turned on the gigantic TV screen and checked all the channels one after the other. Then he asked Harry for some grapefruit juice with ice, and sent and received some text messages.

During a break from one of these activities I said, "I saw Nadine today."

"Ah," he said, going rigid with hostility at the mere mention of her name. "The virus."

"Stop calling her that."

"Where did you see her?"

"In a bar on Via Veneto."

"What did she want?"

"I called her. I wanted to talk to her."

"About what?"

"Well," I said, "this morning a strange thing happened. A guy snuck into dad's old apartment while I was outside on the balcony talking to Luz."

"I know," said Fabio immediately. "Luz called me."

"Perfect," I said, struck by just how important it was to him to keep his information up to date, and to let you know he did.

"Of course I can't believe Luz," he said, "leaving the door open like that. God bless her, but I tried to explain to her that Rome isn't exactly an Ecuadorian village."

"It was to let the smoke out. We forgot the rice was cooking."

"*She* forgot the rice," said Fabio, once again not leaving so much as a second's space. "Don't try to cover for her. In any case I sent somebody over to keep an eye on the place."

"Somebody?"

"Yes," he said, not registering the question behind my question. "This way we're all more secure until we've cleared everything out. The chief of police told me there are thieves who specialize in breaking into homes where there's just been a death. They take advantage of the general turmoil and all the coming and going."

"Actually, I don't think it was a thief," I said.

"What do you mean?" He held his eyelids half-closed.

"I mean maybe he wasn't there to steal anything."

Fabio slowly shook his head and said, "Then what was he doing in dad's house?"

"Maybe he was looking for information." I realized that I wasn't giving much of an explanation, but I wasn't entirely sure what I thought, and even less that I wanted to tell him.

"Wait," said Fabio, "let me understand what you're saying. What kind of information? And what's Nadine got to do with it?"

"Nothing. But maybe the curly-haired guy was looking for something that had to do with dad's work. Reserved medical information or something, I don't know."

"Where do you come up with this stuff?" He laughed, spinning the ice cubes in his glass.

"I don't know," I said. "When I was just about to catch up with him out on the sidewalk, he jumped onto a scooter being driven by a girl who came up to me the other morning at the cemetery.

"What girl?" asked my brother. I could read the disappointment in his eyes at being faced with an unexpected lack of information. For a moment we returned to the same dynamic we'd shared when the two years that separated us had been a barrier between his child's perspective and my young boy's outlook, then between his as a young boy and mine as an almost-adult.

"I don't think you've ever seen her," I said.

"If she came there to see dad then I saw her for sure," he said. "I'm no mountain hermit like you. I know the people dad knew."

"I don't know if you knew her. At least not personally."

"What do you know about it?"

"Have you ever heard anyone speak of a Cardinal Ndianga?" I asked.

His face contracted once again into an almost infantile expression of perplexity. "What do cardinals have to do with this?" he asked.

I had an impulse to tell him more about the girl Mette, but for some reason my impulse quit halfway, and was reabsorbed into a not-entirely explainable or confessable reserve. Maybe I didn't want to betray a personal secret, or perhaps I liked the fact that for once there were a few tiles missing from his constantly updated panoramic vision. I said, "Nothing, I read something in a newspaper, that's all."

"This girl on the scooter," said Fabio, "with the thief. Are you one hundred percent sure that she was at the cemetery yesterday?"

"No. Maybe it just looked like her."

"You seemed pretty sure two minutes ago," he said. He was walking back and forth. One of his cell phones started ringing. He took it out of his pocket and refused the call.

"I wasn't sure."

"Try to describe her," said Fabio, leaning on the French doors that led out onto the terrace.

"I don't know. Blond."

"Tall, wearing a long black coat?"

"Maybe," I said. I had a vivid mental image of Mette with her honey-red hair and colorful jacket.

"And you saw her again on the scooter at dad's house? Together with the Rasta-haired thief?"

"I don't know." I went over to the French doors too.

"Man, what a careful observer you are," said my brother, a rising vein of irritation in his voice. "You know when they talk about the sea wolf's unerring eye?"

Faced with this kind of reaction I'd have been willing to claim I'd never chased any curly-haired guy who escaped on a scooter, but now it was too late. I said, "Is it true you've had a lot of lovers lately?"

"What?" He closed his eyes.

"And that you sent the same amorous text messages to every single one? Just to save time?"

"What the fuck are you talking about?" asked Fabio, with a caught-in-the-cookie-jar expression on his face that I distinctly remembered from when our ages could be measured in single years.

"That's the word on the street," I said, taking advantage of the breach in his defenses. "The honorable serial seducer."

He moved his lips as if to emit some dry, effective retort, but instead his arms dropped to his sides and he said, "What else has Nicoletta told you?"

His sudden vulnerability took away my desire to be cruel. "Nothing else," I said.

"Of course. Nothing," he said, biting on his lower lip. "What did she tell you?"

I punched his shoulder and said, "But that's why people become politicians, right? The women, the recognition, the honors?"

"Cut it out," said Fabio. "What the fuck do you know about how things are between Nicoletta and me?"

"Well, you've always seemed like the perfect couple. Beautiful, successful, close, good, conscientious, dynamic, all the right pieces in the right places. I never would have thought it was just a good marketing exercise."

"Are you finished with the bullshit?" asked Fabio. "Are you finished yet?"

It occurred to me that this had always been our way of talking about personal issues: a stupidly sarcastic, male approach, even well before our lives had begun to diverge. Suddenly it all seemed like an absurd waste of time and feelings to me, a stupid defense of protective shields. "Finished, finished," I said. "But you never talked to me about it either, did you?"

"No, that's right," he said, his eyes on the floor. His cell phone said "message received" from within his jacket pocket, but he didn't even bother looking.

"Why not?"

Fabio shrugged and put his hands in his jacket. "What was there to say? That Nicoletta is a neurotic, implacable hyena, a control freak? Can't you see that by yourself?"

I said, "You always seemed so satisfied. So perfectly organized and successful and well-adjusted. So far above any miserable sentimental messes."

"That's an act she puts on. She works at it so convincingly and assiduously that in the end I wound up believing in it too, for years."

I was struck by the level of exasperation in his voice, and by the fact that he was talking to me openly for the first time in as long as I could remember. "But?" I asked.

"You have no idea what it's like to live with a woman like Nicoletta, day in and day out."

"Maybe I can imagine it a little."

"Well, it's worse," said Fabio in a tone of voice so heartbroken it hurt my tympanums. "It's like having the Spanish inquisition, the CIA, and the KGB all rolled into one person. A person who records your every gesture and word and phone call, writing down times and names and tones of voice, comparing in real time every possible contradiction, then follows you into the bathroom and kitchen to spy on you, and enters into the deepest, most hidden circuits in your brain, while in the meantime continuing to work equally hard at maintaining a façade of matrimonial perfection for the world to see."

"But you're talking about a nightmare," I said, entirely unprepared for this picture.

"Yes, but it's a nightmare that never ends. You wake up the next morning and she's still there, in your bed, smiling at you perfectly and expecting an equally perfect response. And if she doesn't receive it her perfect, endless mental torture starts up all over again."

"But your work as a serial seducer doesn't exactly help things, does it?"

"It doesn't change her attitude one bit," he said.

"How come?"

"Because Nicoletta doesn't give a shit about sex. Neither do I, for that matter."

"What do you mean?" I asked, relatively disconcerted.

"Listen, Lorè," he said. "I have a thousand more important things to do than go around screwing women. Things that are a thousand times more satisfying. And where would I find the time? Do you have even the foggiest idea of the commitments that drop onto my shoulders every time I walk out that door, every damn day?"

"What about the serial messages? What about the TV hostesses and your assistants and the wives of your friends?"

Fabio had an expression that would enable him to continue denying everything all ready to trot out, but instead he said, "What the fuck do you think I should do? Resign myself to sexual stasis with Miss Perfect, who I haven't screwed for more than five full years, or get at least some miserable satisfactions on the fly when I can?"

"So what Nicoletta says is true," I said.

"No, it's not true. And in any case, for her it's always been a control issue. That's the way it's always been, ever since we first got together. Control, control, control. On the outside, in words, in gestures, in your tone of voice. Under all that there's the hot, burning lava of unhappiness, bubbling and boiling, but outside you stay calm, you smile, you keep your poise, you're friendly with the journalists. I can't even say the things I want to say to my son without having to pass through her filter! He's become a sort of privileged pensioner, an alternate me, who can't be contradicted or crossed because he's got mommy's approval now and forever! Can you believe this shit?!"

"Maybe it's your fault too," I said, "that you don't try to communicate with him."

"I try, Lorenzo. I try, but it's no use."

"Maybe you don't try hard enough."

"It's like talking to a wall," said Fabio. "And I know Nicoletta has gone and played the victim and sweet saint and told him all about what kind of monster I am. But she didn't tell you about her Cordati, did she?"

"Who?"

"Sante Cordati, from the state television. That phony scoundrel, with his greased hair and those pointy sideburns and his basset hound eyes. I got the phone records from Telecom Italia; they call each other five or six times a day. Do you get it? And your little sister-in-law plays such a convincing victim!"

"The phone records?" I said. "Wow. Good thing a person's private life is nice and safe in this country."

"She's the one who started it," said Fabio. "Checking my cell phone and reading my mail. Otherwise I never would have done it. It's not my style. And don't talk to me about private lives, Lorenzo. I haven't had one for fourteen years, ever since I got married."

"So get separated. End it."

"Yeah, that's perfect," said Fabio. "Then what? Get a new job? Should I go become a ragman?"

"Why?"

"What am I supposed to tell my voters?"

"What kind of voters do you have?" I exclaimed. "Medieval fundamentalists and extremists?"

"Moderates, Lorenzo. Center-left, but moderates. And who knows why, but I think it's a safe bet they wouldn't be too happy watching Nicoletta weep on Sunday talk shows, telling the world how I broke her heart and destroyed her life."

"Do you think she'd do that?"

"No, of course not. Never in such a vulgar manner. She'd find infinitely more subtle and devastating ways."

We stood there motionless in front of the large glass window. One of Fabio's cell phones started ringing inside his jacket. He didn't answer.

I said, "So you're doomed to stay together even though you hate each other?"

"What do you think?" asked Fabio.

Another cell phone started ringing, the one with the Coltrane ring tone. He took it out of his pocket and read the name on the screen, then answered immediately. He listened for a couple of seconds, then started asking for a series of details about staffing changes in a public agency that produced movies, his tone of voice light years away from the one he'd been using just a moment earlier.

I opened the French doors and went out onto the terrace to look at the lit windows of other apartments on all four sides of the palm-filled courtyard.

I DROVE THROUGH THE
FRENZIED MORNING TRAFFIC

I drove through the frenzied morning traffic toward the Stazione Termini neighborhood, where the address I'd found on the Stopwatch website was located. My pickup was too big and rigid and slow in the continuous play of stopping and starting and zigzagging and braking at the last second, crawling along at a snail's pace and accelerating furiously in order to get through an intersection while the light was still yellow. I slowed down on the narrow streets, stopped outside the jams, got honked at by other drivers, provoked rude gestures from motorcyclists.

When I finally reached the station I drove once, twice, three times around the large island where I wanted to park, but there wasn't so much as a single free section of asphalt among the cars parked bumper to bumper. It occurred to me that I'd been stupid not to walk here or take a bus or taxi; I'd forgotten even the most elementary rules of urban survival. Little by little the sense of oppression that had driven me out of the city and toward the sea and ultimately up into the hills eleven years earlier grew in me: the desire for unoccupied spaces, horizons toward which I might extend thoughts and sensations and limitless gestures. On my third trip around I had the early symptoms of a true entrapment syndrome; I considered abandoning the pickup in the middle of the street, or changing direction and heading for the highway, forgetting Rome and all the reasons I'd come. But at that very moment a guy came out of a drycleaners, climbed into his van and left. I parked crookedly in his spot, one wheel up on the sidewalk.

I walked rapidly toward the street, which I'd already located during my circling. I slowed down as I got close to the building number I was looking for. I thought about the conversation I'd had with my brother the night before, still unable to explain clearly the reasons I'd been reticent about the girl, Mette. I asked myself how I was supposed to approach her in the event she was there: should I be friendly or reserved? Aggressive? Neutral?

The number I'd written down with Tommaso's marker corresponded to an old building with flaking gray paint. It had the dark windows of an old shop or workroom on one side. A poster with the Stopwatch symbol was attached to them, as well as a few pages from newspapers and magazines, and a few printed pages from their website. There was a glass door as opaque as the windows. I tried pushing on it, but it was closed. I cupped my hands around my eyes and tried to see inside: I could make out a table and a few chairs, more posters on the walls. It didn't seem like a very busy place, but it didn't seem permanently closed either. Some of the articles taped in the windows were from just a month or two ago.

I went into a bar at the end of the street and had a cappuccino and brioche. I watched the woman at the cash register, bloated and lost in her thoughts, an alcoholic from the train station who picked up a bottle of grappa in exchange for an enormous quantity of five- and ten-cent coins. The other customers came in and out in various degrees of apathy and anxiety, depending on whether they were headed for a train or for a bank office or shipping company. I felt like I stood halfway between their emotions: one moment I was calm and ready to wait, the next I would almost give in to impatience.

I went back to the Stopwatch headquarters. I wondered what the likelihood was that sooner or later somebody would show up, whether I'd have to hang around there for days, tape a message with my cell phone number to the window, or just drop the whole thing.

Then, when I was still some twenty yards off, I saw a guy with curly hair cross the street and fumble with a bunch of keys outside the dark glass door. I didn't recognize him immediately because while I was running after him down the stairs at my father's former apartment I had only seen him from behind. But the hair was his beyond a shadow of a doubt. They weren't Rasta dreads, as my brother had called them based on the information Luz had given him. They were kinky curls with a rounded, treetop sort of style. He looked like a 1960s rock musician.

I crossed the street in the same amount of time it took him to open the door. I pushed the dark glass door open with one shoulder and went inside before he had time to close the door behind him. He gave a cry of surprise, then backpedaled, bumping into a chair.

We faced each other, standing a couple of yards apart in the half-light and smell of damp walls. We were both extremely tense, our legs trembling, our breathing rapid.

The curly-haired guy said, "Who are you? What do you want?" with what was probably a Brazilian accent.

"I'll ask you the same thing," I said. "Explain to me why you snuck into my father's former apartment like a thief."

I couldn't really make out his expressions, so I closed the door with one foot and flipped the light switch on my right with hardly a glance. A few neon tubes shivered, illuminating the room and the face of the curly-haired guy and the chairs and the greenish Formica table and the posters with red and yellow and blue symbols on the walls with cold light. He made a leap for the door. I cut him off. He came at me with his right arm held out. It wasn't exactly an attempt at punching, but almost. I blocked him with a variation of the move I'd shown my nephew the night before.

He fought back violently, but now I could use his arm as a lever, pushing him over, his head toward the floor. He grunted and panted, saying "Arrrgh, let go of me! *Bolas!*"

"I'll let you go if you'll explain." I wasn't talking that clearly either. Furthermore, I was wondering if some passerby outside could see us, if maybe I hadn't made a mistake by turning the light on.

"Unnngraaargh! Let go of me!" he cried, his voice distorted by effort and frustration.

I tried to calm myself down, as much as was possible smack in the middle of a strenuous muscular conflict. I said, "Listen, I'm not some damn private avenger and I'm not at all interested in taking you to the police. I just want to know what you were looking for yesterday. Do you understand?"

"Grrumph!"

"Do you understand?" I asked, still pushing him down toward the floor.

"Urrrgh, yes!" said the curly-haired guy finally.

I let up the pressure little by little, and said, "Let's talk civilly, deal?"

"Mmph, yes," he said.

I let him go. He straightened up immediately, shook himself, and backed up to a safe distance. We faced each other once again, breathing heavily. The room was filled with the sounds of our breathing, the glass windows vibrating slightly with the passing of cars outside. "I'm sorry," I said, "but I didn't feel like chasing you who-knows-where all over again."

He didn't say anything, looking around, maybe for some object he could use as a dangerous weapon. He had a nice face, soft and boyish.

"Please," I said, "just relax. I'm not an enemy. I even went to look at your website, I read the things you guys write. I agree with you. I think the destruction of earth's equilibriums is the mother of all problems, too."

The guy continued to stay silent, but it seemed like the tension in his face melted into a more uncertain expression.

I said, "Look at me, will you? Do I look like an enemy? Do I look like a son of a bitch to you?"

"How am I supposed to know?" he said finally. "You almost knock down the door and attack me."

"I just blocked you. And all I did was come in without asking for your permission, exactly like you did yesterday in my father's former apartment."

He scratched the tip of his nose and said, "What do you want to know?"

"Why did you come into my father's apartment? And why did your friend Mette come to the cemetery the other morning to ask me if I knew Cardinal Ndiabo or whatever his name is, and why was she waiting for you on a scooter yesterday so that you could escape together?"

The curly-haired guy stared at me. I think he was trying to decide whether or not he should still consider me dangerous.

I extended my hand to him, my arm held out, but kept my feet in place so that I wouldn't be sending him any new danger signals. I said, "My name's Lorenzo."

He hesitated again, then extended his hand and said, "Jorge." He shook my hand with moderate pressure, then quickly took his back.

I said, "I want to understand what's going on. These are pretty strange days for me."

"I didn't go in to steal from your dad," he said. "I was looking for something."

"I imagined as much. What were you looking for? If you tell me, maybe I can help."

He looked around the room and said, "Okay, but not now. And not in here."

"When? And where? Your friend Mette said 'not here, not now' too, and then she disappeared."

Jorge said, "Do you have a cell phone? We'll call you."

"When?" I asked. I felt like I'd already lost the advantage I had when I'd blocked his arm.

He went to pick up a cloth bag lying in one corner and put it over his shoulder. He looked at his watch and said, "I have to run, but if you leave your number we'll call you."

"Are you sure?"

"Yes, yes." He turned off the neon light, reopened the dark glass door and waited for me to go out first.

I fished the receipt from the bar out of my pocket and, leaning on the glass, wrote my cell phone number on the back. I gave the receipt to him.

He put it in his pocket and locked the glass door.

We looked at each other a little obliquely. In the light of day, our earlier scuffle seemed even more ridiculous. I said, "But you have to call me soon. I'm not going to stay here in Rome forever."

"I promise." He'd already started walking away.

At first I let him go, but then I ran after him along the sidewalk. He spun around, a new expression of alarm on his face. I said, "The only thing I seem to understand is that there's some connection with this Cardinal Ndiongo, am I wrong?"

"Ndionge," he said, his eyes shifting rapidly to either side of the sidewalk.

"Come again?"

"Cardinal Ndionge," he said without slowing down.

"Huh?" I asked as we turned the corner of the street. "What's the connection? Can you at least tell me that?"

"I have to go," he said. "Really. I'm already late." He stopped at a scooter chained to a lamppost. The idea that it was the same one he'd escaped on the day before together with Mette made me see it in a curiously suggestive light, as if it were some article from rock history. Jorge opened the lock with a small key, wound the chain around the handlebars, kicked the pedal to start the motor, then got on the scooter and drove it off the sidewalk and away down the street quickly in a cloud of smoke and spluttering.

I shouted, "Hey!", but I knew perfectly well that it would be pointless to chase after him again. I looked up and down the street at the formerly respectable buildings, now decayed and dusty, just a few dozen yards from the train station.

I LEFT MY PICKUP NEAR
DANTE MARCADORI'S STUDIO

I left my pickup near Dante Marcadori's studio on the same street where the political science department building is located. I nodded to the doorman in his little office and went up the stairs into the twentieth-century building. I thought about all the times I had gone up them in the period when I was thirteen to fifteen years old, when for a relatively brief period of time I had experienced the symptoms of almost every mortal disease known to man. Perhaps some of my father's extremely clinical descriptions influenced this recurrent syndrome, or perhaps my transitory age made me particularly attentive to every tiny signal that reached my brain from various parts of my body. Whatever the explanation, for almost two years the smallest peripheral tingling or the most barely perceptible interior tremor were capable of convincing me that my end was near. When I thought I had little time left to live I would talk about it with my mother, and she would call Dante Marcadori so that he could take a look at me (in our family there was a rule that our father wouldn't handle our health personally). Strangely enough, usually it was enough just to know that the appointment had been set up for my symptoms to disappear in the space of a few hours. Whenever this didn't happen, my healing would take place as I climbed the stairs up to Marcadori's office. Only in the case of particularly devastating illnesses would I need Dante to actually take a look at me before the medical situation would start to dissipate. I would stare at him as he listened to me and nodded and in the end smiled, sitting straight up, bristly haired and slim between the mahogany panels of the doctor's office, and relief would run through my nerves in warm waves. I remember the feeling of saying goodbye to him and walking back down the stairs, reemerging into the city's light and noise: the incredible lightness I felt in my legs at the idea of once again possessing a limitless quantity of life.

I pushed the brass button next to the shiny walnut door and heard the same old bell ring inside the office. After a few seconds the door opened and a thin, gray-haired woman wearing a turtle-neck sweater appeared. "Yes?" she said.

"Hello, I'm Lorenzo Telmari," I said.

"Ah," she said. "I'm sorry to hear about your father." She extended her hand to me, dry and nervous like the rest of her.

"Thanks. I'd like to speak with the professor, if he has a few free minutes."

The woman looked at me with an uncertain expression on her face. "He's not here," she said.

"Ah," I said.

She said, "We expected him to be here this morning."

"And he still hasn't shown up?"

The woman shook her head.

"You don't know when he's going to arrive?"

The woman shook her head again. Her look and the lines of her face were wrought with worry. She said, "We haven't heard from him since yesterday afternoon. His cell phone is turned off, there's just a message that says it's not possible to connect."

"What about at home?"

She shook her head even more energetically. "He was supposed to go there yesterday afternoon, after he left this office. But he didn't. I tried again ten minutes ago: nothing."

Several images of Dante Marcadori in his doctor's office passed through my head: the last time I'd been there to have him take a look at the symptoms of my latest mortal disease, a lifetime ago; then just a few days earlier, in my father's former living room. "Maybe he had something important to do outside the city."

The woman said, "He would have told me. And this afternoon at four, he's supposed to be at the virology conference in Fiuggi."

I looked at my watch. It was a few minutes after twelve. "Then he'll probably be here soon," I said.

"Yes," she answered, but she looked hardly convinced. "What did you want to talk to him about?"

"Oh, nothing. I wanted to ask him about something that has to do with my father."

She looked at me from behind half-closed eyelids, standing rigidly in front of the open doorway. "Ah-hah," she said.

I shook her hand once again and said, "In any case, we'll talk again. Thanks."

She said, "You're welcome," but kept staring at me. It took her a few seconds to go back inside the office and close the door.

I went down the stairs, feeling the exact opposite of the relief that I used to feel when I was thirteen or fourteen and Dante Marcadori could free me so easily from even the most implacable pathologies.

I followed the road that flanked the river for a couple of miles, various thoughts interweaving in my mind. I left the pickup in an open spot underneath the plane trees along the busy street, then walked into the old neighborhood of low houses and narrow streets. I had lived in Trastevere for long periods of time. I liked the idea of living in a central Italian village that was part of a major city, and yet at the same time continued to be a village.

I ended up in front of the three-floor, reddish building where Dante Marcadori lived. The building stood in one of the last streets before the hill rose up sharply. I pressed the button for the apartment, then waited. No one answered. I backed up across the street until my back was against the opposite façade, standing up on my tiptoes in order to see the windows on the last floor. I could see neither lights nor movement.

A short, fat woman wearing a kitchen apron stood at the door of a small trattoria on the corner, watching me. "Who are you looking for?" she asked. "Are you looking for the professor too?"

"Yes," I said, relatively surprised. "Has someone else been looking for him?"

"A thin, thin signora," she said. "She just wouldn't give up. I told her that the professor isn't there and it's no use pushing on the door and jamming your finger on the button and shouting like you're at the market. But she wouldn't listen. She even got the woman on the second floor to stick her head out, the one whose nerves are all shot, poor thing."

"And what did she say?"

"That if she didn't leave right away she'd call the police. She really would, you know. She wouldn't think twice. Last summer she said the people in the restaurant were making too much noise, and she called the cops right away, I swear. When the police car showed up, my husband almost had a heart attack, he was so angry."

"Did this woman on the second floor say she'd seen professor Marcadori?"

The woman in the apron shook her finger no. "Even Sister Luciana has already been and gone today. She comes and cleans every morning. She said his bed is still made up. He didn't come home last night, that's for sure."

"And you haven't seen him either?"

"Who, me?" she asked, as if I was trying to get her involved in some dirty business.

"Yes, you."

"No, darling," said the apron woman. "I haven't seen a thing. Not yesterday, not today, and not tomorrow either."

It occurred to me that it would be very difficult to get any more information out of her. I said goodbye and left.

Then, just as I was about to turn the corner of the little street, I caught a glimpse of movement out of the corner of my eye: the rapid movement of a shadow in the light. I turned my head and saw a guy with a shaved head and a tan-colored jacket looking straight at me, and then looking away an instant later. This eye movement disconcerted me as much as the fact that a moment earlier there'd been no one there. The apron woman had already gone back into her trattoria, the street was deserted except for a white and black cat walking slowly along. The bald guy was now talking on his cell phone, he seemed deep in conversation: turning around, gesturing with his hands. I thought that maybe I was being paranoid, or that maybe I was just no longer used to the multiplicity of people and movement in a large city. I turned the corner and walked down an even narrower road, coming out into the paved street crowded with urban tourists in couples and alone and in groups, all moving at different cruising speeds.

I continued toward the little piazza, just a few dozen yards ahead, where I'd lived for four years: I could see the windows of my old apartment. I had a brief flash of a breakfast, a girl's dark looks, an embrace in the bathtub, and the sounds of a summer night. Then I thought about how the girl Mette had disappeared into the fields of the cemetery without explaining anything; of her escape together with the curly-haired guy named Jorge; the abruptness with which Nadine had ended our conversations and took off in the taxi; Jorge's hurriedness as he took off for a second time on his scooter; the alarm in the eyes of the thin woman on the landing outside Dante Marcadori's office. I wondered if there was a common thread running through all these events, or if I was artificially connecting them. I wondered if there were other things I had yet to recognize.

I looked back before turning left at the restaurant on the corner, and among the various people standing still or moving around in the little piazza I saw the bald guy with the tan jacket again. He was unquestionably looking straight at me, but I couldn't tell whether or not this was because I was looking right at him. In any case, once again he moved his eyes away immediately. He looked at his watch, turned his head to look at two girls who might have been American walking past arm-in-arm.

I turned quickly into the alley on the right and stopped further on next to a wall. A few seconds later I saw the bald guy turn left, walking with apparent nonchalance, his eye on the objects lined up on the cloth a phony African craftsman had spread out on the pavement. I followed him, walking quickly and coming out a little behind him in the open space of Piazza Santa Maria. The piazza was filled with tourists and locals seated at little outdoor tables in the pale sunlight, and waiters and dilettante photographers and gypsy jazz musicians and theology students and bums and dogs.

I walked a diagonal line across the piazza, turning around when I reached the southern end. I was sure I'd see the bald guy somewhere to the east, between the newsstand and the pharmacy, but instead he was still standing a dozen yards behind me. We stared at each other for perhaps two seconds, then he turned as if to admire the church façade. The situation was so strange that I experienced a quick whirlwind of feelings, doubt and surprise and formless aggressiveness. The aggressiveness won out, and I headed straight for him.

He stood there, his hands in his jacket pockets. I ended up almost on top of him, but just a few inches before possible body contact, or at least verbal contact, my aggression turned into doubt, and doubt into a sort of compassion. Compassion for the attention he was apparently directing elsewhere and his slightly-too-big-for-him tan jacket, and for his posture, leaning back on his heels. I passed behind him, close enough to smell his department store cologne. I kept walking in a semicircle along the southwestern edge of the piazza. It occurred to me that we were in a well-traveled space, that in all probability we were simply headed in the same direction. I tried to keep track of the distances between myself and other moving people so that I could see whether or not it would seem like they too were following me.

I turned back in a broad circle: the bald guy was still standing there, and still seemed intent on contemplating life in the piazza. I walked through the short street that connected the big piazza with the little piazza, where a boy with a pit bull was playing the guitar terribly and singing in broken English. I forced myself to walk naturally, dissolve the tension in my legs. I came out into the little piazza filled with parked cars, near the fruit and vegetable shop whose owner had come running out many years earlier, shouting like a madman after the Italian national team won a soccer championship. I had a perfectly vivid memory of him running around and jumping up and down, his arms held up straight in the air; the frenetic manner in which he spun the handle to wind up his canvas awning and close the shop so that he could hurry and join the collective celebrations.

Against my own will I turned back again to look. The bald guy was once again ten yards behind me. The thin fog of doubt about whether or not he was following me disappeared in an instant, and a jet of adrenaline shot into my bloodstream.

I dashed back and headed quickly down a side street. But fifty yards later curiosity got the better of adrenalin and I stopped to look behind me. The bald guy was caught running toward me, obtuseness and latent violence and embarrassment mixing together in his eyes and the expression on his face once he saw me unexpectedly standing there, turned toward him. Surprise and inertia prevented him from stopping right away, and he kept running for a moment before he managed to come to a stop. At this point he must have realized that it didn't make sense to pretend anymore: we stared at each other from a few yards away, our attitudes oriented more toward waiting than challenging one another.

I turned back around and started running as fast as I could, swinging my arms and pumping my legs, turning right into a narrow street with a garden wall on one side, the branches of a fig tree extending out over the top. The guy ran after me, his stride energized perhaps by the anger of having been caught. The soles of his shoes went *slackt slackt slackt* on the little square blocks of black paving stone. For a few seconds we maintained the same distance from one another, then I managed to gain a few yards on him. Out of the corner of my eye I could see his pistonlike movements and his labored breathing, his utterly dogmatic determination to catch up with me. I wondered what his precise intentions were: to catch me or stab me or shoot me or ask me something, or perhaps simply not to lose sight of me. I wondered if it wouldn't be better to stop and face him, try to throw him against the wall, talk to him, adopt any strategy that wasn't an attempt at escape.

But I had chosen to be the one who runs away, and I couldn't seem to change: I kept running as fast as I could, riding a wave of self-nurtured reasoning that was truly difficult to stop.

Suddenly I saw a few blue cars parked halfway down the narrow street, drivers standing around them, and a group of people gathered in front of a building. I hit the crowd running flat out. Two girls backed up, expressions of alarm on their faces. A boy said something, others turned around, and a big guy wearing sunglasses and a bodyguard's earpiece stiffened suddenly. I looked back: the bald guy had stopped, gasping, some twenty yards back, his eyes staring into mine. I turned back toward the building, and saw my brother Fabio come out, surrounded by a swarm of photographers and journalists holding microphones and cameramen with cameras and talking, smiling, gesticulating courtiers. We looked at one another from a few steps away, I believe with similar expressions of surprise on both our faces.

"Hey," he said. He gestured to a bodyguard who was about to block me.

"Hey," I said, trying to get my breath back.

"What are you doing here?" asked Fabio.

"Nothing. Just taking a walk." I looked back down the street: the bald guy had disappeared.

The eyes of the excited little crowd around my brother explored the two of us with a blend of curiosity and irritation.

Fabio waved at no one in particular and said, "My brother Lorenzo, the solitary seafarer."

I saw several looks and a pair of cameras converge onto me in a superimposition of questions and observations that I couldn't decipher. I looked back the way I'd come again. There was just an old lady with a cane, much further off.

Fabio moved over to one of the blue cars parked along the wall. The guy with the earpiece and sunglasses created space among the people around him. The driver opened the door. Fabio said, "Go ahead. Get in on the other side."

I walked around the car and got in. A short blond woman with glasses got in immediately after me. I moved into the middle, between her and Fabio. The bodyguard got in up front, and the driver started the car.

The car moved down the little street among the gestures and voices of the little crowd, dampened by the thick windows. Fabio stretched out against the back of the seat and sighed. He asked the blond woman, "How did I do?"

"Great," she said, her voice slightly gravelly.

"Seriously, or just to make me happy?" asked Fabio.

"They were hanging on your words, didn't you see?" she said. "Captivated, mamma mia. You could have done anything you wanted with them." She was wearing little round glasses with clear lenses. Her mouth was small and precise.

Fabio needed more reassurances. "I didn't take things too far, in the beginning?" he asked.

"Just what you needed in order to make your point," said the blonde. "Lower their defenses, get them to expose their throats, right?"

"Then?" asked Fabio.

"Then you went straight as a razor," she said. "A perfect cut. Strong, on target, decisive. One hundred percent efficient. So good it was scary."

"What about the part about the E.U. funds and the ministry?" asked my brother.

"You knocked them out," said the blonde. "You saw their faces, didn't you?"

My brother nodded yes. He was probably going back over his words, the faces he'd been surrounded by. He waved a hand between the blonde and me. "I'm sorry," he said. "Giulia Cerlato, Lorenzo Telmari."

"I figured that much out," she said readily.

I shook her hand. Behind the clear glass lenses, her eyes were utterly devoid of interest in me.

We turned the corner, the big blue car just barely making it through the walls on either side. I leaned toward the window on my right to look out, but the bald guy had disappeared. The only proof left of our chase was my heartbeat, which still hadn't completely returned to normal.

"What are you looking at?" asked Fabio as he punched in the keys on one of his cell phones, responding to a text message he'd just received.

"Nothing," I said. "There was a guy following me." The strange thing was that doubts had come back to hinder my thoughts. I was no longer entirely sure what had really happened.

In any case, my brother was too distracted to hear what I'd said. He asked Giulia, "That guy with the hooked nose, was he Rai Uno or Rai Due?"

"Rai Due," said Giulia without a moment's hesitation. She was focused on Fabio with every nervous fiber and spark of energy in her body. She breathed within his breathing.

Fabio took another cell phone out of his pocket. It was vibrating soundlessly. He looked at the name on the screen without answering. He said, "How come moon-face wasn't there?"

"He's in Capri for the Provenzano award," said Giulia.

"Bummer," said Fabio. "This guy was a little sour, don't you think? The insecure, ambitious type who tries to overdo it, then there's that chicken voice of his . . ."

Giulia shook her head. "No. He's in bed with Rovardi, but they're on our side for this thing." She was wearing a gray wool business suit with a white shirt underneath. She kept her knees stuck together, folding her legs toward the other door so as not to risk brushing up against mine.

We came out into the traffic on the main street. The driver turned on the car's blue flashing police lights and started accelerating, braking suddenly and reaccelerating as he slalomed around the other cars. I wanted to ask my brother if by any chance he'd heard anything about Dante Marcadori recently, but one look at him told me this wasn't the time for questions.

He asked Giulia, "What time are Somaré and Saracco coming?"

"Five minutes ago," she answered, glancing quickly at her watch. "They're already up there waiting for you. Do you want me to check?"

"No, no," said my brother. "God, what a drag." He received another text message; Giulia got one too. They both started punching buttons on their cell phones. I wondered whether or not they were communicating with each other.

When we reached the Tiber I said, "I'll get out here, thanks."

The driver didn't slow down in the least until Fabio said, "Pull over for a minute." Giulia got out in order to let me out, but she clung to my brother's intermittent glances even once we were outside the vehicle.

The bodyguard got out, peering in all directions like he was acting out the instructions from some surveillance manual.

Fabio said, "Where are you going?" But one of his cell phones started ringing. He made a gesture to me that meant, "Later."

Giulia shook my hand almost without squeezing and got back into the car like a fish diving back into water. The bodyguard closed the door and got back into his seat up front.

I stood there in the open air amid the noise of the intersection, watching my brother's blue car move onto a lane restricted to tram cars, his blue lights flashing. Then I walked back along the river toward where I'd parked the pickup. Every so often I turned to see if the bald guy or anyone else was following me, but it didn't seem like it.

I CROSSED THE PIAZZA WITH THE
EGYPTIAN OBELISK IN THE MIDDLE

I crossed the piazza with the Egyptian obelisk in the middle, climbing up the hill above it. I was in a strange state of mind; slow reflective waves in a sea of vagueness animated by sudden flashes of insight. I tried to trace a nautical map of the situation, but there were always some missing coordinates. Finally I let the current of my own footsteps lead me aimlessly through the afternoon, occasionally checking behind and on either side of me.

I walked through the gardens, lost in thought. I knew the distances between one point and another perfectly well, but when I tried to calculate travel times I was overcome by memories of dozens of trips taken in straight and curved lines, accelerating in furious rushes or interrupted by stops that could have lasted forever.

I crossed the asphalted bridge where a few girls and boys were running roller-skate slalom courses around soda boxes, taking sidelong glances just to make sure they were being observed. A boom box on the ground was broadcasting '80s music, all synthesizers and electric drums and falsetto voices. It wasn't a game: none of them were laughing or joking or having fun in any way. They skated back and forth, their jeans cut up and the elastic waistbands of their underpants showing. Their hair was dyed blond and their eyebrows had been brutally plucked and they had fake tans, as if it were all some very marginal and repetitive part of the world of entertainment.

I walked through the wet, humid penumbra beneath the Holm oaks, the shadows populated by a few amorous couples and pensioners and tired, half-lost tourist families. I came out into the open space of the little piazza among mothers with children nearby and a merry-go-round and couples kissing or taking pictures or admiring the cityscape from behind the stone balusters. I went over to take a look too: I stared down into the piazza with the Egyptian obelisk from which I'd come, then at the stretch of roofs and cupolas and terraces and streets and cars that extended as far as the eye could reach into the yellow light veiled with the smoke of exhaust pipes and water heaters.

My cell phone started vibrating and ringing from within my jacket's inside pocket. It took me a few moments to identify it amid the widespread vibrations coming up from the city. The words "private number" were written on the screen, but I answered all the same.

A foreign-accented girl's voice asked, "Lorenzo Telmari?"

"Yes, and who are you?" I said, even though I'd already recognized her.

"Mette," she answered. "Where are you?" There was the noise of background traffic on her end.

I told her where I was.

"Then we'll meet on the steps in Piazza di Spagna in ten minutes," she said.

There were a lot of things I wanted to ask her, but she had already hung up.

I waited at the top of that striking set of stairs among the little trucks driven by the men who sell drinks and sandwiches, and tourists catching their breaths and studying their maps and observing other tourists spread out along the long cascade of clear steps and in the piazza with its palm trees and horse carriages and the swarming streets just beyond. I tried to discern, among the many moving and still figures, the girl Mette the way I remembered her, but the field of observation was too vast and in constant evolution. Furthermore, I didn't know what direction she'd come from, so I kept moving my eyes around from one point to the next.

I went halfway down the stairs, evaluating faces and postures and looks and gestures and voices. Suddenly, further down on the right, I saw the brightly colored jacket and the honey-red hair I knew so well. I caught up with her in just a few steps and said, "Hey."

Mette gave a little start; to me her face seemed at once unknown and as familiar as her expressions.

I tried to decide how to handle myself with her, but it was too late. I said "So, what's up?" with a totally hybrid inflection.

She made a nervous gesture toward Via Condotti, which ran perpendicular to the piazza, saying "Let's take a walk."

We went down the stairs, walking silently in the two-way river of pedestrians and onlookers, past windows crammed with lights and clothes and shoes and handbags and jewelry. We didn't look at each other except peripherally, but we kept an eye on the movements around us.

At a certain point Mette said, "Why did you go attack Jorge, this morning?"

"I didn't attack him," I responded. "I just didn't want him to escape again, and I wanted him to explain what's going on."

She took a black wool beret out of her pocket and put it on. "It's not that simple," she said.

"That much I've figured out." I was embarrassed. My tone of voice seemed stupid, my movements rigid.

Mette lifted her eyes to me as if for one last quick evaluation. Her lips spread out for a moment in a slight smile.

I said, "I want to understand the *whole* thing. For example, why was a total stranger following me around the Trastevere today? That has never happened to me before, as strange as that may seem to you."

She stopped walking. Her eyes were a darker blue than they'd seemed before, and contained other colors. "When?" she said. Dozens of pedestrian-onlookers walked past us, dragged along by the current: faces and coats and furs and jackets and berets and hair and cell phones and mouths and eyes, eyes, eyes.

"An hour and a half ago, more or less."

"Are you sure?"

"Yes I'm sure. He followed me for twenty minutes."

The river of people behind us knocked into us and pushed at us; Mette started walking again. "What did he look like?" she asked.

"Bald. He was wearing a tan jacket."

She appeared extremely alarmed. "What did you do?" she asked.

"I tried to lose him. But it wasn't easy. Then I started running."

"What did he do?"

"He ran after me. Then I ran into my brother and some other people, and when I turned around to look up the street he'd disappeared."

We had reached the intersection with Via del Corso, where the two-way river of people that we were part of flowed into an even greater two-way river of other people. Mette tucked her arm under mine with a quick gesture. We crossed the street and headed into a little side street that curved away to the left.

It was a strange feeling to walk so close to her, to feel the interior rhythm of her footsteps: I liked it, and at the same time I realized I didn't know a thing about her or her intentions. "Would you please be so kind as to explain something to me?" I asked. "For example, what the hell were you looking for in my father's apartment? And is there a connection between the thing you're looking for and the fact that I was followed through the streets of Trastevere? Or am I asking for too much?"

She nodded yes. Her blend of shyness and decisiveness seemed to correspond to the line of her forehead and nose. She looked around and said, "I asked you if you knew who Ndionge was, okay?"

"Okay," I said, leaning slightly into her in order to hear her more clearly in the general chaos.

She pushed her hip into me in order to steer me into the paved street on the left. "He was a cardinal from Senegal," she said.

"Why do you say 'was'?"

"He's dead," said Mette. "AIDS."

"Ah."

"Yes."

"And how did he get AIDS? A blood transfusion?"

"No."

"Ah," I said again.

"Of course," said Mette, "the Vatican tried to cover everything up. They invited him to Rome and locked him up in one of their clinics once he started really suffering. The official version is that he died of pneumonia."

"Right," I said. "I imagine they're not very keen on letting people know they've got a cardinal who died of AIDS."

"No. But that's not the only truth being covered up."

"Why? What other truths are there?"

Mette pulled me even closer and said, "When Ndionge found out he was sick, he had a terrible moral crisis, and he wrote a fiery memorial against the Catholic Church's policy on contraception and its refusal to deal honestly with the AIDS question and the issue of overpopulation."

"Really?" I was equally captivated by her words and their sound in my right ear.

"Yes," she said. "The document was written in total sincerity and passion, and demonstrates in no uncertain terms how criminal it is to preach doggedly against the use of condoms while at the same time standing by and watching as in the space of twenty-five years we've moved from a few dozen cases of AIDS to *forty-eight million* HIV-positive patients and AIDS victims around the world, only a million of whom have access to cures. And *three million* die each year, half a million of whom are *children*."

"I know," I said. "It's monstrous."

"And it says these things not from the outside, across a thousand distances and filters, but from the inside, you understand? At the heart of the issue, from inside a hell in which the number of infected people is increasing at a rate of *five million* every year!"

"Yes," I said. The passion in her voice was being communicated to me like an electric current running underneath my skin.

"But the document doesn't just address AIDS," continued Mette. "Or the dozens of millions of people who die each year from hunger. It talks about U.S. and U.N. policies, the reasons behind the total refusal of states and international organizations to control population growth. It talks about how the very concepts of growth and development that dominate the global economy and world politics are wrong right at the core."

I nodded yes, because I couldn't find words enough to tell her how much I agreed.

She said, "And the fact that all this was written by a Catholic cardinal gives the document enormous significance. A man who had always kept himself in line with the rules of Vatican hierarchy, even though he knew just how frightening the consequences were."

"Of course. And you guys have a copy of this document?"

"No."

"Then how do you know this stuff?"

"We have our own 'sources'," she said with the same mysterious expression she'd worn when she came to talk to me in the cemetery.

"But in this specific case, who was your source?"

She looked at a tall man who was leaning up against a wall, talking on a cell phone, then a lady in a fur coat who pushed her way past us to look at a store window. "Ndionge's assistant," she said. "Maurice. He was a friend of ours. We were part of the same campaign to fight destruction of the South African Bushmen's native areas."

"Why do you keep saying 'was'? He's no longer a friend?"

"He's dead too."

"From AIDS?"

"No. Run over by a truck. In Senegal."

I looked at her closely in the hot lights of a stationery store window. There was the strangest contrast between the clarity of her looks and the relative anxiety of the things she was saying.

Mette said, "He was the one who typed Ndionge's memorial."

"Typed?"

"Yes. They didn't have a computer. He typed it by hand using carbon paper, so that he'd have a copy."

"And he told you what was written in it?"

"Yes," said Mette. "It wasn't a secret document. It was written for all the inhabitants of planet Earth. We had plans to meet Maurice in October and discuss how to get it read by as many people as possible."

"But instead he died too."

"He was standing on the side of a road, waiting for a bus that would take him back to his parents' village, when a speeding truck hit him full on. Then the driver ran away. It happened a week before they brought Ndionge to Rome. It was terrible for all of us, he was a very dear friend."

"What happened to the memorial? Did the Vatican make it disappear?"

She shook her head. "When they went to get Ndionge and bring him here and lock him up in the clinic, they got their hands on his papers, but the two typewritten copies were no longer there."

"Where were they?"

"At your father's house," said Mette.

We had stopped in front of a shop window full of men's shirts. At the corner on the other side of the street there was a guy playing music by Paisiello on the violin. I looked at Mette from just a few inches away, amid the rustling and murmuring of the pedestrian-onlookers moving around us, and meanwhile a part of my brain was busy making its own connections between the apparently inexplicable events of the past few days.

"Why my father?" I asked.

"Your father and Ndionge met at an international convention in Rotterdam a few years ago," said Mette. "When Ndionge found out he was sick, he got back in touch with him, and they started writing each other and talking on the phone while Ndionge was writing his memorial. He thought that a famous epidemiologist like Teo Telmari, somebody who was respected all over the world, might help him broadcast the message in the best way possible, adding all the scientific support and documentation needed."

"Couldn't you have told me all this sooner?"

"We tried. But it wasn't easy. Your father refused to have anything to do with us, and we didn't know whose side you were on."

The violinist on the corner hit a wrong note, and to make up for it sped up the rhythm. Daylight was disappearing at the same speed. "With you guys," I said. "Isn't that obvious?"

"What's supposed to make it obvious?"

"My nice face? Come on. You know, otherwise you wouldn't be telling me all this stuff, right?"

She stared at me through my reflection in the window, stirring up a sort of interior excitement in me. She said, "Then help us get the memorial back from your father's."

"Are you sure the two copies are still in my father's house?"

"No. But we hope so. If your father didn't give them to anyone, then they're still there."

"Of course. And then what do you think you'll do with them?"

She took my arm in hers once again. We turned the corner and took another paved street on the right. She said, "Publish it every way we can. Organize a press conference, publish it on the web, print it, send it around the world just as Ndionge would have. If we pull it off, it could have an enormous impact, maybe really change things. It's one of those incredibly rare opportunities."

There were fewer windows and pedestrians and light to see by on this street, increasing her body heat and presence and breathing and the smell of her wildflower perfume for me. I said, "Then let's go look for them right now. I parked my pickup just ten minutes from here."

Mette looked at me. She had a serious, ready-for-action expression on her face.

A moment later I remembered Fabio and said, "After Jorge snuck in there, my brother had them put a guy outside to keep an eye on who goes in and out. They thought he was a thief."

Mette slowed down. Her almost childlike profile made the situation we'd gotten into together appear even more worrisome. She said, "It'll be better if we go tonight."

"What time?"

"At eleven. We'll meet at the bridge in front of your father's building." She disentwined her arm from mine and moved away quickly, provoking a strange, immediate sensation of loss, abandonment.

There was a scooter waiting in a shadowy stretch of the street. When it moved into the light of a streetlamp, I saw Jorge was driving. He said something to Mette and raised his hand to me in an embarrassed salute. Mette got on the scooter behind him and turned around to wave as the scooter disappeared into the falling dark of the November evening.

I ATE IN THE KITCHEN
WITH HARRY AND EMILY

I ate in the kitchen with Harry and Emily: steamed rice, zucchini and shrimp with flat focaccia bread. We talked about the places I knew in the Philippines, getting stuck on an attempt to reconstruct different itineraries. Fabio and Nicoletta and Tommaso were at the inauguration of an art exhibition: we saw it captured for a moment on television, which was turned on with the sound as low as it could go.

Then we watched a report on the avian virus that was threatening to spread toward Europe from Asia. The narrator's voice described the situation in terms of rising panic, showing images of white-coated men chasing ducks and geese, grabbing them by their wings and stuffing them into plastic bags. In other images the plastic bags were being tossed into freshly dug trenches, still bouncing and flopping with life while somebody submerged them under shovelfuls of lime. Immediately following this a doctor appeared, explaining that while there was no vaccine available as yet, everything remained under control. Then the health minister appeared and with a dazed expression explained that the government had already set aside funds to purchase thirty million doses of the vaccine, and that there was absolutely nothing to be worried about. Then the studio anchorman reappeared, listed a series of even more alarming facts, and concluded by saying that there was absolutely no reason to be alarmed.

I kept thinking about Mette's profile and her words as we walked along the paved streets in the center of Rome; her wildflower perfume, her way of holding onto my arm. Every once in a while I checked my watch, impatience rising.

Fabio and Nicoletta and Tommaso came back, spreading their tension throughout the apartment. Tommaso slipped wordlessly into his room, Nicoletta stuck her head in and said, "How's it going?" with a strained smile, then called Emily out into the hallway.

Fabio came in, had Harry pour him a glass of grapefruit juice, and said, "Well?"

"Well?" I answered, with whatever meaning we were supposed to be giving the word.

"The two of us never have time to talk about anything," he said.

"That's true," I said, even though it seemed like a total cliché.

"Let's go in there," he said.

We went into the living room. I sat down in the armchair and he sat on the sofa in front of the big TV screen. I think we both thought about the many things we could talk about, but we were both preoccupied with our own thoughts. Fabio fooled around with the remote, checking if there was anything about him on. I told him that we'd seen him on TV. He nodded yes, and then started reading and sending text messages with one of his cell phones. I looked at my watch again: it was twenty minutes after ten. My heartbeat increased intermittently.

Fabio put his cell phone back in his pocket, glanced at me and said, "Is everything okay?"

"Everything's fine."

"You didn't seem very calm today," he said. On the plasma screen, two people in the background pretended to fight animatedly while a professional instigator looked on.

"No?" I was surprised he'd paid attention.

"You seemed all worked up." He pushed another button on the remote: an image of a government politician appeared. The politician let a television buffoon hit him in the face with a cream pie, then took immediate vengeance by kicking the buffoon in the ass.

"That's possible," I said. "Seeing as how I had just been followed halfway across Trastevere."

Fabio turned back toward me again. I saw the muscles in his jaw contract. He said, "By who?"

"By a bald guy in a tan jacket. I tried to tell you when we ran into each other, but you weren't really listening."

He had turned off the television and was staring at me.

I said, "And I know why he was following me. I found out this afternoon."

"What did you find out?"

"That among his papers, dad had a memorial written by a Senegalese cardinal who died of AIDS."

"I know," said Fabio, quickly.

"And how do you know?" I asked. I had the feeling I was always a step behind the facts.

Fabio got up from the couch. "It might not all be clear to you," he said, "but this is a story with very serious implications, Lorenzo."

"Actually, it's crystal clear. Don't you think that means you should have told me about it?"

"I didn't want to get you involved," he said.

"Excuse me, but what do you mean by that? It seems like I'm every bit as involved as you are."

"Then let's just say I was more aware of all the implications, okay?"

"Why is that?"

"Because of my job. Because of my role, okay?"

"Therefore?" I demanded, a subtle sense of alarm mixing with my impatience.

"I received certain signals from certain spheres, and I acted as a consequence."

"What's that supposed to mean? Could you please stop speaking in code?"

He gestured for me to lower my voice. He said, "I turned the memorial over, in the interests of everyone involved."

"When? To whom?" I said, stifling an impulse to grab him by his jacket and shake him.

"This evening. To the person who asked for it."

"Who asked you for it? Who?"

"Don't shout," said Fabio. He opened the glass doors and went out onto the terrace.

I followed him outside, into the stale terrace lights. I said, "The guys from the Vatican, right? They're the ones, aren't they?"

Fabio gestured for me to be quiet. He turned toward the living room, toward the courtyard, then back to me. He said, "Listen, they had every right to want it. He was one of their cardinals. It's an internal affair."

"It's not an internal affair at all! It's the *whole world's* affair! Ndionge wrote that memorial because he wanted everybody to read it!"

"Don't shout!" said Fabio again in a throaty voice. "And besides, what do you know about it? Did you read the memorial?"

"No, but they told me about it."

"Who? It wasn't your friends from Stopwatch by any chance, was it? The ones who went into dad's house to try and steal it?"

"What do you know about Stopwatch?"

He smiled a tiny smile. "You're not much of a conspirer, Lorenzo. You were seen."

"By who?" I said, as I tried to rewind the mental tape of my movements over the past few days.

"Let's just say by the same people who asked me for the memorial."

"The people from Stopwatch didn't want to steal it. They just wanted to keep it safe."

"I'm sorry," said Fabio, "but sneaking into someone else's house in order to take something is definitely what I'd call stealing."

"That's exactly what you did!" I said. "You're the thief! And an opportunistic coward to boot!"

"I went into my father's home. And what I took was part of my own legal and moral inheritance."

"He was *my* father too, I believe! You didn't have any right to do that without telling me about it!"

Fabio put his hands in his pocket and came closer, balanced on his ankles in order to make up for the fact that he was an inch shorter than me. He said, "I did what I had to do. The only thing I *could* do, Lorenzo."

"But *why?*"

He shook his head slowly and said, "Do you really think it's a good idea for a politician with nonextremist aspirations to go against the Catholic Church, in this country of all places?"

"Ndionge was Catholic too," I said. "In fact he was a cardinal. His memorial speaks out against the mistaken policies established by the leaders of the Catholic Church and other world powers, not against all Catholics! It also talks about the president of the United States, and about the U.N.!"

Fabio made a motion with his hand like the windshield wiper of a car and said, "Oh yeah? Will you please tell me how your mind works, Lorenzo? Do you still have a few zones of permanent immaturity that keep you from understanding how the world works?"

"What about you? What have you become? Thanks to your pathological search for universal consensus?"

"It's incredible how infantile you can be."

"It's incredible how cynical you can be."

He said, "If a document like that went public it would have a devastating effect! How can you possibly not see that?"

"I can see that it would finally open up a real debate."

"Come down from Mars, Lorenzo! What debate? A cardinal who confesses he's got AIDS, and then writes page after page saying that the Vatican's policies on contraception are 'a tragic error rendered monstrous crime by perseverance,' and that 'rather than leading their flocks to salvation, the shepherds are leading them to the slaughterhouse like butchers'! Those are his actual words!"

"So you did read it."

He wasn't listening. He said, "The Catholic Church would be inestimably damaged!"

"Or maybe it would have to reconsider some of its choices! Abandon its frightening dogma and hypocrisy!"

"Wake up, Lorenzo!" said Fabio. "Stop always putting yourself on the wrong side in the name of God-knows-what abstract principles!"

"It's not an abstract principle! It's a question of not bogging down yet again the one question that contains all the others!"

"And what's that supposed to be?"

"The spread of our species above and beyond every tolerable limit! The definitive destruction of any equilibrium between us and the planet we live on!"

"It's an adaptable planet," said my brother with a small, ironic and defensive smile. "It has survived plenty, and for millions of years. Meteors, glacial eras, and lots more."

"But there's a limit to adaptability! More than half the human beings on the planet already live in unacceptable conditions, and over the next twenty years another *two billion* will be born! Dozens of millions of them will die of AIDS, and dozens of millions of hunger! All the other animal and vegetable species will be irreversibly destroyed! And this amid the total silence of those who could do something about it and instead don't say a word!"

"Maybe you've been playing vagabond and hermit for a little too long, Lorenzo. If you'd done your homework you'd know that there's plenty of talk about the future of the world."

"Who's doing the talking? Oil magnates? The heads of multinationals making weapons and tobacco and powdered milk and who are in desperate need of expanding markets?"

"Politics, Lorenzo. Politics deals with it. And politics tries to provide answers, rather than engaging in useless alarmism."

"Oh, yeah? What kind of answers?"

"Reducing the earnings gap, wiping out debt, targeting assistance, accessing the tools of progress."

"Which don't include population control, right?"

He wasn't listening to me. He said, "Modern agriculture has managed to *quadruple* yields per hectare in the space of just a few decades. If there was an equal distribution of resources, each inhabitant of planet earth would have all the food he needs."

"And just how are you going to achieve equal distribution? Are you going to take half Tommaso's damn snacks away and send them to Africa?"

"What's Tommaso got to do with this?"

"The resources your son consumes are enough to provide a decent life for a few dozen people in another part of the world.

And your parliamentary salary could support *thousands*! But would the two of you be willing to give up even half of what you have? A third? A quarter?"

"What's this got to do with anything? I have an important job, serving people! Working for others! Go read the law proposal I signed together with Langonetti, the one that dedicates one point seven percent of our GDP to developing countries! Read that before you come at me with your fucking demagogy!"

"But the point is that no matter what help you create it won't accomplish anything if humans keep multiplying exponentially in the meantime! You can send all the sacks of rice and bottled mineral water you want, but it will never be enough! And how much more do you think you can increase agricultural yield over the next few years? Enough so that you can feed two thousand million more mouths?"

"It's better than doing nothing, don't you think?" said Fabio.

"Of course it's better! But it doesn't deal with even the smallest part of the problem, unless we try at the same time—using all the energies and means available to us—to stop population increase!"

"Oh, it will stop, sooner or later. That's what all the demographers say, that at a certain point the line will stop rising, and slowly but surely become horizontal."

"And what will our world have been reduced to, by that point? Seeing as how it can't expand beyond its physical limits in space?"

"You're so apocalyptic," said my brother. "Mamma mia. Are you listening to yourself?"

As intolerably arrogant and detestable as I thought he was, he provoked the same blend of anger and pity in me as he had when we were children and he would get stuck on the wrong side of an argument, stuck with too little information and too little mental elasticity to make his way out.

Nicoletta appeared in the living room after one of her disconcerting metamorphoses: she was smiling happily and in a vaguely seductive way, and said, "And just what are the two brothers discussing so heatedly?"

"Nothing," said Fabio.

"Aren't you boys cold?" she asked.

"Yes, in fact," said Fabio.

"Yes," I said.

We went back into the living room. Nicoletta had the air of someone who's expecting some stimulating three-way conversation, but Fabio turned the television back on. I looked at my watch.

"I have to go," I said.

"Where?" asked Nicoletta with a look of infinitely inappropriate malice.

"To see some friends," I said. I went to get my jacket, waved from the hallway and went quickly to the front door.

I GOT IN MY PICKUP

I got in my pickup. It was already almost eleven, and my sense of hurry made me move in leaps and jerks. I dropped the keys on the floor, and at the same time the cell phone started vibrating inside the inner jacket pocket. I took it out with nervous hands, raising it to my ear while I tried with my left hand to reach the keys. I was almost certain I'd hear Mette's voice.

Instead it was another woman, her voice cracking with tension. "Lorenzo?" she said.

"Yes?" I looked at my brother's night guards' patrol car parked next to the main door of his apartment building, some thirty yards away.

"Tell your bastard brother I said thanks a lot," said the voice.

A guy got out of the patrol car, looking in my direction.

I managed to grab the keys, and in the same moment recognized the voice on the cell phone. "Nadine?" I said. "What are you talking about?"

The cop was walking toward me slowly, his machine gun in the crook of one arm. A second guy got out of the car. He was armed too.

"They destroyed my house," said Nadine. She seemed on the verge of crying.

"Your house?" I said. I had a series of impulses to move in various directions all at once. I slid the key into the ignition and turned. The old diesel motor started up.

"Yes, my house!" said Nadine. She seemed as furious as she was scared. "Tell that bastard I really thank him a lot!"

The guy with the machine gun was now just a few yards away, saying something that was covered by the sound of the engine. The second guy had caught up with him in the middle of the street, and was gesturing at me frantically with his free hand.

"Did you call the police?" I asked Nadine.

"No," she said. "What good would that do?"

"Give me your address," I said. "Hurry."

"Turn off your engine and step out of the car!" shouted the second armed officer over the growling diesel motor, waving his machine gun.

Nadine gave me her address, her voice rendered even more unstable by the sounds she could hear through my cell phone.

"Put down that fucking cell phone and get out of the car!" shouted the first armed guy. His small, dark eyes were bright with alarm. He had a goatee that seemed drawn onto his long chin with charcoal.

I hung up the phone and put the truck in first gear, turning the wheel.

The second armed guy jumped to the right and knocked the barrel of his machine gun on the window. He shouted, "Stop right there! For fuck's sake!"

I rolled down the window on the left and said to the first armed guy, "I'm in a hurry, I've gotta go."

He stared right at me, his lip curling to reveal sharp teeth, his body in the grip of a muscular tension that made him vibrate all over. He shouted, "Goddamn it! Get out of the car!" with even more emphasis than his colleague. His right hand flexed around the trigger in a disturbing manner.

It occurred to me that winding up murdered by my brother's guards would be a pretty paradoxical way to go, but in the end also appropriate given the circumstances. I turned off the engine and opened the door, getting out very, very carefully.

One of the two armed guards grabbed me by the arm and pushed me as forcefully as he could against the side of the pickup. The other one patted down my chest and sides and back and legs with his free hand. They said, "What the fuck are you doing here? Where the fuck did you come from? What the fuck were you looking at, huh? Who the fuck were you talking to? Where the fuck were you trying to go?" They were both trembling with tension, shouting and pushing me against the side of the pickup, breathing all over me and hopping back and forth and looking this way and that, clasping their black, short-barreled machine guns, the metal shining beneath the streetlights.

I said, "I came out of my brother's house three minutes ago. My brother is Fabio Telmari."

They backed up a little, almost imperceptibly. One of the two said, "Show us some identification. Take it out slowly."

I slipped my wallet out of a pocket, struggling against the pressure of the hand pushing me against the side of the pickup and the desire to hurry that was coursing through my legs.

He took out my identification card and examined it closely, then showed it to the other guy: the tension drained out of their expressions and their muscles in the space of a couple of seconds, abandoning them to a bottomless sense of disappointment and boredom and discomfort. The first one gave my wallet and identification back to me, saying "Here, take this."

The other one said, "Sorry, but it's our job."

"I'm sure you understand," said the first guy, struggling mightily to put a half-smile on his face.

"Of course, of course," I said, struggling in my own right not to start kicking them for the precious time they'd wasted. I got back into the pickup and started the engine, driving away as fast as I could toward my father's old apartment.

I parked on the southwestern edge of the little piazza, then got out and walked quickly along the banks of the Tiber. There was nobody by the bridge, nor further on. I looked at my watch: it was twenty-four minutes after eleven. Mette had undoubtedly left after having waited for me. I didn't know where I could find her. Now I had to go to Nadine's and see what had happened. I looked around anxiously among the patches of light from streetlamps and shadows of trees and bushes and shrubs. I was trying to figure out if the man my brother had sent was still keeping an eye on the entrance to our father's old apartment building, but I was too far away and there were too many parked cars to tell. Periodically waves of traffic came racing up the big street, driving clouds of cold, humid air through the night.

I felt pressure on my shoulder and whipped around: there was a compact, elastic figure wearing a black wool beret, a short black down jacket and black jeans. It took me a fraction of a second to recognize this new commando version of Mette.

"Hey," I said softly.

"You're late," she said. Her face looked even clearer than before, contrasting with the black of her clothing.

I took her by one arm and dragged her across the street, into the densest shadows of a small garden. We stood still there for a few seconds, catching our breath. I said softly, "There's no point in going up. The memorial isn't there anymore."

"What do you mean it's not there?" she said, close enough that I could feel the warmth of her breath.

"My brother gave those copies to the Vatican."

"Why?"

"He's a politician. I'm sorry." I kept watching the edges of the little piazza in order to try and make out possible figures standing still or moving around the outskirts, but my sensorial centers were overloaded, the information they provided untrustworthy.

Mette moved a little and said, "Jorge." There was more movement and some rustling in the shadows, then I saw Jorge's face in a shaft of light. He came up close to us, breathing heavily.

His arrival made me feel a strange sense of intrusion through the hurry and anxiety already coursing through my blood, tightening my muscles. "Let's get out of here," I said, moving toward my pickup.

"What about the memorial?" asked Jorge.

"It's not there anymore," I said, annoyed. I didn't turn around.

"His brother took it," said Mette.

They followed me silently, putting into practice methods they must have perfected on other occasions. But all the same it seemed to me that we were too exposed to all the edges of the little piazza. I said, "Nadine called me a little while ago. She's my father's ex-assistant. They tore her house apart."

"Looking for the memorial," said Mette instantly.

"Maybe," I said. "She knew more or less everything my father did."

"It was them," said Jorge.

We left the shadows of the little garden, coming out into the open street bathed in streetlight. I pointed to my pickup parked by the curb and said, "Are you coming with me?"

"But the police will be there," said Mette.

"We can't come, not if the police are there," said Jorge.

"Nadine didn't call them," I said. "She doesn't trust them, and thinks it wouldn't do any good, anyway."

They exchanged glances. Mette said, "Okay."

"The scooter," said Jorge, gesturing toward the next corner.

I pointed to Mette. "She can ride with me, you follow us."

There was another rapid exchange of looks between them, then Mette followed me to the pickup and Jorge ran around the corner.

I opened the passenger door for her. She leapt agilely into the cab and put on her seatbelt. Inside the cab her faint perfume and breathing and interior rhythms and thoughts created an aura around her, sending out an irregular electricity to me as I started up the vehicle.

I drove through the sparse nighttime traffic, looking over at her intermittently. The fact that she was sitting just a couple of inches to my right had a surprising, almost miraculous quality. It made me want to change directions and run away with her toward the Apennines or somewhere else, abandon the whole memorial affair and all its obvious and as-yet-hidden implications. It occurred to me that in reality I hardly knew her at all, that we hadn't exchanged any words or gestures that weren't connected with external issues, except perhaps for when she'd taken my arm while we were walking around downtown, or the fact that our bodies had almost touched in the shadows of the little garden just a few minutes ago. I wondered if my feelings were a result of my having lived alone for too long, if perhaps my brother was right when he spoke of perennial immaturity. These were just fragmentary thoughts, in the background with respect to the fact that she was by my side as I drove as quickly as I could along semideserted streets.

Jorge kept up with us easily on his scooter, pulling up on Mette's side at stoplights, nodding to her or waving his hand. Each time I hoped he might lose us and get left behind, but that didn't happen.

"Have you two known each other for a long time?" I asked Mette.

"For a little while," she said. "Ever since we did some work together in the Amazon, three years ago."

"Are there a lot of you?" I asked.

"You mean in Stopwatch?"

"Yes."

"No, there aren't a lot of us."

"How do you get by? How do you pay for things, move around, do the things you do?"

"We get by. We do the jobs that come our way, depending on where we are. Occasionally somebody sends us some money, or makes a donation, but it doesn't happen very often. Most of all we just make do with very little."

"Where do you and Jorge live, here in Rome?"

"At a friend's house, somebody who's in Peru right now," she said.

In reality, I wanted to ask her what kind of relationship she had with Jorge, but I couldn't manage to formulate the question in a way that sounded natural. Instead I broadly summed up the fight I'd had with my brother, his justifications for having turned over the memorial, the religious policy scenarios he'd mentioned to me.

Mette held onto the handle on the ceiling of the cab, looking straight ahead as if she didn't entirely trust my driving, checking to make sure Jorge was following us, only turning occasionally to look at me.

Whenever she did, I felt a little jolt of awareness flow out into my every gesture and expression until I was practically paralyzed: I ground the clutch whenever I shifted gears, and on one curve I struck the curb with one wheel.

"Hey!" protested Mette. Then she laughed, clinging to the handle with the same ready-for-anything naturalness that she might have had at sea in stormy weather, or on a cargo plane flying over the jungle.

It was the first time I'd ever seen her laugh. I laughed too and almost ran into a parked car, making the pickup swerve back and forth with a quick double-brake.

"Be careful!" she said, half alarmed and half entertained.

"I'm sorry, I'm sorry," I said. Most of all I was trying to find balance between nonchalance and control in the way I handled the steering wheel. I had an impulse to touch her shoulder or give her a little shove, but I had no idea how she might interpret the gesture, so I gave up on it. I would have liked to drive for hours with her nearby, sitting there in the noisy cab where every tiny movement we made was amplified all out of proportion.

But a moment later we'd already reached Nadine's house. I pulled up to the curb and turned off the engine. We got out.

Jorge was a couple of yards behind us, sitting on his scooter. He exchanged a few more glances with Mette.

"It's here," I said, pointing to the big door displaying the number Nadine had given me on the phone.

NADINE WAS SITTING ON
THE ARM OF A GREEN COUCH

Nadine was sitting on the arm of a green couch, holding a glass in one hand. I caught a glimpse of her through the half-closed, partially unhinged door. I knocked on the wood and said, "Can I come in?"

A thin, tall guy with gray hair cut close to his temples blocked the entrance, staring at Mette, Jorge, and me with a hostile expression.

"They're friends of mine," I said.

He flexed the muscles in his face even further, as if to say that this meant next to nothing since I was no friend of his. But then he turned to Nadine and she nodded. He let us in.

The floor in the little living room was covered with papers and photographs and CDs out of their cases and envelopes and newspaper cutouts and notebooks and books and pencils and pens and every other kind of object you might find on a desk or bookshelf. Entire drawers had been overturned, a chair lay on one side, an armchair was upside down. Even the paintings had been ripped away or removed, revealing clearer squares of wall.

Nadine got up, the glass of what might have been cognac in one hand. Her face was long and pale, her nostrils bright pink. The stylish design of her glasses and the masculine cut of her hair communicated a specifically urban sense of vulnerability to me. She looked at Mette and Jorge, alarmed.

"They're with me," I said.

She took a sip from her glass, her eyes closed.

"When did it happen?" I asked.

"I found it like this at ten thirty," she said without looking at me. "When I got back from the movies."

"What did they take?"

She made a vague gesture. "Just a bag I kept under the bed, with some necklaces and a few other things."

I looked toward one of the rooms. There the floor was covered with the overturned, mixed-up fragments of her formerly private life.

"They went through everything," said Nadine. "Everything."

I knelt down to pick up a carved, painted wooden fish that my father had probably given her as a gift. Already a moment later I had no idea where to put it. Behind me, Mette had taken off the black beret and was shaking her hair. Jorge was still standing by the door, his hands in his vest pockets.

Nadine sniffed in through her nose. "Your brother will be satisfied," she said.

"I don't think it was his fault."

She wasn't listening to me. "His friends in the Vatican will thank him," she said. "They'll pay him back with their precious support, no doubt."

Mette looked at me as if she'd suddenly discovered she was friends with the brother of a monster.

I said, "It wouldn't take Fabio to know that you were our father's assistant. That information was public."

Nadine said, "He always hated me. He'd do anything to destroy me."

"But not *this*," I said, both for my brother and for Mette.

"Oh, no?" said Nadine. She seemed on the verge of crying again. "If I'd been at home and they had murdered me, he'd be happier now."

Her friend fixed me with an accusatory stare. I was feeling increasingly uncomfortable.

"What happened to the second copy of Ndionge's memorial?" asked Jorge from behind me.

"Was it here?" asked Mette.

Nadine raised her head as if shocked and turned to me. "What do they know about it? Who are they?"

I said, "They're with Stopwatch. They were the ones who told me the whole story."

Mette said, "We had been trying to get in touch with professor Telmari for months. I'm Mette Dalgaard."

"What are you doing here?" said Nadine. "What do you want?"

"We've spoken on the phone a few times, you and I," said Mette. "I wrote you three letters and I don't know how many emails. But there was never any way we could speak with professor Telmari."

Nadine brushed a few papers and envelopes off the couch and sat down. She took another sip of cognac or whatever it was. "Teo didn't want something this important and delicate to be handled the wrong way," she said.

"Or maybe he wanted to keep the memorial locked up in a drawer forever," said Jorge.

Nadine turned red and said, "Teo was the first person to grasp how important the memorial was! And he was Ndionge's friend. He promised to help him spread it all over the world!"

"Then why didn't he want us to help spread it?" demanded Mette.

"Because he wanted it done right!" said Nadine. "In the right context, with the right balance, with the indispensable corollary of scientific fact, verified and verifiable!"

"So that the whole thing would be watered-down?" said Jorge. "Taking away any and all shock effect?"

"Exactly the opposite!" said Nadine. "So that it would have the greatest possible effect and become the focus of everyone's attention! But without stooping to extremist provocation or turning it into a media circus opportunity that would offend millions of Catholics!"

"As we would have done," said Mette, a bitter smile on her lips.

"I'm Catholic too," said Jorge. "My brother is a priest in Manaus."

"I'm sorry," said Nadine, her voice hard. "But Teo didn't agree with your methods, or with your language."

"He didn't know us," said Mette.

"He saw your website," said Nadine. "He read about you in the newspapers."

"What about *their* methods?" said Jorge, sweeping his hand to indicate the small, devastated living room. "What about their language?"

"Look," said Nadine, "it's *my* house they destroyed!" She got up again, trembling from shock and fear and rage and her sense of impotence. "If you've come here to criticize Teo and his decisions, there's the door! And it's already open! You can leave right now!"

Her tall, thin friend stood beside her, his expression even more hostile. He looked ready to throw us out.

I made a gesture with my palms open and said, "Everybody calm down. Let's not start fighting each other now. We're on the same side, aren't we?"

"It doesn't look that way to me!" said Nadine. "Especially not if you're attacking Teo!"

"We're not attacking him," I said, experiencing a secret vibration with the idea that she could consider Mette and I as a collective entity. "He was my father, after all."

Mette hunched down on the floor. "We're not attacking him," she said. "Even though he didn't trust us, Teo Telmari was one of the good guys."

I tried to catch her eye, to figure out if her declarations of esteem extended to me as well.

Jorge crouched down too in what might have been one of their body language techniques: present a low profile in situations of potential conflict. In his singsong accent he asked Nadine, "Did you have the second copy of Ndionge's memorial or not?"

Nadine hesitated, then said "No."

Mette picked up a little book of African songs from the floor, but she was watching Nadine.

"It wasn't here anymore," said Nadine, biting her lip.

Mette and Jorge exchanged glances. Mette said, "Where did it end up?"

Nadine seemed unsure whether or not she could trust them. She looked around, then went and put her glass down on the desk. "I gave it to somebody," she said.

"To who?" asked Mette.

Nadine stared out the dark window and didn't answer.

"I'm sorry," I said, "but you only had two copies of such a fundamental document? Isn't this the age of instant, limitless copying?"

Nadine nodded yes. "Hand-typed on Ndionge's typewriter."

"With his signature on the title page and at the end," said Mette.

"And his initials on every page," said Jorge.

Nadine seemed struck by the accuracy of their information, but it certainly didn't make them any friendlier in her eyes. "My compliments on your spy work," she said.

"We had a friend who worked with Ndionge," said Mette. "They murdered him."

Nadine's muscles contracted and her face drained of color.

"Where's your copy now?" I asked her. "Who did you give it to?"

Nadine hesitated again, finally saying "To Dante Marcadori. I obeyed the written instructions Teo left me."

Mette and Jorge looked at each other, crouched down among the papers and objects strewn across the floor. It was clear that Dante's name wasn't one they recognized.

"But where's Dante?" I asked. "I went to look for him yesterday, and he wasn't in his studio or at home. His assistant hadn't heard from him since the night before."

"I know," said Nadine. "I've been trying to reach him too. Nobody has heard from him or seen him today, either. He didn't go home to sleep, and his cell phone is always turned off."

"Excuse me," said her tall, thin friend. "But if that's the way things stand, somebody needs to file a missing persons report with the police."

"Dante's sister already has," said Nadine. "They're looking for him, but they haven't found anything yet."

"And you don't have any idea where he might be?" asked Mette.

Nadine shook her head and said, "Yesterday afternoon he was supposed to make an initial presentation of Ndionge's memorial at the epidemiology conference in Fiuggi." She shuddered and glanced at her poorly closed door.

Her friend went to take a look out on the landing, then came back inside. All five of us were silent, stealing surreptitious looks at one another. The sound of a garbage truck reverberated along the street, lifting up dumpsters full of trash in order to turn them over and eat their contents.

Jorge stood up and said, "If you had involved us two months ago, we would never have ended up like this, without so much as a scrap of paper in our hands."

"Don't you start!" said Nadine. "You've just made things worse, insisting on coming to Rome and stirring things up!"

"How?" said Jorge. "Tell me how we made things worse! Worse than they are now?"

"Lower your voice!" said Nadine's tall, thin friend.

"You can't accuse us like that!" said Jorge to Nadine. "For no reason! Out of pure prejudice!"

"*Por favor*," said Mette to Jorge, her voice lowered.

"*A culpa é dele!*" said Jorge. "*É falso, não tem razão!*"

"Can't you see you're extremists?" said Nadine. "That we were right not to let you take part in a delicate issue like this?"

"You were dead wrong!" said Jorge. "And look at how things turned out! Thanks to all your prudence and delicacy! Your desire to do things carefully, at the right time, in the right place, with the right people!"

"Hey look, Brazil boy," said Nadine's friend, "we're not at the Rio carnival here!" He stood up to his full height, threatening.

Jorge went up to him, equally aggressive, and said "What does the carnival have to do with anything? Huh? *Imbecil! Vai para o diabo!*"

I went to break them up, but Mette reached out and touched Jorge's arm, saying something to him that I didn't catch.

He backed up, though unwillingly. "He's the one who said stupid, insulting things," said Jorge.

"Yes, but that's enough," said Mette.

Jorge raised up one hand, staring down at the floor.

I felt a tiny, absurd jolt of jealousy for their ease of communication, for the three years in which they'd done who knows what together, in who knows what corner of the world. I said, "In any case, that's the situation. There's no use fighting each other about it."

"Just what do you think we're supposed to do?" asked Jorge. "Give up and drop it? Let them get away with it?"

"Of course not," I said. "Let's wait until Dante Marcadori shows up again. He can't have disappeared forever, right?"

"Fanoué did," said Jorge.

"Who?" said Nadine.

"Ndionge's assistant," said Mette. "Maurice Fanoué."

"Run over by a truck," said Jorge. "Just a few days before he was supposed to bring Ndionge to Italy, as luck would have it."

"Yes," I said. "But here we're in Rome, not in the Senegalese countryside. And Dante Marcadori is a world-famous doctor."

Jorge looked at me without saying anything. The others were silent too.

Finally Nadine moved to usher us out the door, saying "If you don't mind, I need to spend some time alone. It's time for you to leave." She pinched the bridge of her nose, the muscles around her eyebrows tightening with tension.

I said, "But you can't sleep here alone with your front door broken. We'll stay here with you." I had a brief vision of Mette and me lying down next to each other on a clear stretch of floor, Jorge at the other end of the room.

Nadine pointed to her friend and said, "I'm sleeping at his place."

My mental image melted away in an instant. I said, "Then we'll check in with each other tomorrow morning."

"Okay," said Nadine, though it was clear that her first priority was getting rid of us.

Her friend gave me another angry look. It occurred to me that perhaps they had gotten together when she and my father had broken up, and he felt a sort of latent jealousy of me by extension.

Nobody said much by way of goodbyes: Jorge, Mette, and I waved or nodded and headed for the door.

Out in the street we looked around in the cold light from the streetlamps. All three of us were trying to figure out if someone was watching us from some parked car or from behind some corner, but it was hard to say. Jorge took a short jog, his head down, to peer into car windows. I stood by Mette's side: I was hoping she'd take my arm like she had when we'd walked together, but she didn't.

Jorge came running back, breathing hard. "Nothing. But they could be behind any of those windows," he said, pointing to the façades facing us.

"We'll talk tomorrow morning," said Mette.

"Whatever," I said. "I don't know. Personally I'm not really sleepy."

She looked at me, then turned toward Jorge.

I was praying intensely that he'd say he was going back alone, but instead he stayed stuck there with all the physical familiarity three years of close contact could bring, saying "Should we go?"

Mette nodded yes. She gave me a kiss goodbye on either cheek and repeated, "We'll talk tomorrow morning."

"Yes, but how?" I said.

"We'll call you," she responded, still keeping things in the plural. "We have your number."

I realized that it might sound like a loaded question, given the circumstances, but I said, "If you give me your number too, it would make communication a lot easier."

She turned and looked at Jorge. He seemed against it, but she gave me her number all the same.

I stood there on the sidewalk and watched them go over to their scooter and take off, still experiencing the perfectly three-dimensional sensation of my brief embrace with her two minutes earlier.

I WOKE UP EARLY IN THE
OVERHEATED ROOM

I woke up early in the overheated room, following a night of
tossing and turning and bad, fragmented dreams. I did a half hour
of calisthenics in front of the open window, through which the
sounds and smells of traffic floated in. Then I took a shower, got
my clean, ironed laundry from Harry, and put my usual clothes on.

My brother and sister-in-law and nephew were sitting at the
breakfast table, arguing about some homework Tommaso hadn't
finished. When I walked in all three turned to look at me, three
different expressions of suspicion and hostility and indifference on
their faces.

I poured some oatmeal in a little pot, but Emily chased me away,
saying "I'll take care of it, *signore*." I tried to squeeze a couple of
oranges, but she immediately took those away from me as well.

Fabio and Nicoletta went back to chastising their son in what seemed like a periodical recital, interrupted by continuous glances at their cell phones and the newspapers open on the table and the television broadcasting the news. For his part, Tommaso took a stance of semipassive resistance: his arms crossed and his head hung low, an untouched mug of caffe latte and several unopened snack packs in front of him. Every so often he emitted one of his unintelligible mutterings, at one point saying quite clearly, "You two don't understand fuck all."

Fabio retorted, "I already told you I don't want to hear you using that language, is that clear?" But even here he had a false tone of voice, his gaze slipping away toward the screen where images of an attack in Iraq were flashing past: bodies and blood and dust, mechanical detritus everywhere.

Suddenly Nicoletta gave in to her son's moral blackmail. "Tommaso, eat something, please!" she said. "You can't go to school like this!"

He immediately sensed that the situation had tilted in his favor, and said extremely clearly, "Go fuck yourselves, both of you!" Then he got up and left the kitchen, followed by Emily.

Fabio and Nicoletta exchanged looks, then she left, following in her son's wake. Fabio sat rigidly. He glanced at me, saying nothing. He raised the volume on the TV in order to follow the usual rapid progression of declarations by exponents from all the political parties: first those from the governing block, then those from the opposition, then those with the government again, each moving his lips soundlessly before dozens of microphones, his words summed up in a convulsed tone by the narrator.

I finished squeezing the oranges Emily had left behind. Fabio ate his low-fat yogurt in quick spoonfuls. Nicoletta and Tommaso could be heard shouting in the hallway: imploring and inarticulate insults and new accusations and threats of retaliation, doors slamming.

I went back to watching the television on the countertop, and saw a slow, circling shot of a gray BMW stopped by the side of a country road. The voiceover said, "At dawn near Bracciano Lake, following a report filed by a local fisherman, police found the body of professor Dante Marcadori, an internationally famous virologist, inside his car. Marcadori had been missing from his home and work for the past two days, and his absence had been reported by his family and relatives. Investigators are looking into the cause of death, but an initial examination of the body did not reveal signs of violence. Seventy-nine years old, born in Friuli but a longstanding resident of Rome, Marcadori earned numerous awards in both Italy and abroad for his work in . . ."

I slammed the glass of orange juice down on the counter, and half the juice ended up on the floor. Fabio started at the sound, but immediately went back to watching the screen. He only managed to turn away once the report was over.

We looked at each other without any expression, me standing up and him sitting down.

Nicoletta came back into the kitchen, still worked up with motherly demands. She said to Fabio, "Listen, you really should tell him that if he thinks he is going to get away with . . ." Suddenly she saw our expressions and realized that there was something afoot more serious than her son's behavior. She turned her gaze from me to her husband.

Fabio stood up, pale. He put one hand in his pocket.

"Are you happy?" I said, as shock began to change into an oceanic wave of indignity, limitlessly intense and far-reaching.

"What's happened?" asked Nicoletta, looking at the orange juice on the floor.

"Huh?" I said to Fabio. "Do you really think you've put yourself on the right side, this time?"

"What the fuck are you talking about?" he said, all the muscles in his face jumping with tension, his eyes half closed.

"About your dear friends who've murdered him!" I shouted.

"What the fuck are you saying?" shouted Fabio in a disconcerted burst that turned his face red and made him spit white yogurt drool. "How fucking *dare* you make that kind of conjecture!"

"It's not conjecture! It's obvious who it was, and why! I knew yesterday, that it would have to happen, or that it had already happened! Since the day before yesterday, even!"

"Who? Who's been murdered?" said Nicoletta. "By whom?"

"They didn't find any signs of violence!" shouted my brother. "You heard it too!"

"On television?" I yelled. "From those masters of free, liberal investigative journalism you know so well? Besides, there are a million ways to kill somebody, you don't necessarily have to beat him to death with a stone!"

"What's supposed to be the reason, will you explain that?" shouted Fabio. "Can you explain that?"

"Because he had a second copy of Ndionge's memorial!" I shouted back.

He became even paler, moving his lips soundlessly.

"Nadine told me last night. In the middle of her totally devastated house!"

Fabio backed up toward the window, knocking against a shelf.

"Your friends didn't tell you about that part, did they?" I said, though his expression made it obvious they hadn't.

"Will you two please tell me what's going on?" said Nicoletta in a lacerated tone of voice.

"They killed Dante Marcadori," I said.

"Dante? When? Who?"

"Fabio's friends, or somebody who works for them."

She turned to stare at Fabio, her good-girl's face tight with alarm.

He continued to stare at me. He wiped the yogurt drool from one corner of his mouth, took a deep breath and said, "Try to be reasonable, Lorenzo, before you start making arbitrary connections about something so serious! There's no way that can be real!"

"It doesn't get any more real than this!" I said. Once again, against my will, I felt the same compassion he'd sometimes aroused in me when we were children, when facts would unexpectedly destroy some small certainty he'd acquired at great expense. Despite my indignation and sense of alarm, I had an impulse to pat him on the back or on his head, to bring him out of his state of shock, to talk with him brother to brother, find some shared stance we could take together to face what was happening around us.

But I wasn't dealing with the same Fabio as when we were ten and twelve. His certainties had become a thousand times more consolidated; his relationship with the world had become infinitely more real. He took one of his cell phones out of his jacket and typed in a number. "Fabio Telmari," he said, "Good morning. Could you pass me the chief of police, please?" Then he left the kitchen, walking away down the hallway.

Harry passed him coming the other way, dragging Tommaso's backpack and Tommaso behind him. Emily came back into the kitchen, grabbed a rag and started cleaning up the orange juice on the floor.

Nicoletta watched me from between half-closed eyelids. Underneath her nice clothes, her entire body was vibrating with anxiety at her lack of information. She said, "What's happening here, Lorenzo? Can you please tell me what's going on?"

I explained the situation to her, based on the elements I had: I connected the events that had taken place since my arrival in Rome with those that Mette and then Nadine had told me, all the way up to this morning's news on television.

She sat down. She said, "Yes, but this can't be happening."

"It *is* happening," I said.

She shook her head, saying "You're just suffering from some sort of seventies conspiracy theory."

"And you're just suffering from some sort of negation of reality."

"What reality? These are just arbitrary connections, like Fabio said."

"Oh, yeah? We've just stumbled into a sea incredibly thick with coincidences, haven't we?"

In reality she didn't know what to say. She said, "The one thing for certain is that it can't be . . . I mean, you can't . . . Nobody can say . . ."

"He committed suicide," said Fabio from the doorway. His tone of voice was one of intense relief mixed with a slight trace of pain. "He used the exhaust from his car. Trauma or violence have been one hundred percent excluded." He was holding the cell phone in the palm of his hand as incontrovertible proof.

"Why would he do that?" I asked.

"He had prostate cancer. In a terminal phase."

"That's news to me," I said. "And I think it'll be news to his closest collaborators, too."

Fabio said, "The chief of police says that they're waiting for the autopsy results, but they're already ninety-nine percent certain."

"Well, that was perfect timing, wasn't it? Right on the eve of the international virology conference at which he was supposed to present Ndionge's memorial."

"When somebody decides to kill himself, he doesn't spend a whole lot of time worrying over coincidences, Lorenzo."

"It was clear he was really depressed," said Nicoletta, clinging to her husband's relief. "You could see it in his face."

"You mean right after dad's death?" I said. "Who coincidentally had been his best friend for more than fifty years? Do you think he was supposed to be all happy and bubbly? Jump around and spin pirouettes among the distraught family members?"

"Lorenzo, he committed *suicide*," said Fabio again in a tone of artificial calm that he was supposed to save for one of his broadcast declarations. "Accept it and deal with it."

"Fuck accepting it! Where is his copy of the memorial? Where did that wind up? Did your chief of police explain that to you, too? Or didn't he find anything else in the car? Well?"

"Lorenzo," said my brother as if he were dealing with a capricious child, relying on all the patience he'd never had for his own son. "If your source of information is Nadine the Virus, then in all likelihood Dante never even had a copy of any so-called memorial."

"Oh, perfect! That way everything's taken care of. And maybe dad never had any so-called memorial either, right? And you didn't turn anything over to anyone, right? Under no pressure whatsoever, right?"

"Listen, Lorè," he said, retreating even further into his act of balance and sensibleness. "I don't know what idea you've given yourself of that memorial, but I can guarantee you that it wasn't the revolutionary document you and your Stopwatch buddies imagine it to be. Those things have already been said over and over again, and they're mixed with a healthy dose of African irrationality, and the bitterness of a man who knows he's going to die of an illness that isn't exactly, let's say, *appropriate* for someone in his public position."

"Then how come your friends are so afraid someone might read it? How come they'll stop at nothing, not even murder, in order to make it disappear?"

"It wasn't murder, Lorenzo," said Fabio. "Dante committed suicide."

Nicoletta nodded yes, but no matter how hard she tried, she

couldn't bring herself to look as sure as he did.

I looked at the pair of them. As early in the morning as it was, they were both well dressed and well groomed, standing there in their kitchen full of designer objects and the finest home appliances: they seemed like two aliens intent on playing human roles, but using a script that was devoid of any sense of the ridiculous or doubt or uncertainty of any kind. "Have a nice day," I said. Then I walked out.

They followed me into the hallway, almost identical expressions on their faces. My brother said, "Where the fuck are you going?" Nicoletta said, "Lorenzo . . ."

"I'll see you around," I said. I opened the double-deadlocked, steel-reinforced door to their apartment and ran away down the stairs.

NOBODY PICKED UP THE PHONE
AT NADINE'S APARTMENT

Nobody picked up the phone at Nadine's apartment, and her cell phone was turned off. I drove over to her house and tried ringing the door, but nobody answered.

I stood there on the sidewalk at the precise point where I'd stood next to Mette the night before. The sensations I'd had when she was nearby returned as if they still hung there in the air, increasing my heartbeat. I looked up her name on my cell phone menu: it seemed almost incredible to me that I could read it there among the others. I pressed the button, listening to the faint, wailing sound of her cell phone ring arriving from who-knows-what point in the city, vibrating and scraping and screeching all around.

She answered cautiously, "Yes?"

"I need to see you," I said, my heart racing even more rapidly. I watched cars and pedestrians pass by along the street and in the piazza on the other side. Even the most innocent-looking faces seemed like potential hit men.

Mette said nothing. There was the sound of a piano in the background. From her silence it was clear that she didn't know anything about Dante Marcadori yet.

I realized that my words might sound dictated by purely personal motives. "Something serious has happened," I said. "Something connected with you know what."

"Okay," she said immediately.

"When?" I had a growing sense of urgency, my head full of anticipations and accelerations.

"One hour from now. At our place, okay?"

"But I don't know where you are," I said, experiencing a small, irrational jolt because of that "our."

"Where you attacked Jorge."

"I didn't attack him."

"Whatever. You know where."

"Okay." I glanced at my watch. It was nine a.m.

"Bye," said Mette.

"Bye," I said, though I would have liked to talk to her some more.

I walked back and forth for a few minutes in front of Nadine's door, then I saw an old lady arrive carrying shopping bags. She took out a set of keys. I slipped in before she closed the door, ignoring the diffident look she gave me, and went quickly up the stairs.

I thought I'd find the landing deserted, but instead I encountered Nadine's tall, thin friend fooling around with a screwdriver outside the door. He turned around instantly, retreating into a defensive crouch before he even recognized me.

"Nadine?" I asked him.

He was even less friendly than the night before, nodding toward the apartment. He was attaching an external latch on the half-unhinged door, and reluctantly moved aside to let me pass.

Nadine started when she saw me too: her face was drawn, with marks around her eyes. An open suitcase lay on the green couch, while another closed suitcase sat on the floor, which was still littered with papers and objects of every shape and size just like it had been the night before.

"Did you hear about Dante?" I asked.

She went back to picking up papers and books and fliers and putting them in the open suitcase, giving me nothing more than a couple of quick glances.

"Do you think they killed him?" I asked.

She remained silent, moving from one spot to another in the room like a seashell collector on a beach with very little time left.

I said, "Fabio talked to the chief of police. They said he committed suicide."

Nadine's lips drew back in a sort of weak smile. She looked at me, then moved her eyes away immediately.

"Are you leaving?" I asked, pointing at the suitcases.

She collected some other objects from different points in the room and tossed them into the suitcase. Suddenly she stopped, dropping a few CDs she was holding. "If I had been at home last night, I'd be dead right now too!" she said.

I said, "Nadine."

Her friend immediately stuck his head into the living room, extremely unhappy to find me there.

I pretended I hadn't seen him. I said, "Luckily you weren't at home."

"What luck, huh?" she said, her French-speaker's accent breaking free of her Roman accent as if through an osmosis of traumatic origins.

"Where are you going?" I asked.

"To my parents' house, in Geneva. Don't tell anybody. Promise me you won't tell anybody."

"I promise."

"Not even your brother." She bit her lower lip.

"Of course not."

"Not even your friends at Stopwatch."

"Nobody."

She stooped to the floor and picked up a fountain pen, a photo of my father sitting on a low stone wall, a spiral notebook, a little kangaroo stuffed animal, a Jimi Hendrix CD, and a butterfly-shaped sequined hair band. She threw them all into the suitcase in such a convulsed way that I couldn't tell whether she'd made a deliberate choice or if it was all by chance. She closed the zipper, reopened it, went to take a watercolor of a mackerel off the wall, stuck that in the suitcase too, then closed it back up. She pressed her hand on her forehead, dilating her nostrils to breathe. She looked at me again and said, "It's just that I don't trust this country, Lorenzo."

"I understand," I said. It was a feeling I knew all too well, although I certainly didn't enjoy hearing it from a Swiss citizen.

"I've lived here for fourteen years, and I was sure I'd adapted, especially thanks to your father's help. But it's not true. The thing I can't get used to is the *flexibility* of your rules. In the beginning it was a thing I liked, compared to Switzerland. It made me feel free. But it's a horribly dangerous flexibility, one that continuously erases the line between good and evil and between true and false and between licit and illicit, between full rights and concessions that are temporary and revocable at any time."

I nodded yes. I felt partly responsible as an Italian, my father's son, I don't know.

"What scares me is the *ambiguity*," said Nadine. "The atrocious lack of definition."

"Passed off as the lightness of living," I said against my will. "The ability to adapt and creatively improvise."

"Your father used a beautiful image to define it." She made an effort to remember it exactly. "Beautiful Italy where, against a background of ancient, ruined rules, the swamp reeds of reinterpreted rules wave."

It occurred to me that over the years I'd probably felt more a foreigner than she had, and more often.

"That's how *this* happens," said Nadine, her lips trembling. "And you know right from the start that it's completely pathetic to expect justice, or even clarity. Because the connections are dark and complicated, and because everything depends on the arbitrary will of each single, individual judge or policeman or traffic cop who can move and bend rules according to the prevailing winds."

"Yes."

"You know right from the start that they'll even doubt that what has happened actually took place! That they'll suspect it's the fruit of your pathetic imagination!"

Both of us looked at the window and door in turns, listening to try and distinguish the sounds that came from the street or the landing or the stairwell.

Nadine gathered up a few colored glass marbles, then let them fall. She said, "At this point, I'm starting to wonder how Teo actually died."

"What?" I said, because of course I'd asked myself the same thing. "There are no doubts about his death, are there? He died at home, of a heart attack. He was eighty-three."

She didn't answer, pale in her natural wool sweater: the formerly beautiful Swiss-French girl who had fallen in love with a famous

Italian epidemiologist who was married, with two sons.

Her friend came back into the living room holding the screwdriver in one hand. "I'm finished," he said. "Are you ready?"

Nadine put her coat on. She looked around at the chaos and objects spread everywhere. She picked up a gold-capped pen from under the desk and slipped it into one pocket.

I said, "So there's nothing left that can be done, for the memorial?"

She shook her head. She picked up a small compass, then a gray silk scarf lying near the window.

"It's gone forever? Melted away as if it never existed?"

Nadine wound the scarf around her neck, lifted her face up.

"Can we go?" she asked her friend impatiently.

She picked up one suitcase. I tried to get the other for her, but her friend ripped it out of my hands as if he wanted to prevent me from stealing it. Outside on the landing, he closed the latch he'd just finished installing with a lock and gave the key to Nadine. She pressed her hands against the door, perhaps to say goodbye, or perhaps just to register its fragility with respect to whoever had broken in through there and devastated her home.

We said goodbye out in the street while her friend was putting the suitcases into the trunk of his car. Nadine already looked like a refugee. She repeated again in a half-whisper, "Don't tell anyone anything about where I'm going."

"Nobody," I repeated, moving my head to reinforce my words and cancel any possible impression of Italian moral flexibility.

She laid her hands on my forearms, leaning her head forward and brushing her cheekbones against my own. Then she took a photo of my father out of her pocket and gave it to me.

"Thank you," I said, surprised by her gesture. I slipped it into the inside pocket of my jacket, hardly even looking at it.

Nadine tightened her lips barely and turned around suddenly, getting into her friend's car. He stared at me through the windshield, unfriendly.

I went back to my pickup, casting surreptitious glances to either side in order to identify the glances of killers or spies among the torrent of looks exchanged along the sidewalk.

I PARKED ALMOST A MILE AWAY FROM
THE STOPWATCH HEADQUARTERS

I parked almost a mile away from the Stopwatch headquarters, walking a tortuous route in order to reach the station on the south side and cross the arrivals hall heading north. I knew these were relatively useless precautions, since the place I was going to was almost undoubtedly being watched, but I wanted at least to make life more complicated for my possible follower. This desire made me whip suddenly around after every turn, backtracking for dozens of yards, knocking into strangers, fighting my way diagonally across groups of travelers leaving or arriving.

At five minutes to ten I was at the corner of the street where the Stopwatch headquarters were located. I kept checking my watch to make sure I didn't arrive early or late. There were unexpected slowdowns and accelerations in the flow of cars and pedestrians.

There was an acrid smell in the air and the sound of sirens wailing at various frequencies.

I turned the corner, and from a few hundred yards away saw black smoke, police cars, a red fire truck, and police barriers to keep curious onlookers back. I crossed over to the other side of the street, walking more quickly even though incredulity tended to slow me down. But I knew the smoke was coming from the Stopwatch headquarters, even before I got close enough to see. The sweat from the walk froze on my back. My head filled with senseless, hypothetical images that overlapped those in front of my eyes.

I reached the point where I'd seen Jorge open the dark glass door, and on the other side of the red and white barriers and blue police uniforms and brown uniforms with yellow stripes worn by the firemen who were coming out rolling up hoses, there was nothing left but a blackened, smoking hole.

I stopped among the onlookers. The stench of burned plastic was making everyone cough, our feet on the sparkling, crackling fragments of glass spread all around for dozens of yards. The sense of alarm and indignation I'd felt up until a few minutes ago flowed out through my bloodstream, leaving space for a sort of essential anxiety into which faces and figures and gestures and looks and sentences and names dove and became minuscule in an instant, only to return larger than before a moment later.

I took my cell phone out of my pocket and called Mette, my fingers so nervous that I had to start over twice. A computerized voice said, "The number you have called is not in service at this time" in an unbearably upbeat tone. I had mental tapes of images and sounds that were constantly playing out and rewinding: Mette's sleepy and maybe self-absorbed voice when I'd spoken to her an hour earlier; the slow camera pan around Dante Marcadori's car; the looks on the faces of my brother and Nicoletta in their well-outfitted kitchen; Nadine's speech in her little, overturned living room; the dozens of body expressions and exchanged looks and perfectly foreign mechanical movements I'd collected along my convoluted walk.

I looked at the black tongues of soot along the building façade, a little burnt-out truck parked just beyond, the cars with broken windows that had contributed to the spread of glass. I tried to make something out inside the former Stopwatch headquarters, but the crowd was too thick and I didn't want to get too close to the police.

I turned around toward a guy who was holding a scarf up to his face to combat the smoke and asked, "Was there anybody inside?"

"No idea," he said without looking at me, entirely concentrated on the other side of the street.

"They took one guy away," said a craftsman standing in the doorway to a frame shop. "In an ambulance. But it was no use."

"Why was it no use?" I asked, clinging to the lines of his face.

"He was dead as a doorknob," said the man, his emotional detachment complete and total.

I made an effort to talk to him again. "Was it a man or a woman?" I asked.

"How should I know," said the craftsman. "It was a piece of charcoal."

"When did it happen?" My heart had slowed down to the point of stopping.

"About twenty minutes ago," said the guy with the scarf.

"A half an hour," said the craftsman without looking at me or the other guy. "There was this explosion and I thought it was an earthquake or Islamic terrorists or the Third World War, goddamn it."

I desperately tried to calculate how long it might have taken Mette to take the piano CD out of the stereo and call Jorge—assuming he wasn't already standing alongside her—and get ready and put on her scarf and jacket or her coat, and go out and get on the scooter and travel across the city from who-knows-where in order to make it here. I was missing too many elements in order to form even the vaguest hypothesis. I looked at the craftsman again, but I didn't want to ask him anything else.

He said, "The smoke was so thick and black I couldn't even see over there, and it stunk much worse than it does now. Then the firemen and the cops came and chased everybody off."

The firemen seemed relatively calm now, but the policemen continued to move around restlessly, going in and out of the old shell that was formerly Stopwatch headquarters and up and down the sidewalk and all across the street. There was a plainclothesman, who might have been an officer, talking into his cell phone and giving orders to uniformed cops, accepting or dismissing photographers and television crews. He was also scrutinizing the crowd of onlookers I was a part of with a highly specialized predator's gaze. I realized it wasn't a very good idea to stand that close and visible, but I couldn't even consider leaving without at least attempting to gather some more precise information.

I asked some other onlookers for news about injured or burned people. They all had completely contradictory versions. I crossed the street and asked a fireman who was drinking milk out of a pint carton. He looked at me suspiciously, sweaty and filthy with soot, and said, "Who do you work for?"

"Nobody." I tried to move out of the plainclothes cop's view.

The fireman shrugged, turned around and went back to drinking milk out of his carton. A few yards further on the police chief had someone bring him a walkie-talkie, talking and casting aggressive looks around.

I slipped in among the people standing still and moving around, walking along the sidewalk with a terrible sense of emptiness, without even the faintest idea what to do. Then, just past a little curtain shop with dusty windows, I felt someone touch my back. I spun around violently, dozens of anticipatory moves and countermoves running through my mind in a single instant, and found Mette standing before me.

My surprise and relief at finding her there were so intense that they overwhelmed in a single instant all the negative feelings permeating every fiber of my being.

"But . . ." I said.

She shook her head quickly to warn me not to talk, then walked very quickly toward the next intersection. I followed her at the same speed, trying to perceive without turning around whether or not someone was following us.

We turned the corner and sped up, first one behind the other and then side by side. We switched sidewalks, turned into yet another street without once looking at each other or saying anything. I think we both felt the same impulse to start running, but we knew that this would only make us more visible, and so we continued to walk quickly against the flow of cars and taxis and buses.

When we reached the trees near the wall on the edge of the piazza we slowed down, finally looking each other in the face. I asked, "Jorge?"

"I don't know," said Mette. Her pupils were dilated with worry, her lips almost colorless.

We sped up again, looking over our shoulders occasionally. I kept thinking of the craftsman's words about the piece of charcoal, but it was too terrible to share with Mette or even think about. I asked, "Didn't you two come together?"

"No, I took the bus. Jorge left first on the scooter because he had to pick something up in Testaccio."

"Can't you call him?"

She glanced at me quickly. "That's the stupidest way to get caught. They can trace any call or movement, immediately."

I realized my cell phone was still turned on. I took it out of my pocket and turned it off. I said, "Maybe Jorge saw the chaos on the street and took off right away."

Mette shook her head slowly. She said, "His scooter is parked where he always leaves it."

"Where?" An ugly character wearing sunglasses stood outside a car dealership, watching us.

"On the side street, chained to a streetlight."

"That doesn't mean he was inside the building when it blew up."

She didn't answer, but it was clear she thought he had been.

"He didn't even have enough time to get there," I said. "It was nine o'clock when I called you. The explosion took place around nine-thirty."

"Jorge is incredibly fast," she said. "He can get anywhere in ten minutes on that scooter."

We kept walking, looking at each other only peripherally. Our eyes were busy evaluating the faces of passersby, identifying bars and shops that seemed like possible refuges or potential traps. I felt a new desire to ask her what her relationship with Jorge was, but I realized that this certainly wasn't the right time. The uncertainty of the situation made me register details indiscriminately, speeding up or slowing down according to totally random signals.

We reached a big, very busy street, crossing it quickly amid the multiplication of sounds and movement. We slipped underneath the trees lining the parallel side street, turning right onto the first street we encountered. My pickup had a parking fine stuck underneath the windshield wiper. We got in and sat there, catching our breath and staring ahead. Despite the anxiety I felt, having Mette beside me provoked an even more intense electric buzz than the night before. I thought that if she had known she probably would have hated me, but I couldn't control it: it was a phenomenon activated by receptors spread out across my body and the imagination centers in my brain, producing little concentric waves around my heart.

I made an effort to concentrate on the practical aspects of the situation, but it didn't seem like there were any that could be considered reassuring. "What are we going to do now?" I said.

Mette turned and looked up the street. She said, "I have to know what's happened to Jorge."

"Yes, but how?" I was aware that I didn't have any specific experience in clandestine activities, unless you counted the relationship I'd had some eight years earlier with a married woman and an extremely jealous husband.

Mette rubbed her index fingers against her thumbs and said, "We have a system for communicating. Through a chat line."

"Then let's go look for an Internet spot."

She nodded yes. She was entirely consumed with anxiety.

I turned the engine on, driving along secondary streets in a blend of caution and risk.

I KEPT MY EYE ON THE DOOR
OF THE INTERNET SPOT

I kept my eye on the door of the Internet spot, while a few feet away
Mette typed on a computer keyboard. There were only a few other
clients, most of whom were Asian or Middle Eastern. Outside the
window, traffic flowed along the big commercial street. I wondered
if in a case like ours it was safer to be in open, busy spaces or in
shadowy side streets. Instinctively neither one appealed to me. But
it was a relatively abstract instinct that increased my sense of hurry
and reduced the time for reflection, suggesting images of escape in
the most diverse directions. For example, it made me retrace my
steps along the street I'd traveled a few days earlier, from Rome
along the highway and then the interstate and then up and down
the peaks and valleys of the Apennine mountain passes and regional
highways and local roads all the way to the little carriage gateway

that led to the top of the snow-covered hill I'd started from. Other instincts put me on guard against this mental path: the result was a continuous oscillation of impulses and sensations. One moment my little stone house seemed the safest place in the world to hide with Mette, the next it seemed like a trap in which even the least agile of our faceless enemies could find us. Clearly defined images of the two of us getting on trains and airplanes passed through my head, only to melt in the sudden light of elementary considerations.

Mette moved the mouse and struck the keys, sitting in a corner seat far from the windows: a foreigner's face, her hair gathered back and hidden underneath her black beret; an agile body that seemed ready to leap away at the first warning sign.

In the end she got up, her face expressionless, and went over to pay at the register. She passed alongside me, saying, "Nothing."

"Maybe it's too early," I said.

She shook her head and went out into the violent noise of the street.

We got back into my pickup. I turned it on, but the contradictory impulses coursing through my body robbed me of any sense of direction. Once again I asked, "What should we do?"

Mette seemed as lost as I was. "I don't know," she said.

"Don't you have some emergency network, for when things go wrong?"

She looked me in the eye and said, "We're not a terrorist organization!"

"I know, I *know*. I meant, don't you have safe houses or people you can contact, in cases like this?"

"There've never been any cases like this! At most we risk being arrested and charged with hindrance or damage, or violating private property! Not being *murdered*!"

"Of course." I had a desire to hug her shoulders tightly.

She brushed one hand underneath her nose in a little gesture of anger. "And in any case," she said, "when something goes wrong the rule is to keep anybody who isn't directly involved out of it."

I nodded yes. Discovering that she had no experience with the sort of danger we were now in made me considerably more anxious. It seemed to me that between us we had very few tools with which to face the situation closing in on us, apart from our survival instincts and good physical condition and the ability to make quick mental connections. For everything else we were defenseless and exposed, with increasingly less time available. I said, "The important thing is to keep moving," though I realized just what a generic idea this was.

"To go where?" She looked at me, then back at the traffic.

"Let's start by getting out of Rome," I said, four or five different, simultaneous itineraries floated through my mind, lighting up in my head like colored lines on a map, none of them with an adequate destination.

"I'm not leaving until I know something about Jorge. I'm staying here."

"Where? On the street? At your house, where there will definitely be somebody waiting for you?"

"I don't know. You go if you want. I'll figure something out."

"I'm definitely not leaving you." I knew just how mixed up my personal and general reasons might appear, but I didn't have the time or desire to think about it.

"You aren't involved," she said. "We were the ones who dragged you into this thing. You can explain that to them, they can check. Your brother will help you, I'm sure of it." Her fingers were on the door handle, her body already containing all the movements necessary to open it and get out and walk quickly down the sidewalk, disappearing among the passersby.

Suddenly an unbearable sense of emptiness rose up in me at the idea that she might go away and leave me to my former life: I said, "What do you mean, I've got nothing to do with it? I've got as much to do with this as you or Jorge, by now! And you weren't the ones who dragged me into this thing! I became a part of it the first time Ndionge contacted my father!"

For all she was shocked and scared, she had an ironclad core. "You don't have to feel obligated to help me," she said. "I can take care of myself."

"I don't feel obligated. And I'm sure you can take care of yourself. But we're in this thing together, do you understand?"

She watched the movement out in the street, unconvinced.

"Would you please look me in the eye?" I said.

She turned her head toward me, but only for an instant.

I looked at the lines of her forehead and nose and chin. I asked myself if her words were the product of altruistic reasons, or a desire to be free of me in order to make her decisions without any hindrance. I couldn't figure it out, and meanwhile I could perceive the pressure increasing with the passage of time, reducing our options one second after the next. I knew that we couldn't sit there in my pickup, motor running, on the edge of traffic forever. I put on the turn signal and shifted into first, saying, "Let's get out of here."

Mette reached out and turned on the radio. She went through station after station after station, but all that came out were the standardized voices of ultra-gleeful disc jockeys and ads and little ditties distorted by my dusty, mud-caked speakers. She turned the radio off and asked me, "Where are we going?"

I was stopped at a stoplight, watching a police car coming down the opposite lane. As soon as the light turned green I made a quick left. "To my brother's house. It's three minutes from here."

"But your brother is against us!" said Mette, clinging to the handle above the door. "He turned the memorial over to the Vatican, maybe he even sent them to your father's assistant's house!"

"That's exactly why we're going. It's the safest place for us now, at least until we've decided what to do."

"I'm not going," she said, her face tense with a totally determined expression.

"Oh yes you are!" I shouted, "because for now we don't have any valid alternative, and I don't think you want to be shot on the street or run over by a car or dragged away lord knows where!"

She seemed surprised by the determination in my voice. I didn't say anything else, and she hung on to the handle while I shot past parked cars and swerved sharply through the streets that led to my brother's house.

I left my pickup in a parking space left miraculously unoccupied. We went to the main building door trying not to look around us in any obvious way. The guards had driven off at daybreak. The doorman nodded to me from behind his glass, casting a long look at Mette, who was holding one hand up to her temple.

The only person at home was Emily, who was vacuuming with slightly maniacal dedication. She told me that Nicoletta was out but that she'd be back for lunch. Mette moved like a wild animal in enemy territory: she had a cautious way of placing her feet on the floor, avoiding touching the walls or furniture. I asked her if she wanted something to drink or if she needed to use the bathroom; she shook her head no. She didn't even want to take off her jacket or beret until I insisted, and when she did she laid them on an armchair in the living room as if she needed to be ready to put them back on on the fly while escaping. Under her jacket she was wearing a gray turtleneck sweater that softened her curves. I turned on the large screen on the wall, but there were no news programs on. I turned it off.

My familiarity with the house embarrassed me, my frustrated impulse for movement made me feel trapped. I wasn't even sure that it had been a good idea to come here, and yet I couldn't seem to think of anything better. There were a thousand questions I wanted to ask Mette, but I was almost certain she wouldn't want to answer them. We kept quiet, staying in distant points in a room that was too big and too bright. We looked around at the paintings and furniture and designer objects like two fish in a semideserted aquarium.

I went into the kitchen to squeeze some fresh orange juice. Emily tried to keep me from doing it on my own, but I turned one shoulder to her and told her I'd do it myself. I filled two glasses with the cold, intense orange juice and went back into the living room. Mette was leafing through a book of photographs of the various forms of water: she put it away immediately, stepping a safe distance away from the bookshelf.

I brought her a glass. She shook her head no, but I kept holding it out to her until she finally took it. She raised it to her lips and drank slowly and continuously.

I drank too. It seemed like a sort of small, silently shared ritual.

By then it was one in the afternoon, and I turned on the plasma screen to watch the news. We saw new images of terrorist attacks in Iraq and new declarations by the pope about citizens' private lives, new alarms and reassurances about the avian flu, a new blend of declarations from the representatives of every single different Italian political party. I heard voices in the hallway and a few seconds later Nicoletta stuck her head into the living room.

She said "hello" to me, but her gaze immediately swept across the space to Mette, who was staring at the screen from far away. Her territorial instincts and feminine sense of competition came instantly into play.

I made a vague wave of presentation: "Mette, Nicoletta."

Mette said hello in barely more than a whisper.

"Hello," said Nicoletta in the coldest possible tone she could muster.

I thought that it was difficult to imagine two women more diverse in looks, colors, style, and movements: the contrast even seemed to be so obvious to the two of them that it locked them both into expressions of intense reciprocal diffidence.

Now the news displayed a sweeping shot of the blackened, smoking cavern that had been Stopwatch's Roman headquarters, the street outside blocked off and full of curious onlookers and policemen and firemen milling about. Mette and I moved closer to the screen. I used the remote to turn up the volume.

"Lorenzo?" said Nicoletta.

"Shhhhh," I said.

The voiceover said, "This morning at nine-thirty near Stazione Termini a fire broke out due to as-yet-unidentified causes at the headquarters of Stopwatch, an organization that has been suspected of ecoterrorism activities for some time . . ."

"Excuse me, Lorenzo?" said Nicoletta.

"Let us listen!" I said, making a gesture that was as sharp as my voice.

The images on the screen zoomed in amid the smoke and burned detritus of the room where I'd blocked Jorge. The voiceover said, "The body of a man who may have been a part of the organization was found at the scene, killed by what investigators believe may well have been a bomb he himself was preparing."

"Jorge," said Mette in a shattered tone. She stepped forward.

"*Bastards*," I said. I was unable to translate my sensations into precise feelings, and even less into words. But I felt a new, powerful urge to embrace her.

Nicoletta looked back and forth between us. She pointed one finger at the screen. "Was that someone you were involved with?"

Mette walked over to the glass doors that led onto the terrace. She laid her forehead on the glass.

Nicoletta took me by the arm, her woman-girl and wife and well-balanced professional figure vibrating with incomprehension. "Lorenzo," she said, "would you please be kind enough to bring me up to date with what's happening? What do you have to do with this affair? And who is she?"

A report on the hijacking of an armored car in Puglia was now playing on the screen. Mette was crying, her forehead against the glass door. I pulled away from Nicoletta's grasp and said, "It was Fabio's friends."

"What are you saying?" said Nicoletta. "How dare you say that?"

"You asked me what's happening."

"I wanted to know what's happening to *you*! What you've done, what kind of mess you've gotten into! Who is she?!"

"Leave her alone!" I said, my voice breaking violently, a protective instinct running through my entire body.

"No, I'm not going to leave her alone! Seeing as how you brought her into my house! If you think this is some sort of seaport, you're wrong Lorenzo!"

"Can we talk alone, you and I?" I said, trying to push her into the hallway.

"Let go of me!" shouted Nicoletta, red in the face. "We're going to talk right here, and right now! With that young lady present!"

The house phone started ringing from atop an eighteenth-century console by the door. Nicoletta froze in a state of temporary suspension until the answering machine turned on. Fabio's voice issued forth from the little speaker saying, "Nico? Are you there? Hello?"

Nicoletta picked up the phone, listened for a few seconds and then said, "He's here. I was just trying to tell him that he's behaving in a criminally irresponsible manner, without the least consideration for you or me!"

I looked at Mette on the other side of the room. She was already putting on her short jacket. The expression on her face broke my heart. I said, "What are you doing?"

She didn't answer. She picked her wool beret up off the armchair and put it on, then got her bag.

Nicoletta handed me the phone. "Your brother." She went out into hallway. I could hear her high heels clacking nervously on the tile.

"Lorenzo?" said Fabio. His voice was tight with tension.

"Yes." I made a gesture to stop Mette, who was headed toward the door.

"Listen to me," said Fabio. "I don't even want to know the reasons behind the company you've chosen to keep recently, but I can guarantee you that they are *extremely* dangerous, and that I don't have any intention whatsoever of getting involved on any level."

"Nobody is trying to get you involved."

"You know damn well what I'm talking about!" he shouted. "Stop acting like a carefree little boy!"

"And why don't you stop acting like an opportunist willing to wheel and deal with the worst of the worst in exchange for Lord-knows-what! I don't think your voters elected you in order to see you serve a bunch of fundamentalist fanatics and assassins!"

"I won't allow you to spout such bullshit! I won't allow it!"

Mette tried to get by, but I blocked her with one arm. She looked at me, her eyes furious, her cheeks reddened. The beret was sloping across her forehead.

"And for your information," said Fabio, "just this morning the Ministry of the Interior inserted Stopwatch into the list of highly dangerous organizations! They're wanted all over the country, Lorenzo!"

"Fantastic!" I shouted. "First they kill them, then they black-list them!"

"They're killing themselves, Lorenzo! That guy blew himself up today with his own bomb! Who knows where he meant to detonate it!"

"You have incredibly accurate information!" I shouted. "The same identical information that shows up on the news, just a dozen minutes later!"

Mette pushed hard against my extended arm. It wasn't easy to stop her with one hand still holding the phone. We pushed each other back and forth in an interplay of muscles and panting until I managed to turn to one side and shoulder the door jamb.

"Hello? Hello?" said Fabio. "What the hell is going on over there?"

"Nothing," I said, trying to catch my breath. "Nothing that has anything to do with you."

"That's *my* house! Every goddamned little thing you do in there is my business! Put Nicoletta on the phone!"

"She's not here."

"Put her on right away!" shouted my brother. "IMMEDIATELY!"

I stuck my head out into the hallway. Nicoletta was just a couple of steps away. She walked over, grabbed the phone out of my hand and started talking to her husband, the indignation coursing through her making her stammer.

Mette took advantage of the moment to slip out of the living room. I dashed out and blocked her with one arm in the hallway, pressing her against the wall. I said, "What does it take to make you understand that we're in this thing together?"

"I don't need your help. You don't need to get into a fight with your whole family over me."

"I don't give a shit about my whole family. Let's just try and decide what the best thing to do is. Please. My brother just told me that Stopwatch has been blacklisted by the Ministry of the Interior."

She looked away, panting slowly. She said, "Do you think that changes anything? After what they did to Jorge?"

"Maybe it does. If you're being hunted by the police, something changes. They'll have pictures of you, or something."

She tried to look indifferent, but it wasn't easy. She bit her lip, looking to one side.

From the living room I heard Nicoletta say to my brother, "Okay, okay, *okay*, you don't have to tell me a thousand times." She hung up the phone and walked up behind me.

The three of us looked at each other in the hallway, me standing between two incredibly different women.

Nicoletta pointed a finger at Mette and said, "I hope you realize that you can't stay so much as another minute in this house."

"That's right," said Mette. "I was just going."

"And I'm going with her," I said.

"But you can't!" said Nicoletta, an expression of damaged good sense on her face that made me feel a moment's compassion.

"Why not? It's my business, isn't it?"

"It's your brother's business too! And mine! Don't you realize what the consequences would be, if you got yourself arrested along with her?"

"Listen, there's no problem," said Mette. "I'm leaving alone." She pushed me aside in order to head for the front door. I tried to stop her. Nicoletta grabbed my arm and we all grappled with each other and spun around in the narrow space, desperate intentions and gestures overlapping.

"I'm going with you," I said. "I'm going with her."

"Where?" said Nicoletta. "To get yourselves picked up at the first roadblock? So that you'll be all over the evening news, the two ecoterrorists, one of whom wouldn't you know it just happens to be the brother of Fabio Telmari of the Democratic Myrtle Party?"

"Listen," I said, "I'm sorry about any damage to your and Fabio's image."

"You're *sorry*? You know what I'd like to do with your 'I'm sorry'? And it wouldn't be damaging to our image, my dear! It would be infinitely worse than that!"

"I don't know what to tell you. I'm leaving with her."

"For fuck's sake, Lorenzo, think about what you're doing!"

"I've already thought about it."

"*Please*. Just once in your life."

"What do you know about my life? Why are you bringing my life into it?"

She looked back and forth between Mette and me. There was a burning light in her nut-brown eyes. She said, "Then at least try to go somewhere where they won't catch you five minutes from now like a couple of fools!" She pushed her way past us and went toward the front door, rummaging around in a bronze plate full of keys.

Mette and I followed her, both equally perplexed. Nicoletta took a bunch of keys with a green tag out and gave them to me.

I stood there staring at her, the keys in one hand, failing to understand the significance of her gesture.

"The beach house," she said. "You know where it is, right?"

I nodded yes. I couldn't make out any clear thoughts.

"Try to go straight there, and lock yourselves in. Don't use the telephone and don't turn on the outside lights and don't do anything else stupid. You've already done enough."

"Uh-huh."

She dug around in her purse and took out another key, handing it to me. "And take my car. It's down in the courtyard. Don't even touch your pickup. It's undoubtedly been identified."

I hesitated again. "Thank you," I said, although I wasn't sure it was the appropriate expression given her motives.

Nicoletta opened the heavy door and said quietly to me, "Try to be reasonable, Lorenzo."

I looked at Mette and didn't answer her. Mette made a small, unrecognized gesture of goodbye, then started down the stairs.

I remembered my backpack. I went to get it out of the next room, then turned back to the front door as fast as I could.

Nicoletta blocked me at the door and said, "Let her go, Lorenzo. Forget about her."

"Let me through," I said.

"Don't act like a child. Try to be reasonable. Please."

"Move." I pushed her aside as gently as I could given the sense of hurry devouring me.

She said, "If you can't bring yourself to think it over right now, at least think it over tomorrow!"

"Okay. Thanks!" I went dashing down the stairs through the respectable building inhabited by lawyers and notary publics, my eyes glued on Mette's black beret two and a half flights below.

I DROVE NICOLETTA'S EXTRA-SMALL CAR THROUGH THE CITY

I drove Nicoletta's extra-small car through the city, heading west. It was strange to be sitting so much lower compared to the cab of my pickup, on minuscule wheels, with no hood in front and no bed in the back. I felt both more vulnerable and more agile, and I was certainly much closer to Mette inside this tiny interior. She looked straight ahead without speaking. She breathed through sensitive nostrils, all her features tense.

I was all too aware of the risks of our position, and yet this didn't keep me from feeling a sort of intense happiness at the thought that we were running away together. We didn't talk for fear that our words might be listened to. We paid attention to even the smallest shifts in movement on the streets and along the sidewalks.

My attention was so hyped up and fine-tuned that every sensation was amplified; the slightest contact between our shoulders or arms or legs sent tiny jolts through my anxiety and into internal areas.

We got onto the ring road, winding around the city in invasive light, centrifugal force pressing on us with each curve. Then we got on the highway that followed the coast, speeding up on the straight strip of asphalt. We looked at the glimpses of pale sea on our left, out beyond the lines of oleander and eucalyptus. Further ahead on the right stood brownish mountains. We traveled among glass and plastic greenhouses, warehouses, ugly random constructions, and groups of suburban buildings. The car and truck traffic was relatively thin, but I couldn't decide whether this was an advantage or disadvantage.

We stopped in a service station to get gas. Neither one of us got out, although we were both hungry. There was a police car parked outside the restaurant, a dozen yards away. Mette and I said nothing to each other, we just slid slightly back in our seats until the gas station attendant had finished filling the tank.

When we got back on the road heading north I felt an unjustified sense of relief. I touched Mette's knee and said, "We're out."

"Yes, but now what?"

"Now we'll see."

We said next to nothing over the next sixty miles. We were tense and self-absorbed, sitting there in the constant hum of the engine and the sound of wind blowing across the small canvas roof.

We reached the road that led into the bay when the sun was already low over the sea. Banks of grayish-blue fog were rising inland. I followed the route I remembered toward the southeastern edge of the promontory. As had already happened other times, I lost my sense of direction on the road and went too far; I had to turn around and go back. Mette looked outside: at this time of day and state of mind it certainly wasn't a serene landscape, the low water reflecting in what little light there was, the dark mass of the mountain looming on our right, the profile of two ugly, possibly military towers sticking up amid the vegetation.

I went back and took the narrow road that curved its way up toward the vacation homes wedged into the cliff. We went slowly past the façades and balconies and gates and lattice of parking spaces carved out of tiny spaces until we reached the steep drive that led up to Nicoletta's parents' old summer vacation home. I got out and opened the gate with *Buen retiro* engraved on it. I had to rev the engine to drive the little car up the driveway. "There," I said before going back down and closing the gate. Mette got out and looked around at the little stone walls and the Mediterranean pines, the hydrangea bushes and the rough corners of the cement walls. She contrasted with the scenario in a way that under normal circumstances I would have found amusing. I tried to smile at her, but she didn't see it. The muscles and nerves in my face hurt.

I opened the door, turning off the alarm in the entryway like I'd seen my brother and Nicoletta do the two or three times we'd opened the house together. I pressed the central circuit breaker on the electric panel. It was a strange arrival compared with those I'd experienced before: no baggage or hosts, no summer, no heat, no boredom, no expectations of food or wine or conversations that had already been had, no time to let slip away like water that doesn't cost a dime.

Mette came in behind me, moving cautiously. The air was intensely cold and humid, with a salty, vaguely moldy smell. I turned on the lights one by one as I moved further down the hallway. I lit up the big living room with its couches and armchairs and 1970s interior design magazines, Italian Pop art paintings on the walls. Nicoletta's parents' tastes blended with those of Nicoletta and Fabio to produce a chilling effect in this bourgeois vacation home with intellectual aspirations. I watched Mette as she looked around, and I felt like I had some responsibilities that I didn't want to shoulder given where we were. After the silence and closeness of the little moving car we had to struggle to adapt to this wide open, still space. We were two strangers in territory foreign to us both, made awkward by embarrassment and diffidence, uncertain even of the next move to make.

It seemed to me that actions or at least decisive words were needed in order to facilitate a transition. "Make yourself at home," I said. Immediately afterward I realized what an absurd thing it was to say, given that I myself hardly felt at home. My words were absorbed by the damp cloth of the curtains and couches. I went to open the sliding glass doors, but then I remembered what Nicoletta had said about keeping any signs that we were here to a minimum. I closed the handle again and let go.

I showed Mette where the closest bathroom was, taking a pair of towels out of a closet for her. I turned on the electric water heater. Then I went outside to turn the heat on, but the iron door to the heater shed was closed. I went back inside and rummaged around in the drawers in the kitchen and living room looking for keys, but couldn't find any. I thought about breaking the lock, but I could imagine the noise it would make in the still night, so instead I went back outside to gather some firewood from beside the barbecue and bring it back into the living room. I took two colored, metal horses and a marble mortar out of the fireplace, then pulled the chain to open the flue: a hail of sand and pine needles came raining down. I put the wood on the andirons, then went into the kitchen to look for newspapers I could wad up and some matches. Everything was in impeccable order: I could imagine Nicoletta making final rounds with Harry and Emily in order to make sure that the house's wintry state of suspension corresponded to her mental standards. Seen in this light, the fact that she'd given me the keys seemed extraordinarily generous, as long as it wasn't the product of self-protective prudence.

Mette came back into the living room as I was lighting the fire. With all traces of make-up gone from around her eyes, her face seemed even clearer, its lines evolved through countless generations in distant lands and climes. She asked me, "Can you light it?" Her accent sounded even more foreign than it had in Rome.

"I hope so," I said. "At my house I spend roughly a quarter of every day lighting fires this time of year."

"In Rome?"

"In the countryside. I haven't lived in Rome for years." The wood was damp just like everything else, but I put some more newspaper underneath it and blew forcefully. Little by little the flame caught on.

Mette sat down on the stone lip of the fireplace, watching my technique closely. "We light a lot of fires at my house, too," she said.

"In Norway?" I asked, not looking directly at her.

"Denmark."

I was struck by the thought that we were running away together, fleeing considerable danger without even knowing what part of the world the other was from. It occurred to me that perhaps it was better this way: I was scared to consider a sudden inrush of all the information available about our two lives.

We watched the fire and smelled the wood smoke, absorbing its initial, weak heat. I went back outside to get another armful of firewood, checking that there weren't any sounds or lights beyond the fences. The air seemed immobile, dark and full of heavy, purplish hues.

When I got back inside Mette had rearranged the fire using the poker in such a way that it drew better, the red of the flames reflecting on her face.

We sat there without talking, hardly even moving, for a while. Every now and then we added some wood or shifted the burning logs. The silence made my ears ring, highlighting every little crackle and hiss of the fire. I felt totally inside the moment, with no before and no after. And yet I was totally overwrought by what had happened before and full of apprehension by what might yet happen. These three levels coexisted: all I had to do was separate my thoughts from my sensations in order to pass from semi-immobility to the most convulsed mental maneuverings. I tried to hold myself in semi-immobility, with all the unasked and unexplained elements that contained. I made minimal gestures, listened to minimal sounds, looked only at Mette's hand or ear, or a length of her hair. Whenever I extended my field of vision against my will and looked at the whole, one or two mental images would detach themselves from the calm of the moment and send my heart racing. Then I would have to move my eyes elsewhere and breathe deeply in order to return to my earlier calm. I couldn't remember ever having experienced a similarly dense or unstable condition, except perhaps when I was fifteen or sixteen years old. I had no desire to leave it.

Then from one moment to the next the hunger that had subsided for hours rose up inside me with uncontainable violence. I jumped up and said, "Are you hungry?"

I startled Mette: she jumped up too, ready.

"I'm sorry," I said, though I was endlessly attracted to her every movement or change of expression. "Don't you want something to eat?"

"Yes. But what?"

"I don't know. We can go see."

I walked around the French countryside-motif tiled walls of the kitchen, past the shelves upon which the espresso coffee machine and blender and centrifuge and juice press and toaster and deep-fryer and grill were all hibernating in good order, each one's electrical cord gathered up and tied with a rubber band. Away from the heat of the fireplace I had to move much more energetically in order to beat the cold and dampness and emptiness of the house: I spun my arms, did a few squat-thrusts, jumping once or twice.

The big refrigerator was unplugged just like the other appliances, and perfectly empty. There were a few packages of pasta and rice in the pantry, as well as cookies, cans of tuna, jars of tomato sauce, a little jar of capers, packets of coffee, salt and sugar. I took out a pot and filled it with water, placing it on the stretch of black glass atop their German electric stove. I turned the knob, but no lights turned on. I knelt down and stuck the plug in, feeling the icy floor tiles through the cloth of my pants.

When I turned around I saw Mette watching me from the doorway, silent. She had a peculiar way of standing, her head slightly to one side and her arms along her sides, one leg straight and the other slightly bent at the knee: it seemed like she would be able to stand that way for a long time without getting tired.

"Hey," I said as I got up. Her look and her body communicated a subcutaneous heat to me that transcended any state of anxiety or winter cold.

She seemed lost in thought, but a few seconds later she started trembling just a little and taking short, quick breaths. Faint throaty sounds came out of her mouth. She covered her eyes with one hand.

I went over to her and stood there looking at her from just a few inches away, unsure what to do or say. Then she started weeping and I embraced her. I felt dragged along by an irresistible force that compressed the space between us and the thickness of our clothing and the air in our lungs.

It was such an unexpected event that I almost immediately had to loosen my hold on her and back up, unbalanced and breathless, overcome by the sensations coming from my face and neck and hands and arms and chest and stomach and groin and legs; sensations that worked their way into my bloodstream a few seconds behind my movements.

Mette slipped away. She took a paper napkin out of a package on the shelf, opening it with trembling hands.

I followed her at a distance, shaken by what had happened, totally unsure of our ability to communicate verbally. "I'm sorry," I said. "About Jorge."

She continued to cry and sob, her face hidden behind the white paper napkin, her body shot through with a continuous tremor.

I tried to rein in my urge to embrace her again, ignoring the feelings that were hammering me from within. "Really. I liked him, even though we barely talked."

Between one sob and the next she said, "He liked you too."

"Really?" I even felt a little guilty, because my dislike for Jorge had a vein of jealousy, and was less intense than the vertigo of deep contact I'd felt a moment before when embracing her. I wished I could reestablish a more appropriate order for my emotional priorities, but no matter how hard I tried they kept rolling over in favor of the irresistible pressure that had crushed us one against the other.

Mette said, "He was a wonderful person. Wonderful."

"I know."

"But you hardly knew him."

"It seemed like I knew him. After our first, difficult encounter. Maybe it was because he was so close to you."

She turned around, her eyes full of tears. "Jorge and I weren't together."

"Ah, no?" A small wave of relief that I would never have confessed to washed over me, soaking all my different sensations.

Mette shook her head. "He was my best friend."

"Of course. You two had such a natural way of communicating. Very instinctive. That's why I thought he was your boyfriend."

"It was better that way," said Mette. "There were no emotional power games between us. What we had could never be broken. Never."

I said "Of course" again, making a supreme effort to try and share in her pain rather than think about my unexpected opportunity to enter into what might be the open space in her heart. It was the kind of thinking that made me feel like a sort of emotional jackal. "Bastards," I said.

"It's just so horrible, so horrible," she said.

I went and opened and closed a closet twice so as not to give in to the urge to embrace her and hug her with all my strength, cover her with kisses and caresses.

"And the fact that they're passing him off as somebody who made bombs," she said. "He was the least violent person I've ever known. He couldn't even have violent *thoughts*, despite the fact that he grew up in a troubled environment, with an alcoholic mother and sick brother, a father who beat them and who ran away with another woman when Jorge was just six."

"He was a fantastic person," I said, now that my retrospective relief enabled me to be generous.

"Yes." She blew her nose on a paper napkin, drying her tears with one hand.

"And you two met in the Amazon?"

She nodded yes. "His brother ran a small center that helped the *indios* against the colonists and *garimpeiros* and thugs working for the American and Japanese timber companies. There was a plan authorized by the Brazilian government to destroy five square miles of forestland where three tribes lived. That's when we met."

"In the forest?" Even though I had no more reason to be jealous of Jorge, I still felt a sense of irreparable loss at the thought of everything she had seen and done and felt and thought before I even knew she existed.

"Yes."

"I was in the forest too," I said. "But not when you were there." It seemed like an absurd waste of time, seen in this light: the energy and attention and enthusiasm spent on nothing, the millions of gestures and steps and thoughts consumed back when my life and hers still hadn't come close to contact.

She put her hands in the pockets of her jacket, standing there near the door.

The pot was hissing on the stovetop, almost no water left in it. I grabbed it with two potholders with leopard-skin designs and filled it up again in the sink. The contact between cold water and the burning hot metal created a burst of steam. Then I took out the tomato sauce and tuna and capers, mixing and heating everything up together in a pan.

Mette took out another paper napkin, drying her eyes and blowing her nose again. Our breath produced little clouds. Even wearing our jackets and sweaters we had to keep moving constantly in order not to become paralyzed.

I gave her a wooden spoon and said, "You stir it a little." I went around opening cupboards in search of something alcoholic to drink. In one low cupboard there were a number of well-ordered bottles, important wines that had probably been received as gifts and set aside for guests, seeing as how neither Fabio nor Nicoletta drank alcohol. I rifled through the *grand cru* champagnes and Barolos and Brunello di Montalcinos and Château Lafites, taking out a bottle of Brunello. It was ice-cold. I opened it and put it near the fireplace, throwing some more firewood on.

When I went back into the kitchen, Mette was stirring the sauce in the pan with the wooden spoon. She had stopped crying. I was struck by how our hunger could coexist with the unhappiness and uncertainty and preoccupation that were assailing us, maintaining its own perfect, intense autonomy. I wondered if this was a form of recklessness, or a self-protection mechanism developed by a species that urges individuals to stockpile energy for when they have to face dangerous situations. The one thing I knew was that my brain was rife with anticipations of the taste and consistency of our meal, to such a point that I had little space left for rational thought.

I poured more than half a package of penne into the boiling water, standing there to watch it foam up. Mette came close. We both scalded our faces in the starch-flavored vapor.

Then we drained the pasta and mixed in the sauce. I brought steaming plates over near the fireplace, into the small semicircle of heat at the center of the big room. I dashed outside to get some more wood from the garden, then put it on the fire. Mette sat down cross-legged on the edge of the stone lip and plunged her fork into the dish. I did the same. The pasta was turning lukewarm. The wine was still cold and had the tannic taste of old smoked velvet, but we sent it down in sips, our fingers curled around the stems of glass to keep them from falling out of our hands. The penne in tuna sauce seemed incredibly delicious to me, filled with complex tastes on multiple levels. I couldn't believe we'd made them so simply and easily. Mette used her fork as if she had to harpoon the essential supplies of life as long as she could, chewing intensely and occasionally taking a sip of wine. We seemed like two thieving children in somebody else's house, hounded accomplices, isolated in the bubble of our shared sensations. We didn't speak, holding our plates on our legs, our heads bowed low, uncomfortable and ill at ease in our own clothing, infinitely aware of every little signal.

Once we'd finished, our movements became much more fluid and slower than before. I gathered the plates, poured the rest of the wine into our glasses, and added more wood to the fire. We looked around so as to avoid looking one another in the face, but my entire nervous system was busy with perceptions of her. I hesitated for a long time between a number of possible words and gestures, finally nodding toward another part of the living room and saying, "Should we watch something on television?"

Mette nodded yes. I saw worry in her eyes.

I went and plugged in the television, then went back to take refuge near the fireplace with the remote in one hand. I changed channel after channel after channel, watching the images run behind the glass from several yards away, like signals from some distant world.

At a certain point a wide view of the street near the train station appeared, with the former Stopwatch headquarters transformed into the blackened, blocked off cavern. I turned up the volume. The voiceover said, "In Rome, investigations continue into the explosion this morning in the hideout of the ecoterrorist group Stopwatch. Authorities are still trying to identify the body of the person found on the scene, while other members of the organization are being actively sought by officers all over Italy, with all airports, train stations, and principal travel arteries under strict surveillance."

Mette and I looked at each other: I experienced an almost physical sense of an invisible net closing in on us in the darkness outside the house. I wondered how many traces we'd left behind, just how strict the surveillance was, what elements the people searching for us had available. I also wondered whether or not my brother would be willing to turn me over to the police in exchange for support and political favors, the way he had with Ndionge's memorial. I wondered if he'd already done so. At the same time I completely regretted having turned on the television: I wished I could go back a few minutes in time to when Mette and I had looked around with our glasses in our hands, caught in the slow flow of undefined sensations and thoughts.

"Do you think your sister-in-law won't tell anybody?" asked Mette. "That we're here."

The renewed anxiety in her voice cut me like a razor. I half-closed my eyes. "I hope not."

"She must have told your brother."

"I would think so." I didn't have any desire to think about my brother and Nicoletta, nor to entertain hypotheses about them.

"What about your brother? What will he do?"

"I have no idea. Evaluate his opportunities, I think."

Mette took a look around and said, "So we're not at all safe here."

"I don't know. But in any case we're not going to find anything better for tonight." Once again my head filled with escape routes, but they all wound up in front of police roadblocks. I turned off the television, and the big room filled back up with dense silence, interrupted only by the hissing of the fire.

Mette stared at the tips of her shoes, her profile communicating an almost unbearable expression of vulnerability.

I jumped up to my feet and said, "For tonight we're sleeping here, and that's that. Let's not think about it until tomorrow morning."

"And what about tomorrow morning?" she asked.

Immediately after that the phone started ringing, sending out an uncertain trill that struggled to take shape in the room's silence. We both stiffened, looking at the little table where the sound was coming from as if we could intuit who was on the other end and what his intentions might be. At the end of each trill I hoped it would stop, but it kept going on and on. Finally it stopped, but after a dozen seconds it started ringing again, even more insistently.

"Are you going to answer?" asked Mette.

"No, I'm not," I said, though this course of action seemed too passive to actually be right.

When the telephone stopped ringing again we went back to silence and immobility for minutes on end, our eyes pointed toward the phone, all our muscles tensed to absorb the shock of a new ring. But no more came and little by little we started breathing again. Now every curtain at the window and every corner of the wall had taken on a disturbing look.

"Who could that have been?" said Mette, her hands plunged into the pockets of her jacket.

"Maybe Nicoletta. Or my brother. I don't know."

She looked at the phone again and said, "I wonder what they wanted to tell you."

I scratched my head, wondering whether it had been an attempt to pass me some vital information, warn me of some imminent danger, convince me to come back, involve me in some pointless discussion.

We sat there a while longer, outside the heat of the fireplace, blocked by our uncertainties. The telephone did not ring; the house remained immersed in silence.

I went over to a window and moved aside the curtain in order to look between the slats of the roll-down shutters and see if there were any lights or movement. I strained my ears to catch any possible sounds. It didn't seem like there were any, but it was hard to be sure from inside. I said to Mette, "I'm going outside to take a look, you stay here."

"I'm coming too," she said immediately, following me toward the entrance.

We went cautiously out into the garden, peering left and right into the darkness. There didn't seem to be movement anywhere.

The air was as cold as it was in the house, just a little damper, its salty marsh smell shot through with smoke from our chimney. The little yard on the eastern side of the house was wet, sinking underneath our feet at every step. There was no moon and no stars; the only visible light came from the house through the metal slats of the roll-down shutters outside the living room, but you had to be really close in order to see it. "Don't go far," I said to Mette.

"No," she said from just a few inches off. I could feel her lukewarm breath in the darkness.

We walked down the hill to the gate, bumping into each other two or three times. Even after we'd had two or three minutes to adjust to the dark, all we could make out were the denser shadows of the wall around the property, the pine trees above our heads and some other houses on the right. The rest was impenetrable night, broken only at its furthest limits by the whine of a distant airplane descending.

We walked back up to the house following the wall. At a certain point I bumped into a bench and Mette ran into me. We breathed even closer than we had in Rome, moving about to disentangle ourselves. Without thinking about it I ran my hand down her arm until I found her hand, and then dragged her along behind me. I pressed her fingers between mine and felt the same sense of vertigo I'd felt when I'd held her in the kitchen, increasing every step with the pressure of her response.

We took another walk around the house in the strangest blend of vigilance and distraction, feeling the wine we'd drunk as much as the effects of our continuous contact. Despite all the reasons for alarm competing for my thoughts, I wouldn't have wanted to be anywhere else in the world if not there and with her.

WE LET GO OF EACH OTHER'S HANDS IN
THE SUDDEN LIGHT OF THE ENTRYWAY

We let go of each other's hands in the sudden light of the entryway. The marvelous dreamy naturalness we'd shared while walking outside in the dark fell apart into angular movements. The fire in the living room had almost completely died down. I gathered the last little burning bits into the center; it would only last a few minutes more.

I didn't feel like I was lucid enough to reflect on the uncertainties and decisions that awaited us in the morning. I said, "We should go to bed, if we have to get moving early tomorrow."

"Yes," said Mette.

I tried to overcome my mental resistance. I asked her, "Where would you like to go?"

"To France. Then I'll see once I'm there."

It occurred to me that one of the many things I didn't know about her was where she'd lived, but I couldn't think of a good way to ask. I said, "There's a Stopwatch office in Lyon, right? I saw it on the website."

"Yes," she said. "And we have friends in other cities."

"But where do you live?" I asked finally.

She looked away. "For the past few months I lived in Rome, with Jorge."

"Before that?" Now that we'd started, I was being dragged along by a hunger for missing information.

"Before that in London. Before that Manaus. Before that Cape Town. Before that Copenhagen. Before that, Rome."

"Rome?" I said, surprised.

"Yes, after high school. I lived there for almost a year. I worked as an au pair girl."

"That's why you speak Italian so well. But originally, where were you born?"

"Lemvig. It's a small city on the coast, in Jylland."

"Which is Jütland?"

"Yes."

"And you grew up there?" I was trying to imagine her as a little girl with honey-red hair.

"Yes. Then I went to study in Copenhagen, at the university."

"What did you study?"

"Anthropology."

"And that's how you ended up in South Africa?"

"Yes. I was doing research for my thesis in a village in Swaziland."

"What was that like?"

"One inhabitant out of three was HIV positive or had outright AIDS, including the children. The forest behind the village had been completely destroyed by a North American timber company. The cows and other animals had almost all died of thirst or illness. There was nothing left."

"What did you do?"

"I did my research," said Mette. "Even though I felt like a monster, recording interviews and writing my observations instead of *doing* something. Immediately after I got my degree I went back to Africa to work for Stopwatch."

"What kind of work?"

"A contraception program in the villages in Swaziland and Lesotho. But as soon as we managed to build the tiniest bit of faith and achieve some minuscule result, the Catholic missionaries would show up and say that condoms were the devil's handiwork, and that chastity was the only way to avoid becoming sick."

"What did you do?"

"We did what we could. Against everybody."

"How many of you were there?" I asked, my brain struggling to create arbitrary images of her in Africa.

"Just a few." But she didn't want to talk about herself anymore. "What about you? Where do you live? Where is that place in the countryside you told me about?"

"It's in the hills," I said, though I had a thousand other questions I wanted to ask her. "In Umbria, in central Italy. But it's just a temporary home base."

"Where did you live before that?"

"In Ancona. Before that I was sailing the seas. Before that São Paulo, in Brazil. Before that London. Before that Rome." I was struck by how we'd been in the same places at different times, by our possible missed connections—everything that could have filled the years and months and days and hours and minutes and millions of seconds now compressed into simple city names.

Mette stretched out toward the center of the fireplace, but even the last flames had gone out by now. The weak wash of heat had finished, and we were both stiff with cold.

I said, "Should we go to bed?" and went to unplug the phone cord.

"Yes," she said, walking past me in order to collect her bag from the couch where she'd left it.

"Tell me where you'd rather sleep," I said as we walked toward the bedrooms. I opened the door to Harry and Emily's room, which was white and bare as a jail cell. Then I opened the door to the guest bedroom where there were two twin beds. The bedcover and curtains and lampshade were all the same yellow tone. I walked ahead of her upstairs, opening the doors to other rooms in a state of wintry suspension: Tommaso's room, where a life-size shark outline decorated the wall and children's toys and books still sat on the shelves; Fabio and Nicoletta's room, where a large bed with a rounded headboard stood beneath an abstract painting with multicolored shapes.

We peered into each room as if they were hypothetical reconstructions of distant living environments, sniffing at the air to gather traces of what was left behind.

"Well?" I asked Mette.

"It doesn't matter," she said. "You decide."

"No, you choose." I realized that it was like asking her to choose between sleeping separately or together, but on the other hand my nerves were shot and my ears were buzzing, and I didn't think I could trust my own impulses alone. I had mental images of she and I in the same bed, she and I in different beds, in different rooms, on two separate floors. I couldn't figure out if having held each other's hands in the darkness implied a natural choice in favor of the first option. The overly intense light from the lamps and ceiling seemed to be working against us, accentuating the empty space separating us.

We were standing halfway down the stairs. Mette went back to the ground floor, pointing to the guest bedroom. "This one," she said.

"Do you mind if we both sleep in the same room?" I asked. The words of my question came out tight-lipped in part because of the cold, in part to skip at least some of the implications.

"Sure," she said with a naturalness that didn't make me any more certain.

We went into two different bathrooms. I left her the one with hot water. I looked at myself in the mirror, and found my face corresponded with how I felt: I had the expression of a thirteen-year-old overwrought by the circumstances.

In the guest bedroom I took what bedding there was out of the closets, throwing two on each bed. I took off my coat and boots and slipped into the bed by the door, pulling the covers up to my nose. The pillow and sheets had the smell of ancient detergent, and seemed to have absorbed all the humidity in the room in order to share it with my legs and back and arms and head, behind the ears.

Mette came in two minutes later, barely glancing at me. She went and put her bag on a chair, took off her jacket, sat down on the bed, unlaced her shoes, took them off and placed them in a corner. I perceived her movements in the left edge of my field of vision, never turning my head yet following her with acute intensity. She got under the covers dressed as well, saying "There. Brrrrr."

Finally I turned to look at her. "Are you comfortable?" I asked.

"Yes," she said, though I could see her trembling in the cold, damp bed.

I wished I could extend an arm toward her, but there were almost two yards of space between us. "Relatively," I said.

"Relatively," she said with a smile that was too brief.

"Do you think we'll wake up on our own," I asked, "or should we set an alarm?"

"That's probably better. Even though I'm sure we'll wake up."

I got out of the bed and took the seventies-style alarm clock off the dresser at the wall, turning its little alarm dial. It was only forty minutes past nine in the evening. "Six o'clock?" I asked.

"Yes," said Mette.

I went back and slipped under the covers. "Should I turn off the lights?" I asked.

"Yes."

I turned off the main light. The little goblet-shaped lamp on my nightstand remained on. "Do you want me to turn this one off too?"

"Yes."

We lay there silently in the dark, divided by the space between our beds, by the motionless house. The only sounds came from us turning from one side to the other, stretching and folding our legs under the hard-to-warm bed sheets.

I tried to think about the best thing to do in the morning, but I could only get fragments of ideas, intuitions that were too brief to be useful. None of my thoughts lasted long enough, and it was no use thinking about anything else: the images of roads and places that I focused on disappeared almost immediately. My own ability for mental organization seemed nullified, each attempt to choose a plan of action simply increased my restlessness. I tossed and turned in the bed, shot through with continuous jolts and flashes, suffering an almost painful awareness of Mette's breathing and her movements such a short distance away.

In the end I realized that two blankets weren't nearly enough, and as tired as I was there was no way I was going to get to sleep like this. I turned to Mette and said, "Are you sleeping?"

"No," she said.

"Are you cold?"

"A little."

"A little, or a lot?"

"A lot."

"But shouldn't you be used to the cold? I mean, as a Danish person?"

"I'm used to cold *outside*. Not inside the house."

"Right," I said, a few images of Scandinavian interiors passing through my mind.

"What about you, then?" she said. "You live on wild hills and spend a quarter of the day lighting fires in the fireplace."

"I'm used to *dry* cold. Not this damp, creeping stuff. It's like zombie swamp cold."

Submerged, breathy sounds came from the other side of the room.

I thought that she had started crying again. I raised myself up on one elbow, full of apprehension. But she was just laughing. It seemed like a miracle, after entire days during which every single little exchange we'd had had been hardened and interrupted and made difficult. I started laughing too, out of relief and contagion and the same reason she was laughing: the desperate, electrifying absurdity of our situation.

We kept laughing for minutes on end. Occasionally we'd stop, then start up again in an even more convulsed manner, rustling the sheets and covers, setting the beech wood slats underneath us creaking.

When we stopped we were quiet again for a few minutes, breathing in the darkness. Then, without thinking about it I said, "You know that two people exposed to the cold are supposed to sleep huddled together, to unify their body heat? That's what the survival manuals say."

"I know," said Mette.

"Then why are we sleeping separately like two idiots?"

"Dunno."

I turned on the little light on my nightstand. We looked at one another in that yellow light, both sitting up, our covers piled up around our knees. I got out of my bed and pushed it over to hers in a single wave of thought and movement, without taking my eyes off her. It seemed like an imagined gesture, one that didn't cost the least bit of effort.

I turned off the light again and got under the covers, sliding over toward her as if I was swimming through the sea at night. I found one arm with my hand, a leg with my leg, a hip with my hip. I hugged her waist and turned her around, pulling her in close. She was marvelously warm and solid. Her wildflower perfume made my heart race; being this close after having just been separate was stupefying. I kissed her hair and forehead and temples with quick, infantile smacks. "Hey, hey, *hey*," I said.

"Hey," she said, hugging me in turn. She pressed her body against mine, hard. Her forehead was tucked into the curve between my neck and right shoulder, her hair touching my chin and nose, tickling me. Her breasts and stomach and legs created constantly shifting friction, the backs of our feet overlapping one another in elastic interplay. We were so totally absorbed in our embrace and the infinite sensations it produced that there was no space for thought. Our body heat combined and multiplied much more than it says in the survival books. I had never experienced such an intense embrace, yet there was no specific sexual intent: ours was the essential, vibrating joy of a male and a female of the same species pulled one into the other in a safe corner of the planet, all around us the dense darkness of night extending out to the known ends of the universe.

———

After an indefinable length of time I said softly, "Mette?"

"Huh?" she said, her voice close enough to cause a shiver to start from my temples and run through my whole body.

"Who are you?"

"You?"

"I asked you first."

"What do you want to know?"

"How you came to be the way you are. How we got here. The how and why of everything." It wasn't the first time that words struck me as inadequate instruments for communication, but at that moment the feeling was so strong that they melted away before my very eyes as I searched for them.

"Right now I don't know," she said. She moved her head against my shoulder, producing another endlessly deep shiver in me.

THERE WERE ELECTRIC DOORBELL
SOUNDS IN MY DREAM

There were electric doorbell sounds in my dream, so penetrating and insistent that they crossed over into real life. I woke up with a start: I was still lying next to Mette, threads of light filtered through the roll-down shutters to touch the floor. I looked at my watch, it was twenty minutes past eight in the morning. The doorbell rang again. I moved the covers and jumped to my feet.

Mette woke up too. She sat up immediately, her face swollen with sleep, her hair in disarray. "What's happening?" she said.

"There's someone at the gate," I said, my sense of urgency conflicting with an instantaneous nostalgia for when I'd still been sleeping alongside her.

"Who?" she said. She was already sitting on the edge of the bed.

"I don't know." I took the traitorous alarm clock off the nightstand and shook it. I went to the closed window and then came back. I put on my boots. There were too many simultaneous gestures in my head, too many contradictory impulses. It was impossible to choose a single, efficient sequence of movements.

Mette got her shoes from the corner and put them on without lacing them up. Out in the hallway the bell rang again: an unbearably invasive *rrrrring rrrrring*.

Near the front door I touched her on the shoulder. "If something happens," I said, "go out through the sliding glass door in the kitchen and jump over the little wall. Run away as fast as you can." It wasn't a very comprehensive or promising escape plan, but I couldn't think of any others.

"Wait," she said, trying to hold onto my arm.

"You stay here." I pushed her back. I opened the door just a little and looked outside. There was cold light, the sky covered with whitish-gray clouds. A metal segment of the gate blocked my view: I could only barely see a pair of pants and a head of gray hair through the joint where the gate met the column on one side. My muscles were tensed for battle, my blood full of adrenaline, my head busy with guesstimations about potential weapons inside the house, the front door's potential for resistance, possible escape routes inland and toward the sea.

"Who's there?" I shouted.

"Giacomo!" shouted a voice from behind the gate. "I'm the caretaker!"

My battle tension melted into partial relief, then the partial relief into irritation. I went down the cement drive set with sunken decorative stones and said, "What do you want?"

"Hello." He was peering through the narrow crack, surrounded by oleander leaves.

"Hello," I said to the small blue eye and narrow mouth in constant movement.

"Miss Nicoletta called me. She said that you have to call her right away. It's extremely urgent."

"Thank you very much." I couldn't believe I'd slept this late.

"She said you're not answering the phone. That the phone just keeps ringing. She tried more times than she can count."

"Alright. I'll call her." I was trembling with impatience.

The caretaker continued to move his head about in order to try and see things on the other side of the gate. "You should have told me, last night. I'd have turned the heat on! I told Miss Nicoletta."

"Oh, that's alright. We got by without it."

"What do you mean without it? All night? What about that poor young lady there?"

"What young lady?" I turned back toward the house. Mette was standing in the doorway, watching me. I motioned for her to go back inside, moving my lips to say, "Go!"

"I'll turn it on now, don't you worry," said Giacomo. He already had the keys in one hand. It was clear that he had rung the bell rather than coming straight in only because Nicoletta had instructed him to do so.

"Don't worry," I said. "We can do without it. But thanks anyway."

"What do you mean? It'll be freezing in there!"

"We're fine just the way things are. Really."

He didn't want to give up, and said "If the senator finds out I left you in here to freeze, he'll tan my hide. Tan it!"

"I'll explain things to him. I'll tell him that I preferred the cold air. Don't worry about it. Thanks again, you've been very kind. Thank you."

He continued to stand there, peering in toward the entrance.

"In any case," he said, "the key to the heating shed is in the kitchen closet, hanging behind the cupboards. Call me if you need anything. Do you have my number?"

"I've got it, I've got it," I replied. "Thanks again. You've been very kind. Have a nice day, thanks."

Giacomo finally moved off, very reluctantly. I waited until I heard his car engine start up, further below, then I went quickly back up the drive.

Mette was standing in the entryway, tense. "What's up?" she asked.

"That was the caretaker," I said. "Nicoletta sent him. She wants me to call her immediately, says it's urgent."

She stared at me, her eyes full of alarm.

I tried to fight off the urge to embrace her, but was unsuccessful: I pulled her in close forcefully, inhaling her breath and body heat and smell, absorbing the feel of her body. I wanted to keep holding her forever; I had to check my watch in order to let go.

She followed me into the living room, stopping by the cold fireplace while I plugged the phone back in and called Fabio and Nicoletta.

Emily answered, saying "Senator Telmari's house" as if they were the words to an enchantment.

I asked her to put Nicoletta on the phone. I watched Mette, who watched me.

"Lorenzo," said Nicoletta. Her voice was very strained.

"Nicoletta."

"I tried calling you more times than I can count. You never answer."

"I know." I was struck by her tone of voice. She sounded like a jealous woman.

"Your brother tried to reach you too. On the cell phone, on the home phone. Nothing."

"What did you want to tell me?"

"That the situation is serious, Lorenzo! It's not a game! It's not an adventure!"

"I never thought it was," I said. I had to make an effort to control my irritation and sense of urgency and all the other unsettling impulses running through me.

"I don't think you do!" she said. "A person died in that explosion near the station yesterday!"

"I know."

"They're looking for these people all over Italy! Fabio says that they'll catch them soon, it's just a matter of time!"

I tried to smile at Mette in order to release some of the tension from her face, but without any success. "So what?" I asked.

"So you have to do the only intelligent thing you can, Lorenzo!" said Nicoletta. "Stop playing Knight of Lost Causes, dump that poor girl who's clinging to you and come back to Rome immediately!"

"Poor girl? Look who's talking."

The quip passed right over her head. "Fabio says that your position can still be cleared up," she said. "But you have to hurry up and get back here! Before things get so bad they can't be fixed!"

"I'm already beyond the fixing point."

"Lorenzo, cut it out!" shouted Nicoletta in a gravelly tone of voice that she wouldn't have liked to hear played back to her. "Don't invent some inane higher mission for yourself! This is just a stupid infatuation of yours!"

"My personal feelings have nothing to do with it. It's something that has to do with my father, with the subterranean traffic of this rotten country, with the imbalances of this world."

"Who do you think you're talking to, Lorè? You've known that girl, what, three days?"

"Long enough."

"You can't ruin your life without at least stopping to reconsider! And you'll be ruining your brother's life too! And mine!"

"I've thought about it, don't you worry."

"For fuck's sake, Lorenzo! I can't do anything *but* worry!" she shouted, beyond control now. "I've got every reason in the world to worry! And I want my car back, right away!"

"Never fear, I'll leave it parked here. Thanks again for everything." I ended the conversation, smashing the phone down on the table. I looked at Mette, my ears still ringing with Nicoletta's words and all the reasons contained within and behind her tone of voice.

The expression on Mette's face was closed, distant. "Go back to Rome, Lorenzo," she said.

"What are you talking about?"

"Leave me here. I'll take a train. I can take care of myself."

I went over close to her. The idea that she might exclude me from her thoughts and plans turned my blood cold. I said, "First Nicoletta, now you? Are you in this together, conspiring to drive me crazy?"

"Don't think you owe me some kind of debt," she said.

"Don't you start up with that again. I'm not doing it for you, I'm doing it for me!"

A different light came into her eyes. She looked away without responding.

I said, "If you have to go to the bathroom, then go now. Move it. We have to leave. It's already late."

I took a quick shower in cold water, then dried myself at hyper speed with a towel to warm up. I got dressed again, hopping from one point to another on the cold tiles. Against my will, I kept running Nicoletta's words over through my mind like a bad, clingy pop song I'd just listened to on the radio. I wondered if maybe she was right when she defined my feelings for Mette as an infatuation, if I'd gotten into this thing for Mette, or if I'd been in it even before I'd met her. I wondered if it made sense to keep hoping that truth could somehow be established, when the truth had already been wiped out by the erasure professionals. I asked myself if maybe what I found attractive in Mette were things I didn't know yet, if I was willing to jump back into that game of self-depiction and expectations and offers and demands that had caused nothing but disappointment and assertions and accusations—enduring disenchantment—in my previous life.

These were not real questions, but rather fragments of questions, running one on top of the other and blending in with fragments of escape plans and a million different images: my father dead on his bed, Nicoletta's gestures in the entryway to her home, the empty, snow-covered landscape outside my house, Jorge's bushy hair, the way the tan jacket chased after me, Mette's face when she was shocked awake. It occurred to me that in the end, I didn't expect certainties, not even relative certainties. I realized that I was a thousand times happier letting destiny and my own instinct guide me through dangerous territory, rather than make an effort to cultivate results devoid of common sense.

And there was no time left: I went into the kitchen, filled up the coffee maker, and put it on the stove. I walked back and forth without stopping for one moment to run through possible routes and calculate distances.

Mette came into the kitchen just as the coffee was ready. She was already wearing her short jacket and her bag was over one shoulder. She held her black beret in one hand. I filled two coffee cups, then took a package of sugar-free Swedish cookies out of the cupboard. The boiling coffee burnt our lips and tongues. We nibbled on moist, tasteless cookies.

"Do you think we're going to be able to get away?" asked Mette.

"Away from here?" I asked as I continued to consider new routes and plans.

"Out of Italy."

"It depends. Depends on the road we take, and what kind of vehicle we use." I realized that I didn't have much I could reassure her with, but I couldn't even imagine being anything but completely honest with her.

She, however, didn't seem at all panic-stricken. She was organizing herself for travel given the circumstances. "Is there a train station near here?" she asked.

I nodded yes, but I didn't like the idea of taking an international train at all. It seemed like a stereotypical Hollywood trap: Mette and I sitting in our seats, two pairs of police officers coming from opposite ends of the car to block us just before the train reaches the border. I opened the door to the kitchen closet, searching behind the broom and cleaning supplies and vacuum cleaner for the key box the caretaker had spoken of, attached to the wall. There were a lot of different keys inside, each one hanging from its own hook and with its own colored tag. I took them all out and tossed them on the table in a heap. I started rummaging through them.

"What are you looking for?" asked Mette, following my actions, perplexed.

"The keys to my brother's boat. He keeps it at a marina near here. It should still be in the water. He had pictures taken of himself and Nicoletta on it just a few weeks ago."

"Why the boat?"

"We're going to France over water," I said. "We'll dock in Nice, then we'll take a train from there."

"But it's an incredible distance by sea. And it's *December*, Lorenzo."

I liked the way she pronounced my name, especially the R and the Z. And I liked her feminine prudence: she made me feel a desire to challenge any form of judiciousness in order to strengthen it. "I've sailed the *Atlantic*, in December. And it's better to sail for a few days than to get ourselves arrested on the train at the first station."

She shook her head. "I know how the sea can get in the winter. I grew up next to the sea."

"But you're used to the North Sea. This is the Mediterranean. It's a sort of lake, by comparison." The fact was I knew she was right, but I was completely taken by the idea of going by boat all the same: my head was full of images of the two of us out at sea, free of land and all its commitments and pressures, outside the net that was tightening around us minute by minute. Everything else tended to fade into the background, practical considerations and organizational needs included.

"It's absurd," said Mette.

I went into the living room and took an old, framed nautical map off the wall. I carried it into the kitchen and set it on the table. I ran my finger over it in a line toward the northwest until I reached the French coast. "You see?" I said.

"Yes, it's absurd."

"You're hardheaded." But with the map lying before us it was impossible to deny the evidence. I traced a line west and said, "Then we'll go to Corsica."

Mette's gaze followed the nervous movements of my finger. I could read the different considerations that were passing through her mind by the look on her face.

"Corsica is reasonable," I said. "Trust me."

She wasn't convinced. She said, "Besides, we don't have any of the things we need for a sea voyage."

"What do we need?" The blood ran through my body increasingly quickly, transporting pure impatience everywhere.

"I don't know. Supplies. The right clothing." She pointed to what she was wearing, an outfit that I had come to care for intensely over the past few days.

I took her by the hand and led her upstairs, into Fabio and Nicoletta's room. I opened their mahogany, navy-style clothes bureau. Inside there was nothing but a few summer clothes, completely inappropriate for a winter crossing. I took out a light jacket, a pair of shirts and a pair of colorful bikinis all the same.

Mette laughed, but worry proved much stronger than amusement. "Come on, Lorenzo," she said.

I put everything back into the bureau and we went back downstairs into the kitchen. I went back to searching through the keys on the table. I asked her, "Do you trust me, or not?"

"I don't know," she said. "We don't even know each other. You said so yourself, last night."

"You know that's not true. We've known each other for a long time, you and I, and you know it."

She cocked her head to look at me from a different angle. I liked that, too.

"Just tell me if you trust me. Instinctively, without thinking about it." Immediately after that I found a pair of keys attached to a yellow tag with *Aqualuna* written on it. I showed them to her.

"Yes," said Mette.

I stuck the boat keys in my pocket, put all the others back into the key box, and left the keys to Nicoletta's car on the table. I rinsed the coffee cups in the sink and grabbed a plastic bag from the closet. I filled the bag with a few bottles of water, two packages of pasta and a couple cans of tuna. I said, "Let's go, let's go." I couldn't wait to be outside, in movement.

WE WALKED ALONG THE DESERTED ROAD

We walked along the deserted road flanking the closed villas clinging to the hillside in the veiled light and fog rising off the sea. A few dozen yards below us on the left lay the beach, on the right wet fields and road and marina warehouses, the rolling waves of the forest of white and silver sailboat masts.

We held our breath as we walked past the gates and doors and balconies and shuttered windows of the other villas, past the agaves and oleanders, past the latticework and the wisteria pergolas and the naked grape vines, past the big metal T's set into the ground in order to guarantee parking spaces for owners who didn't have somewhere to park inside. There were neither sounds nor smoke nor lights turned on, nor any other sign of human life. We walked along silently, lightly, with nothing but our bags over our shoulders and the plastic bag of supplies, but silence and simplicity were the only advantages we had. If a police car had come rushing up at full speed ahead of us or from behind on that narrow road it would have been difficult to jump off and down the hill in time, or continue our escape in any useful direction. I tried to concentrate on the invisibility techniques I had learned during a ninjutzu course I'd taken in São Paulo before the instructor was arrested, but they had been conceived for nighttime or the jungle much more than for an off-season vacation spot on the Tuscan coast. My eyes were constantly drawn to Mette walking alongside me: the blend of attention and apprehension that she aroused in me was so dense it slowed down my other reflexes, save those that had directly to do with her.

"Don't think about yourself walking," I said, "but about what's around you. Become one with your surroundings."

"I know, I know," she said with a half-smile.

I realized I even liked her way of not giving in to enchantment, and her ability to remain equally enchanted when she felt like it: her variable equilibrium of practicality and absentmindedness.

We reached the beach, walking between the small wood and cement buildings of the summer clubs. We crossed the wet sand, where we were more exposed but also more difficult to reach. Every once in a while we glanced toward the woody, vaguely sinister hills in front of us, the two forts on peaks at the far ends of the bay.

"How did you sleep, last night?" I asked.

"Fine," said Mette. "Too well, apparently. What about you?"

"Me too. And it was the first time I've slept with somebody else in quite a while." I didn't know why I said that: maybe it was an attempt to open up, and to get her to open up too.

"Oh yeah?" She didn't look at me.

We walked along silently for a while. I looked at the algae and seashells and driftwood and pieces of plastic on the beach, then up toward the houses. "What about you?" I said.

"Me too."

"Really?" The uncertainty in my voice was easy to identify.

She nodded yes and said, "Except with Jorge, of course."

"You two slept together?"

"When there weren't two beds. He snored so hard that he'd wake me up twenty times every night. I had to blow on his nose or pinch his ear to get him to stop."

It certainly wasn't an exhaustive exchange of information about our sentimental lives, nor did it clarify if we'd slept together as wonderful instant friends or as something else the night before. But the caution with which we were walking along the beach seemed to reflect an even stronger interior caution; we were trying not to break any of the equilibriums that kept us together. We were careful about how we moved our thoughts as much as our feet.

It took us less than ten minutes to reach the marina. We walked between temporary warehouses built of white plastic and big boats suspended in wheeled, tubular structures, underneath a fake galleon with three masts, alongside what seemed like a gigantic golden bathtub with dark windows and double propellers, the words *Gran Nirvana* written on its stern. It was a sort of storage yard for adult toys, weekend dreams and ostentatious desires in the form of hulls and superstructures that cost millions of euros and weighed dozens of tons and occupied hundreds of thousands of square feet. Mette and I silently pointed out the most grotesque names and most vulgar shapes, turning our heads left and right as we walked along among them. I could imagine the attitudes and gestures and gazes and tans and swimsuits and hair and wraparound skirts and sunglasses and empty words and cocktail glasses and throbbing bass music and dance moves and laughter and games of seduction and the sordid or stupid or worrisome conversations that these hulls must have hosted for the two or three months of the year during which they were put in water: I entertained brief hallucinatory flashes, contemplating upward from down below.

We slipped beneath the white bar and warning signs and the guardian's empty little office. We walked along the dock. I looked at the sailboats docked along the piers, their gaff-sails and jibs wrapped in protective coverings or naked, their cockpits closed beneath tightly clasped canvases. The water was grayish-brown, stirred by a light breeze. Out beyond the jetties the sea was frothy. Mette looked out in the same direction. I was almost certain I could guess her thinking. I asked myself if this was really a reasonable plan, not a stupid, risky idea. But I didn't really want to spend time considering the pros and cons; I was too impatient.

My brother's boat sat a little further on, docked halfway down the pier between two other similar boats. I pointed it out to Mette. We stole along like thieves, down the concrete to the white, squared stern with *Aqualuna* written across it. It certainly didn't possess the elegant lines of the old English sloop built of carvel iroko on oak with mahogany topsides and a teak deck on which I'd traveled so many seas before being forced to sell, but its fiberglass hull had certainly done less damage to the world's forests. The corner of the gaff-sail stuck out of the self-winding boom, the jib was rolled up on the mainstay, the tiller was tucked beneath its sky-blue canvas. There was no more than an inch of stagnant water in the cockpit.

I glanced toward the road and the dock: they were deserted, aside from a little white dog trotting up to a black dog standing further on. I put down the gangway and went aboard. As soon as I felt the hull rock beneath my feet I felt almost completely free. I smiled at Mette, who stared back perplexed. I had her pass me the backpacks and the plastic bag with our supplies. The keys worked; I went below to check the engine compartment. The tank was almost full of gas, the batteries were charged, and the boat's various instruments all seemed okay. There was a good selection of sea maps in the cupboard above the map table. It was a vessel full of automatic equipment and servomotors, built for lazy city dwellers with no desire to tire themselves out at sea. I took the canvas off the tiller and pressed the starter button. The motor started up almost immediately, chugging regularly.

We continued to look around, but there really didn't seem to be anyone anywhere in the marina registering our sounds or movements.

I extended one hand to Mette. She jumped aboard without taking it. Judging from her movements it was easy to see she knew how to move around in a boat.

I went back out on the pier and untied the two stern mooring lines, then got back aboard. I pulled in the gangway. I found a bag with oilskin jackets and boots in a pile down in the hull. I tossed them out onto the dinette couch. I put on my brother's pair and told Mette to do the same with Nicoletta's.

The boots were a little tight for both of us, but the rest fit relatively well. We looked at each other in our red and yellow outfits, barely smiling.

We went out on deck. Without my having to say anything, Mette gathered up the fenders and went to pull in the bow rope.

We slid slowly down a corridor between the other docked boats, silent and almost immobile at our posts, gliding over water veiled by a haze that grew increasingly thick the closer we got to open sea.

Out beyond the jetties the breeze suddenly grew stronger. The waves came one on top of the other and began to spray the hull. I pressed the button for the gaff-sail winder and jib winder: the sails opened slowly, crackling in the wind and then filling and drawing tense. The boat leaned to one side, picking up speed little by little. I breathed more deeply once the first sprays of water started hitting my face.

Mette joined me in the cockpit. Her oilskin and boots and black beret gave her the look of an ancient mariner. "The weather?" she asked.

I looked up at the sky covered with gray clouds shot through here and there with darker veins. "Well," I said, "it's not great."

"What's your forecast?"

I glanced at the barometer. It showed low pressure. But I didn't feel like going down below to listen to the radio forecasts, nor making any pessimistic mental calculations. "I have no idea," I said.

"What?" she said. "Aren't you supposed to be the one I can trust?"

"And aren't you supposed to be the one who trusts me?" I touched her shoulder, laughing. Holding the tiller wheel and looking out toward open sea gave me a feeling of pure euphoria.

Mette didn't respond, but she smiled, even if only for a moment.

I hauled the gaff-sail aft. We moved ahead at good speed toward the southwest, then tacked northwest.

By One the Wind Blew
at Fifteen Knots

By one the wind blew at fifteen knots. Giglio Island had long since disappeared behind us. Mette shouted to me, "I'm dying of hunger!"

"Me too!" I yelled. The sailboat cut quickly through the medium-sized waves. Both our faces were wet with spray from the choppy, foamy water. I checked the compass and GPS. I wondered if anyone had realized the boat was missing and warned my brother or alerted the coast guard, or if the marina was still as empty and deserted as it had been when we left. I looked back from time to time, but I didn't see any threatening motorboat outlines.

"I'll make something!" shouted Mette, going down below.

Visibility wasn't good and there were some stratocumuli coming in from the northwest. To make matters worse, I didn't know the boat very well. But I liked the idea of sailing along secretly with Mette so much that I didn't feel like worrying. The very thought of prudence seemed to contradict the vagueness of our plans and the feelings that ran between us. All I wanted to do was to let the sails drag me along with her as far as possible from land, and that was it.

She stuck her head out of the hatchway and looked at me.

"What's up?" I shouted.

"Nothing!" She went back below.

I thought about the intense pleasure of when we had clung to each other in bed the night before; the inexpressible feeling of completion that breathing on and warming each other in the dark had provided. I continued to be blown away by the idea that we were still together in the light of day, sharing a degree of familiarity that we hadn't enjoyed in the least the day before.

Ten minutes later she came back up to me with two plates of spaghetti. The pasta was a little overcooked and flavored with nothing but olive oil, but we devoured it greedily all the same, hunched over and clinging to the boat so that we wouldn't lose our balance or control of the tiller, barbaric forkful after barbaric forkful right to the last strand.

When we'd finished Mette took the plates back below, then came back up and sat down next to me, propping herself up on the bench seat. She had a sad expression, looking from side to side. She wiped her eyes with the back of her hand, but I couldn't tell if that was because of the spray, or because she was crying.

"What's the matter?" I asked.

"Nothing." She took her eyes away again.

"Is it because of Jorge?"

She nodded yes and said, "It's unacceptable that he died like that."

"I know," I said, competing with the noise of the wind and sea.

"Unacceptable."

"I know."

"That they win. Once again."

I looked at her and at the sea over the bow, tightening my hands on the tiller. The hull crashed and rang in the waves.

"That they murdered somebody like him," said Mette, "and then go around saying it was his fault."

"Yes."

"It's as if the memorial never even existed. They stole the truth, and spread something else around in its place. Jorge died for nothing. It's unacceptable."

Three-quarters of me was listening to her words, the rest concentrated on the sails. The wind seemed to be rising, although not uniformly. "Then let's refuse to accept it," I said.

"What are we supposed to do?"

"We should take back the stolen truth."

"How? By now they've surely destroyed both copies of the memorial."

"We'll hold a press conference. We'll tell Ndionge's story and everything about the memorial and my father and Dante and Jorge, every detail."

"Do you think there are a lot of people willing to believe us, just based on our word?" she asked. "Or even any willing to come to our press conference?" Sitting there in her seafaring oilskins she seemed to oscillate between unawareness of the rules of the world and awareness of the rules of the world, exactly like me.

I asked her, "Are we totally sure there were only two copies of the memorial."

"Maurice only typed two," said Mette. "He said so several times. Your father's assistant confirmed that there were only two copies, didn't she?"

"Yes."

"Did she say anything else, when you saw her yester-day morning?"

"No."

"How was she doing?"

"She was scared. She was filling two suitcases with stuff to take away with her. Her tall, thin, hostile friend was there too."

"What did she tell you?"

"That she was scared. That she didn't trust Italy."

"That's it?"

"More or less." I remembered the photograph of my father that Nadine had given me right before she got in the car. I opened the zipper of the oilskin and reached into the inside jacket pocket while holding the tiller with the other hand. I felt around for the photo. In the end I pulled it out together with my cell phone, but a large wave came along and hit us sideways and I lost my balance. I tightened my fingers more around the photo than the cell phone, and the phone flew out of the boat.

Mette leapt after it, but it was no use: the cell phone sank like a little silvery fish.

"Don't worry about it," I said. "It wasn't important to me anyway. It's better this way." In fact, the event seemed symbolic, cutting all ties with my very limited life of relationships to leave me unequivocally with her and the situation we were living through together.

"Really?" said Mette, looking at the water behind us.

"Really. There's nobody I'd like to call right now. Nobody."

She smiled, a little uncertain. She hugged herself tighter.

The photograph was still in my hand. I looked at it closely for the first time, trying to protect it from the sea spray. It was relatively recent: my father wearing a straw hat and shorts. His shirtsleeves were rolled up.

"Who's that?" asked Mette.

"My father. Nadine gave it to me yesterday morning, just before she left."

She took the photo out of my hand and stared at it for a while. She said, "He doesn't look anything like you."

"No? Maybe he was more like Fabio, at least his looks."

She continued to stare at the photograph, trying to protect it from the sea. She held it up for me to look at, asking, "Where was he?"

There was a palm tree and a dilapidated wooden hut in the background. "I have no idea," I said. "Maybe in Africa. Or South America."

Mette turned the photo around, studying the backside.

"What?" I asked.

"I don't know. A poem, I think." She held the backside of the photograph up so that I could see it: there were a few ordered lines written in blue ink.

It wasn't easy to hold our course and decipher my father's oblique calligraphy at the same time, but I read:

For Nadine to keep safe at hand / What without Faolo she won't understand. / For that which passes at all costs / From your knowledge to my thoughts: / The fantastic August fish / Of distant 1976.

"What does it mean?" asked Mette.

"I have no idea." I felt a measure of embarrassment for my father's limping rhyme, inspired by a web of feelings that had long since faded away.

"Who is 'Faolo'? Do you know him?"

"Paolo," I said.

"Here it says *Faolo*," said Mette. "With an F."

"Faolo's not a name. He must have made a mistake."

"But the F is really clear. Look at the two horizontal lines.

It can't be a mistake."

"It must have been a private thing between the two of them. A lover's code."

Mette cocked her head to one side. "How's that? Wasn't Nadine his assistant?"

"They were together for a long time," I said. "She was a sort of second wife, after my mom. That's why my brother hates her."

Mette smiled a little. I liked her lips, the way they accompanied her line of thought. She held herself propped on the inclined bench, continuing to study the back of the photograph, protecting it with a cupped hand.

"What about this writing down here?" she said, holding it up to me again.

In the right hand corner, written in pencil and in handwriting different from my father's, stood the words *Rua do Sol 53/b*.

"An address?" asked Mette.

"It sure seems like it."

"In Brazil?"

"Maybe. Or in Portugal. Who knows?" I wished she would stop focusing on the photograph and go back to what we were talking about before.

But she didn't stop turning it over in her hands. "Why did Nadine give you this specific photograph?" she said.

"I don't know. Maybe because it was one of the most recent." A big wave hit us before I could prepare for it, making the hull ring with a *schlunk* that wasn't entirely reassuring.

"Where did she get it?" asked Mette.

"Out of her jacket pocket. She took it out as we were saying goodbye."

"In the house?"

"Outside in the street. Right before she got into the car with her friend."

"Did she have other photographs too?"

"I don't know. She had some others in her suitcases, but maybe just that one in her pocket."

"So she must have put it in her pocket before she went out. In order to give it to you."

"Maybe." I tried to remember, but I couldn't.

Mette looked at both sides of the photo again, using her left hand to try and shield it from the salty sea spray. She asked me, "Did she say anything when she gave it to you?"

"No. Maybe 'Here, take this.'"

"Nothing else?"

"No." I was watching the waves grow larger.

Mette gave the photograph back. She too stared out at the oncoming sea.

I put the photograph back in my inside pocket, closing the oilskin zipper back up. The wind was changing direction and kept getting stronger. I bore up to cut across the wind. We sped along quickly over the vast lead-colored expanse amid explosions of white foam.

Toward five o'clock it grew dark and we had twenty-two knots out of the northeast. The crests of the waves rose and then broke into surf, the boat danced and smacked the water and shivered and tended to sag to leeward. I reduced the sails, and we kept flying forward full speed all the same. Mette clung tightly to the handrail. She had a good way of leaning and setting her feet. She was looking ahead, her eyes half-closed against the wind and sea spray, absorbing the blows to the hull with the muscles in her legs and arms.

I shouted to her, "Do you want to go down below?"

"Why?" she shouted, as if she couldn't understand the reasons behind my question.

"Nothing!" I was all too happy to have her stay and keep me company.

A wave bigger than the others slammed against the side, submerging the wheelhouse, breaking into foam and splashing over us in the cockpit. The wind grew even stronger, changing direction every few minutes. The boat was buffeted and leaned over and responded to the tiller in a completely different way than my old fishing sloop had. In these seas, this boat's light hull and thin, short keel made it behave like the gigantic plastic toy it was.

Mette worked her way over to me and shouted, "What can I do to help?"

"Tie yourself down!" I shouted, because it wasn't the kind of boat the crew could do much with.

She ran a rope around her waist, double-checking her knots. She did everything with careful precision, and didn't seem particularly worried.

I reduced the sails again, but we kept going too fast all the same. I kept checking the onboard instruments, trying to outweigh the risk of capsizing with that of being caught by even worse weather halfway through our trip.

Mette untied herself and went down below. She came back up wearing a lifejacket and carrying another one for me. She helped me put it on, one arm at a time without letting go of the tiller. The light was disappearing rapidly. We kept sailing northwest between the cutting waves, our eyes half-closed against the wind.

At two in the morning we were sailing at almost thirty knots, flying along among endless gusts and whistles and roaring and blows and buffeting in almost total darkness, save for a vague, milky lunar halo that appeared occasionally. The sea grew even stronger and the wind came in violent blasts that forced me to work the tiller constantly. I was clinging to it so tightly and the air and water were so cold that I almost lost circulation in my hands, but I didn't dare let go, not even to shake them one at a time. I reduced the sails yet again. By now all we had was a portion of the gaff-sail and jib, and yet we were still at the limit. Mette sat beside me on the bench, tied to the handrail just as I was.

Occasionally I would shout to her, "Everything okay?"

"Yes!" she would shout back. "What about you?"

"Me too! Sure you don't want to go below?"

"No!"

I could barely see her, but her closeness filled the space with substance and heat, voiding my worries as we went up and down through the black, furious sea in a tilted shell that boomed with every wave. Much more than in other moments of my life, I had the precise feeling that I was not the one who had chosen the route, but had to use my greatest powers and best abilities and intentions just to stick to it. We were carried by the wind, against and over and beyond the waves.

At a certain point I limited myself to checking the compass, abandoning the wind gauge and nautical log and GPS and clock. My bodily sensors were synchronized solely on Mette to my left and our shared movement. There was no space for any other measurements.

After an indefinable stretch of time, when we were exhausted and frozen and banged up and almost blinded by the salty water and practically deafened by wind whistling so ceaselessly in our ears that it seemed like a permanent condition, Mette shouted, "Lights!"

I looked too, catching a glimpse of barely perceptible luminous dots that were high enough up that they couldn't be lights on another boat or ship. The very idea produced a mix of relief and incredulity in me, then fatigue, urgency, patience, lightness, exhaustion. I turned on the motor and rolled the jib and gaff-sail up almost completely. The boat straightened partially and the propellers drove us forward.

WE SAILED INTO THE PORT IN BASTIA JUST BEFORE DAWN

We sailed into the port in Bastia just before dawn, amid a furious blowing and crashing sea. As soon as we got behind the big jetty it took just a few seconds to pass from blows and roaring to the almost complete silence of calm waters. I maneuvered slowly, searching for a free spot in the boat marina. It took me almost fifteen minutes to slip in between two big boats that I thought would at least partially hide us from view once the sun was fully up.

Mette and I looked at each other in the early light: I think we both wore the same bewildered expression, the same salt on our eyebrows and eyelashes, the same constricted movement in our facial muscles.

She untied her safety line, then went to the bow to check the anchor while I ran the chain out and backed the boat up toward the pier.

I jumped out onto dry land and tightened the stern lines: my hands struggled to hold the line, my feet were unstable, my leg muscles still tense from the constant struggle to adjust.

Mette watched me, looking at the city emerging more and more clearly behind me.

I jumped back onboard. We helped each other take off the lifejackets and the oilskins, our fingers and movements so rigid we had to laugh.

At that point it seemed too early and too late for anything: we went back down below with the idea of trying to get some sleep. I got out the only blanket I could find aboard; it was made of thin, damp wool. Our clothes were even wetter, but we didn't have anything to change into, or even the strength to do so. We lay down on the little V-shaped bed in the bow, bringing our legs and feet gradually closer together. We pulled the blanket over ourselves and hugged each other tight the way we had the night before. But our nervous systems had been too overworked and our clothes were too uncomfortable and our hair too full of brine; we had too many muscle tremors and flashes of thought and hunger pangs in our stomachs to actually manage to get to sleep.

At a certain point I realized that we were both trembling, but even this feeling was very clear one moment and already confused with others a moment later. I closed my eyes, then opened them. I closed them again, squeezed Mette's arm, and everything grew distant.

I heard the sound of aggressive voices. I threw the wool blanket aside, banging my head on a shelf, and tumbled out of the little bed before I could even remember where I was or how I'd gotten there. Mette woke up too, propping herself on one elbow and looking at me. I said, "Wait here, I'll go see," but she was already slipping out from underneath the thin blanket.

I walked across the boat, my steps uncertain. I opened the hatchway as gradually and cautiously as possible. The light was blinding, but it turned out to be just a pair of technicians a few moorings further down. They were talking as they worked on a little pole with electric outlets. The boat marina and the commercial port full of big ships on my right and the streets and houses of the city immediately after that appeared much more defined and rich in detail than they had when we'd arrived. But it was a view entirely too extensive and concrete for my current mental state. It seemed I could only adapt to things in degrees.

Mette stuck her head out, diffident, her hair mussed up.

I smiled at her, suddenly deeply moved, and said, "Hey."

"Hey," she said, still bewildered.

"It was nothing," I said. I could barely hear my own voice, still too dazed by the noise of our voyage and our attempt at sleep.

She looked at the two technicians by the pole. "I can't get to sleep anyway," she said.

"Me either."

"So what should we do?"

"Let's go get something to eat." I felt like I was in a permanent state of hunger: it wasn't a bad feeling, and it was connected with an equally intense need for her looks and words and movements.

"Hmmm. Yes," she said.

The two technicians by the little pole stared at us, perplexed by the idea of two sailors arriving so far out of season. I waved to them with one hand; they nodded back.

We walked along the pier and then along the dock, both of us with partly closed eyes and weaving steps. I wondered if we could dispose of at least part of the sense of alarm we'd acquired in Rome and which had followed us to the sea and driven us across the water, or if it wasn't better to keep it active and as close to the heart as possible. I couldn't decide, and it seemed that things were the same for Mette, judging from her way of moving around and looking this way and that. We were also extremely tired and confused. The lack of sleep and food certainly wasn't helping us evaluate things.

We left the marina, crossing a street that I remembered as a continuous flow of cars and trucks and buses in a distant August long ago, now walking against the flow of very little traffic. The sound of each motor and gust of air knocked me for a loop. My head would spin, I registered strips of colored metal passing me by, blinding red lights that turned on at intersections.

Near a square with trees and a statue, we went into an old bar filled with dark wood and tenuous yellow lights. We sat down at one of the tables surrounded by mirrors, ordering cappuccinos and brioches from an ancient, stuttering waiter. We looked at each other only intermittently, our senses reverberating with all-too-recent memories of wind and sea and blows and waves and darkness, recurring tremors still in our bones and skin.

We sat there silent and immobile until the waiter came back with his tray full. Then we held the mugs of cappuccino in our hands in order to absorb their heat. We took sips of the boiling liquid, dunking our brioches and devouring them, almost in tears.

It wasn't enough to satisfy our hunger or our need to get warm. We ordered two more cappuccinos, brioches, and a little dish of chestnut jelly.

We drank and ate these too, still without speaking. We asked for two more cappuccinos and a couple of cream pastries. The ancient waiter nodded yes, staring at us as if we were a pair of strange animals. When our stomachs and internal thermometers started sending us reassuring signals, we smiled. I touched her arm, and she brushed a little salt from my cheekbone. Our familiarity was neither consolidated nor permanent: it came and went with each new glance and thought, pushing us back and forth in a continuous shift between naturalness and embarrassment. We were in uncertain territory, caught between sleep and wakefulness and stasis and searching and feeling lost, general reasons and personal reasons fighting one another and constantly overlapping between electric urges and traces of doubt.

In order to break free of all this I sent down another sip of boiling cappuccino and sat straight up in my seat. "What next?" I said.

Worry returned to Mette's clear gaze, dilating her pupils in an instant.

"You can think about it while you finish your pastry."

But instead she put it back down on the little plate, cleaning her fingers with a paper napkin. She extended her hand toward me. "Could you show me that photo of your father again?"

I fished it out of the inside jacket pocket, my movements poorly coordinated: it was wet and sticky, the blue ink on the back had haloes where the seawater had diluted it. I passed it to Mette, enchanted by the sensitive, nervous whiteness of the hand that came close and then drew back.

She studied it very closely, first one side and then the other, as if she were looking at it for the first time. There were crumbs and traces of powdered sugar on her chin, her jacket and on the gray sweater underneath.

I extended a hand to brush it off, but too brusquely: she was startled. I said, "The sugar," but it didn't seem like my voice contained much sound; my ears were full of whispers and creaking and the roaring of the surf.

She went back to studying the photograph of my father. She put a finger on it and said, "There's writing here, too."

I could smell the sugar and salt on her as I leaned in to look at my father in colonial garb, standing with his arms crossed in front of the broken-down hut. It was a little hard for me to concentrate or even focus, but it was true: the words *Cão que ladra não morde* were written in white paint on the rough wooden sign behind him.

"What do you think that means?" said Mette.

"A barking dog doesn't bite? It means that somebody who makes a lot of noise and a big scene usually doesn't have much to say or the will to act."

"I know *that*. What's the second level of meaning?"

"What makes you think there's a second level?" I couldn't decide if such a persistent interest in the photo of my father was a sign of functioning lucidity or total exhaustion; whether I should keep analyzing every little detail together with her or try to convince her to let it go.

"There is one."

"Why should there be?" I admired her and was worried about her in almost equal measure.

"Your father had a picture taken of himself standing in front of it," she said.

"He probably thought it was a funny idea. Instead of the usual "beware of dog." This is relatively surreal, don't you think?"

Mette shook her head. She looked at the photo, obstinate. "Doesn't it remind you of something personal?" she said.

"No." I took a spoonful of chestnut jelly.

"Think about it carefully, don't get distracted." She took a bite out of her cream pastry, getting more powdered sugar on her chin and throat and sweater.

I made an intense effort to follow her train of thought, but my attention kept getting lost along the way. I felt like I could have spent the whole day watching the movement of her lips and well-defined jaw while she chewed, her clear throat as she swallowed. "Nothing," I said.

"Did your family ever have a dog?"

"A Bedlington terrier," I said, drawing an image from a corridor of images complete with names and backgrounds. "When Fabio and I were kids. Its name was Oraf."

"Olaf? Like the King of Norway?"

"No. Oraf, with an R."

"What kind of name is that?"

"Originally it was Olaf. But when my father brought him home Fabio was in a phase in which he had only just learned to pronounce the R, and he was so proud of himself that he used it instead of the L too. That's how the dog ended up being named Oraf."

"What was he like?" asked Mette, taking another bite of her pastry.

"He seemed like a lamb, all white and curly and innocent-looking. But in reality he was a pretty ferocious hunter, like all terriers. One summer we were on vacation in Tuscany and he tore the throats out of three real lambs, one after the other. Fabio was shocked."

"What about you?" Her attention was incredibly pure, concentrated on me in a way I'd only seen a few times in my life.

"I was too." I didn't want to hide behind my brother, not with her. "Because of the screams and the blood, the idea that an idyllic situation could turn into something so horrible."

She nodded yes, slowly. She turned the photo over and went back to studying the verses my father had written for Nadine. She brushed her chin with two fingers in order to clean off the powdered sugar. Then she said, "Maybe it's not a poem at all, and not a secret lover's code. Maybe that's why Nadine gave it to you, before she left."

"What makes you say that?" I was still enchanted by the variety of her expressions.

"I'm just trying to imagine. Maybe it's a hint that leads to a third copy of Ndionge's memorial."

"Where would that come from? Isn't the one thing we know for sure the fact that Maurice only typed two copies?"

"Exactly," said Mette. "Two *copies*."

"You mean?"

"Maybe Maurice meant that he made two carbon paper *copies*. In addition to the original."

"You mean *three* copies in all?" Now we were moving forward with our own mental abilities, moving beyond the fatigue that had almost entirely consumed our physical strength. It was a strange feeling, intense and feverish.

"Yes. It's just that we got used to the idea that any text we're dealing with is a copy. Everything is a copy."

"That's true."

"We never see the original," she said. "And in any case it doesn't matter for us."

"Because it's identical to its copies. Indistinguishable."

"Yes. But Maurice belonged to a culture in which there's still a substantial difference between an original and a copy."

"So when he said he made two copies of the memorial, he meant two *copies*."

"Yes. Different from the original and different from each other, given that they were made with carbon paper."

"The second clearer than the first, right?"

Mette nodded yes. She blew a little powdered sugar off the photograph.

"How can you be sure?" I asked.

"I'm not sure," she said with a perfectly disarming expression. "It's just a possibility."

"One among an infinite number of possibilities."

"Yes. But possibilities have a strange way of growing smaller once you reach certain crucial junctures. Infinite can turn into just a few. It's surprising."

"And when did you think of this possibility?"

"An hour ago. While we were trying to get to sleep in the boat but couldn't."

It was a strange conversation, the closest thing to a telepathic exchange I'd ever experienced. We moved our lips and used our vocal cords to enunciate words, but it seemed to me that our thoughts were traveling independently of sound, bound up in the way we looked at each other and our breath and the smallest movement of our bodies. I tried to figure out if it was a feeling created by the fact that we were close to collapsing. I propped myself on one elbow to achieve a minimum of stability, but it slipped off the edge of the table. I said, "But if there were a third copy, then why didn't Nadine tell me about it? Why give me a photograph with enigmatic writing?"

"Maybe because she couldn't figure out how to decipher it. At least not entirely. Your father knew as much, seeing as he wrote *For Nadine to keep safe at hand, what without Faolo she won't understand.*"

"And he thought I would?"

"Maybe," she said. She picked up the last piece of cream pastry and put it in her mouth. We had finished everything the waiter needed three different trips to bring. There was nothing left on the table but empty mugs and plates and crumbs.

I leaned my head back, grabbing a hold of the table so that I wouldn't lose my balance and fall over on the floor. "I've never been very good at riddles," I said.

"Me neither," said Mette. "But we can try."

I grew a little alarmed, because the door to the bar opened and a wave of daylight rolled in, bringing with it a man wearing a long coat and a round hat. But then the door closed again and the light immediately dimmed and the man went very slowly over to the bar and asked for a drink.

Mette watched the scene too, but she held on to her train of thought. She said, "It's the only chance we have of not losing the memorial forever."

I said, "But there might be similar things written behind every other photograph of my father Nadine has in her home."

"Not behind the ones I saw the other night."

It occurred to me that when it came to women, at heart I was full of contradictions: in being surprised, but also in feeling vaguely threatened when I received an unexpected demonstration of their perceptive, intuitive, and deductive capabilities. I wondered if what I was really looking for was an absurd equilibrium between inertia and resourcefulness, or if I could blame my exhaustion for my desire for a conversation limited only to the feelings that were still flowing in my bloodstream.

"You're perplexed?" asked Mette.

"Just exhausted."

"I know," she said with a smile of intense companionship.

"But you're right. We have to give it a try."

"But right now you're distracted."

"That's not true," I said, distracted by the light in her eyes and the brilliance of her skin and the way she pushed one hand through her hair and the shape of her fingers and the structure of her wrists and her sweet and salty smell and the thousands of other simultaneous details emanating from her person that tended to almost completely occupy my attention.

"For starters, who is this Faolo without whom Nadine won't understand?" asked Mette. Her tone of voice was that of a woman who is accustomed to facing difficult climatic or environmental situations, snow or cold seas or ungallant men whose desires are anything but subtle.

I made a supreme effort of willpower in order to send my thoughts along rational pathways; as soon as they began moving I said, "It might be: without Fa *or* Lo."

She stared into my eyes. "What do you mean?"

"Fabio or Lorenzo," I said, almost solely in order to prove to both her and myself that I was still capable of rational thought.

"You or your brother?"

"Yes."

She smiled and wrapped her hand around my wrist, radiant with enthusiasm. "So your father meant that only you or your brother have the key."

"The key to what? And what key are we talking about?"

The ancient waiter continued to watch us from behind the bar, apparently curious so see two people talking so intensely after having eaten so voraciously. I asked him if he could make us some scrambled eggs and a couple of glasses of fresh-squeezed orange juice. He said he didn't have eggs or oranges. The customer with the round hat finished his glass of wine and left, letting a new wave of light in through the doorway.

Mette brought her hand to her forehead and said, "My head is spinning."

I took the photo of my father out of her fingers and put it back in my pocket. I got up, but it was hard to keep my balance and I knocked my chair over. I put one arm around Mette and said, "Let's go."

"Where?" she asked.

"Somewhere to sleep. We're burnt out." I helped her get to her feet and took her with me to the cash register. I paid for breakfast and asked the waiter if he knew of a hotel nearby.

The waiter seemed even more curious and perplexed than before. He said, *"Quel niveau? Haut, bas, médium?"*

"Un hôtel," I said, *"N'importe quel."*

He came out from behind the register and pushed us outside into the sunlight in the square. The light made us squint, although the sky was covered with gray clouds. Using gestures, he explained the way to a hotel. He had to repeat himself twice because it was very hard for me to follow his directions.

We walked along the sidewalk like two shipwreck survivors, our footsteps dragging behind us. I held Mette up with one arm around her waist, but I wasn't doing much better than she was. Each time we crossed a street I had to look left and right four times. Our mental efforts with the photograph had exhausted us both. Every sound or movement or signal from the outside world came crashing down on us with entirely disproportionate violence.

The hotel the waiter had recommended was just five minutes from the bar, an old, gray, formerly glorious edifice with *La Petite Ourse* written over the entrance in 1960s lettering. There was no one behind the reception desk. I rang the bell and we waited, closing our eyes and then reopening them to look at the garishly colored photographs hanging on the walls. In the end a guy with bristly hair arrived, diffident of our exhausted looks and lack of luggage. I told him that we didn't have any identification, but that we could pay in advance, using the firmest tone of voice I could muster. He said that it was still the morning, and that the rooms would only be available after noon, continuing to glare at us as if we were two potential criminals. I told him that we were extremely tired and had to sleep immediately, trying not to let my voice crack. He thought about it some more, then wrote down a price on a piece of paper, turning it around on the counter so that I could read it. I didn't have anywhere near the strength or lucidity to argue with him, and gave him the amount he wanted. He put the money in his pocket, took a key off the rack behind him, and led us upstairs. We followed him, moving slow as molasses, our feet sticking to every step.

On the second floor the bristly-haired fellow opened the door to a room with creaky floorboards. The room was warm, and had a large bed with flowery covers. The man left only after giving us a last, long suspicious stare.

Mette and I looked around, both equally incredulous at finding ourselves in a stable, protected space. I took off my jacket, boots, and socks, went into the bathroom and turned on the showerhead sticking out over an old bathtub. I asked Mette if she wanted to go first. She shook her head no, but then came toward me like a sleepwalker, taking off her shoes and jacket and tights and socks along the way.

I took off my clothes too as if they were a damp, salty, unbearable snakeskin, letting them drop on the floor. I could feel a wavy vibration rising up within me over and over again. Mette took a toothbrush and a tube of toothpaste out and began brushing her teeth incredibly slowly, standing there in front of the mirror in her underpants and a t-shirt. I realized I'd forgotten my bag on the boat, but I couldn't even imagine going back outside to get it. I got under the shower, turned the hot water faucet until the jet of water became boiling, then absorbed the heat with the voracity of a true reptile. The bathroom filled with steam and my heartbeat slowed back down. I watched Mette go pee through the white clouds. It felt like I would never manage to get out of the shower ever again.

She left her underpants and shirt and t-shirt and bra on the floor, stepped over the edge of the bathtub and pressed herself against me. We held each other tightly underneath the scalding water, turning around and around so that the water covered our heads and backs. We kissed: sweet kisses that were so liquid they gushed out of our mouths and ran down into the tiniest free spaces between our pressing bodies. Our tongues slid around one another like marine creatures with lives of their own, our lips stuck together then separated then immediately started searching for one another again. The multiple complications that had brought us together and then laid siege to us at every step up until this very moment melted away like the salt clinging to our hair and throats and foreheads, running down across our stomachs and legs and feet and onto the cracked porcelain of the bathtub until they finally disappeared down the small drain, leaving us pressed close to one another for incredibly simple reasons. We didn't even look at one another: we kept our eyes shut or just barely open to see one another filtered or faded through the steam. But then our hands were gathering every possible piece of information about shape and feel and function and closeness, our body surfaces betraying everything that we could have possibly thought or said. We spent an immeasurable period of time washing away resistance, diffidence, uncertainty, and hesitation. When we finally turned off the faucet and got out of the tub and grabbed two rough cotton towels, we were a totally naked man and woman, each vibrating with urgent need for the other.

We dried ourselves off with all the energy we could muster, then ran into the bed and got underneath the covers still wet and scalded. The sheets were cold by contrast. We pulled the fabric over ourselves and slowly moved together and embraced and kissed once again, almost unconscious from fatigue. Then we crossed over the limits of closeness, into a dense, semiliquid depth that amplified heat and the meaning of every tiny movement a thousand times over. All I had to do was brush a finger across Mette's temple for my fingertips to register an incredible amount of information. They in turn produced an incredibly fine web of sensations that captured images and expectations and dreams and desires all lost and rediscovered, dragging them up to the surface of my skin. Each close-up look I took of her had the ability to excite a deep emotion originating in some part of Mette that contributed to creating her whole: the structure of an ear, the curve of an eyebrow, the color of her lips as they almost touched mine, the continuous mixing and remixing of real and imagined consistencies. The gestures that produced friction multiplied, the sensations produced by that friction began to shoot through us to the point where they became almost uncontrollable. It was as if the force generated by our extreme closeness encompassed all our bodies' perceptive and elaborative capacities: we let ourselves be dragged in, barely catching our breath or moving our heads, feeding a process that drew upon our shapes and thoughts, stretching them out to the point where they were almost completely erased.

At a certain point, we were so incredibly close to one another that I couldn't have said where I ended and she began. Our hands and arms and legs and feet and gazes and hair all mixed together in the same breath at an increasing depth until we were melded together in a sort of whirlpool of feelings that grabbed us up high in the most vertiginous manner and dragged us down on top of one another to slide between the heated, mussed-up sheets toward the extreme edges of the bed.

Then we looked at one another, underneath the Arabic tent the sheets formed over our heads, and we started laughing at the irremediable surprise and marvel of what had happened.

Mette said, "Why are you laughing?" Her face was colored by the lamplight filtering through the covers.

"What about you?" I raised myself up on one elbow, trying to look into the depths of her eyes, but I couldn't.

"I asked you first."

"Out of surprise."

"We were so mortally tired," she said. "I thought we would have crashed immediately."

But we *were* mortally tired, and a second later fatigue broke over us like a wave. We gathered up the covers with the last bit of energy we had left, pulling them over our bodies just a moment before abandoning our senses. I turned out the lamp, we kissed each other three more times, then we went to sleep.

THE SOUND OF A CAR WOKE ME UP

The sound of a car woke me up. I couldn't figure out where it came from, and jumped up in bed with my heart racing. Like every time I happen to fall asleep during the day, I was sweaty and I'd lost all sense of place and time. The hotel room was almost entirely dark, apart from a triangle of weak yellow light on the floor in front of the window. I turned on the light on the nightstand. Mette was sleeping next to me, her honey-red cloud of hair spread out over the pillow and a sweet expression on her face. Her breathing was a barely perceptible whisper. My heart returned to a normal pace. On the nightstand, my watch displayed six-forty in the evening.

I went to the window, peering out into the almost nocturnal street where a small truck was turning around. A bottomless hunger rose up in me that didn't take the breakfast we'd eaten in the bar a lifetime ago the least bit into account. I wondered if I should wake Mette up before going out, but that seemed criminal. On the other hand, I couldn't even imagine waiting. My body desperately needed refueling.

I gathered my cold, rigid clothing up off the floor in the room and bathroom and got dressed. I wrote *I'll be right back* on a piece of hotel letterhead, placing the note on Mette's nightstand. I stood there and looked at her. I felt deeply shocked by what had happened between us, by what she had moved and sensations that couldn't be translated into words. I couldn't believe that such a simple thing could also be so complex, beyond our limits and outside our form, impossible to contain.

And yet my shock did not lessen my hunger in the least. On the contrary, it seemed to be increasing it by the minute. I put on my boots and tried to open the door without making any noise. At the reception desk, the bristly-haired guy was watching television. I nodded to him and rolled my index finger around to indicate that I'd be right back. He watched me with the same diffidence as before.

I walked along the sidewalks underneath the streetlights. The seaside town was practically empty now that it was the off-season. I felt a mix of hurry and absentmindedness that accelerated and slowed down my footsteps at turns. I looked into shop windows, signs above the windows confirming their contents. Finally I found a store selling food. I went in, looking at the food on display on shelves and behind glass counters with a foreigner's uncertain greediness. Every shape and color filled me with a desire to extend my hand, touch and taste. I bought a two-pound loaf of simple baked bread, soft goat cheese, black olives, sun-dried tomatoes soaked in olive oil, some salad, a little jar of chestnut honey, two apples, and two bottles of dark Corsican beer. I pointed these foodstuffs out to the shop owner, he took them down from where they sat and placed them on a piece of wax paper lying on top of the scales. Every time he did this it felt like I'd made an extraordinary acquisition.

As I walked back to the hotel with our worldly supplies in two plastic bags, I stopped in front of a lingerie shop window. I stood there, enchanted, staring at the undergarments on mannequins and half-leg statues and shelves. They struck me as wonderfully ordinary and modest. They were unanswered questions suspended in space, suggestions made of distances that were too great to be entirely understood. In the end I went in, buying a pair of boxers and a t-shirt and socks for myself, then a pair of underpants and a bra and t-shirt and socks for Mette. My hands still contained a micrometrical memory of the shape of her body; I couldn't understand the saleswoman's insistence on knowing the precise sizes I was looking for. All I had to do was look in order to know, with the same naturalness we'd exhibited in the hotel room. I was full of memories and anticipation: instinct and waiting, anxious need to be together again, extreme closeness that takes the breath away. These things caressed my thoughts and skin, the insides of my forearms, the space between my neck and the base of my skull.

I hurried back to the hotel, part of me afraid that I wouldn't be able to find my way back. I crossed the lobby followed by the bristly-haired guy's stare and ran up two steps at a time until I reached the second floor.

Mette was sitting on the bed, her legs gathered under her and her hands around her knees. She started slightly when I came in.

"It's me, it's me," I said, more for myself than for her. I went over and kissed her hair and cheekbones, her lips, the tip of her nose.

"I woke up and you weren't here," she said. The tone of her voice made my heart ache for the way it revealed that she'd missed me and needed me.

I lifted up the bags I was carrying in one hand. "I was dying of hunger." I emptied food out onto the mirrored bureau against the wall, watching Mette's reflection as she stretched out to see what I'd bought. I went back to her and emptied the bag from the lingerie store onto the bed.

She ran her hands over the t-shirt and socks and bra that I'd bought for her. They were made of simple white cotton. She dropped the covers and held the t-shirt up to her chest: it was right. She held the bra up to her chest and laughed.

"It's not the right size?" I asked.

"It's fine," she said. "It's just a little big."

"Are you sure?" I couldn't believe that my memory of her breasts could be anything less than perfect.

"It's wonderful. That always happens."

"Really?" I asked, experiencing a tiny, unexpected fit of jealousy. "Do you have a line of men out there buying you bras every morning?"

"No," she said, laughing. "It's a universal fact. When a man buys a woman a bra, he always gets one that's one size too big."

"I didn't know that. Clearly I haven't kept up with the universal facts." That wasn't all: it truly seemed to me that everything that happened between the two of us was without precedent.

"Well, it's the truth."

"I've never given anyone a bra as a gift before."

"I've never gotten one as a gift."

"I just thought you would like to change," I said. I didn't look at her because we were far from any kind of consolidation of feelings based upon which it was worth being jealous, or even owning up to being jealous.

"*Very* much," she said, a tone of sincerity in her voice that turned her eyes a couple of shades darker.

I went over to her: her breasts were small and even whiter than the rest of her body, placed with soft delicacy on her chest. Her naked body seemed at once ancient and entirely contemporary. I gave her a kiss on the lips. She opened her mouth and closed her eyes and leaned slightly backwards. I hesitated, drawn between my hunger for the food behind me and my equally intense desire to wrap my arms around her and squeeze her into my embrace. But I had a hole in my stomach that ran through my heart all the way to my head. "Don't you want something to eat?" I said.

She laughed again, looking at my lips.

"We haven't eaten in *days*. Aren't you hungry?"

"Yes." She got off the bed and walked across the room to the bathroom: naked and light over the old, creaky wooden parquet.

I went over to the bureau with the mirror and opened the various food packages, careful not to spill oil or whey on the wood. I took the loaf of bread out of its paper bag, squeezing and sniffing it covetously. I thought briefly of the little knife I had in the backpack I'd forgotten on the boat, then I broke the golden crust with my hands and started tearing out pieces of its soft, spongy interior.

"Wait," said Mette. She had a white towel wrapped around her and under her underarms like a little ancient outfit. She rummaged around in her pack and took out a little knife that was exactly like mine, only with an olive wood handle.

"Is that yours?" I asked, because it seemed like too much of a coincidence.

"Yes," she said. "Why?"

"I have one exactly like it. The only difference is the wood on the handle. Isn't that strange?"

She shrugged her shoulders, less amazed than I was.

I cut slice after slice after slice of bread, then slices of soft goat cheese. With each cut I thought of the time that had passed since each of us had bought his or her knife or received it as a gift, never knowing that the other had an identical one, never even knowing the other existed. I took a few sun-dried tomatoes out of the olive oil and laid them on the cheese, adding a few olives. Then I used the tip of the knife to pop the cap off a bottle of beer and pass it to Mette.

We sat facing each other on the room's two chairs, eating and drinking silently and with a frenzy even more intense than when we had eaten breakfast together in the bar that morning. We ate with our eyes and hands and mouths, completely absorbed by the taste and density of every single bit of food, as well as its combinations with other tastes and the miraculous nutritional properties of the whole. We prepared garnished slices of bread and exchanged them, passing the bottle of beer back and forth like special offerings, chewing and swallowing and feeling endlessly thankful for the fruits of nature and for those who prepared them.

When we were as full as humanly possible we cleaned our mouths and hands with the bread bag and sat on the edge of the bed, overcome with languor. We drank the last small sips of beer, now tepid and bitter.

Some subterranean thought or maybe even a purely mechanical reflex made me turn on the television. I changed channel after channel after channel until I located a news program that spoke of events taking place far, far away from us. But just reestablishing this connection with the world's flow was enough to bring the external tension back to our glances and gestures. I turned the television off, but it was too late. I laid a hand on Mette's shoulder, leaning over to give her a kiss on the side of her neck; the external tension was still there. I went into the bathroom to wash my hands and face, then went back and started walking back and forth in the room. I turned off the lights and pulled the curtains aside to stare outside. The street noises had all been turned into alarm signals and urgency; it was no longer possible to ignore them.

"Tomorrow morning we'll take a ship to the French coast," I said.

Mette nodded yes. She took off the towel and put on the underwear and t-shirt I had bought for her, sitting down cross-legged in the middle of the bed. "Then what?" she asked.

"Then we'll see. Let's try to figure out if the third copy of the memorial really exists, and where it's ended up."

Mette bit her lip. "Could you give another look at that picture of your father?" she said.

I wanted to go back with her to that hot, borderless proximity we'd shared earlier, but I knew it was no use. I went and took the photograph of my father out of the jacket pocket: it was even damper and more worn than it had been that morning when we were looking at it in the bar. And now it was dusty with powdered sugar as well.

Mette took it out of my hand and blew on it. She moved across the bed toward the light on the nightstand. She studied it again for a long time, looking at both sides.

"Can you read anything new?" I asked. I looked at her well-drawn knees, her strong walker's calves.

"I don't know," she said. She was lost in thought.

"Let's talk about the parts we've already deciphered."

"Okay. Nadine can't understand without Faolo, in other words without Fabio or Lorenzo."

"Yes, but understand what?"

"The key is in the following sentence. Only you and your brother are capable of resolving it."

"The key?"

"*The fantastic August fish / Of 1976.*" She was staring hard at me, her face tense.

I swept other thoughts that were trying to get in the way aside, then without thinking said, "A *spigola*."

"A what?" said Mette, who didn't know the fish's Italian name.

"A bass," I said. I made a gesture with both hands to give her an idea of the size and kind of fish. "My father caught an enormous one in Sardinia, using a dragline. Four of us sat down to eat it, and we still couldn't finish it."

"In August of 1976?"

"Maybe. It could be. It was definitely August, and that bass was unquestionably a fantastic fish. My mother refused to cook it; she said it was so big it was scary."

"Who cooked it?"

"My father. On the barbecue grill of the house we'd rented, with olive oil and rosemary and juniper and laurel leaves." Several different mental images of the situation floated back to mind, joined by memories of smells and temperatures, the intensity of the sun and wind.

Mette moved her head slowly as if she was seeing and feeling the same things, then she said, "So that's the key. '*Spigola.*'"

"What's this key supposed to open?"

"I don't know."

"A safe deposit box?"

"Maybe. Or a luggage storage locker, or a notary public's drawer, I don't know."

"Where?"

She pressed her thumb on the right margin of the backside of the photograph and said, "This has to be the address. *Rua do Sol 53/b.*"

"But in which city?"

She shook her head.

"Which country?"

"Which continent? Who knows how many Rua do Sols there are spread out around the Portuguese-speaking world."

"That's right," I said. "We could travel for years before we found the right one." I looked at her naked thighs, the white cotton of her new underpants. No matter how hard I tried to keep it on one thing and one thing alone, my attention was constantly moving from one level to the next.

Mette waved the photo of my father back and forth like a tiny fan. "The name of the place has to be here, too," she said.

"Maybe it was on another photograph. Maybe the complete message was divided in half."

"Then why would Nadine have given you just one photograph?"

"Maybe she didn't understand, just like she may not have understood what was on this one. Or maybe she was just too shaken up by what happened."

Mette shook her head, unconvinced.

"Maybe we'll think of it tomorrow," I said.

"How?"

"We'll see a sign. Or we'll manage to decipher one we don't understand yet."

"You're a fatalist," she said, looking at my lips.

"No. But I agree with your theory of infinite possibilities that get reduced to just a few at certain key points."

"Yes, but you can't just to sit around and wait for them."

"Of course not. You have to keep moving."

"Change your perspective."

"Develop your skills and abilities."

"Don't get complacent."

"Learn to read the signs."

"Cut down your reaction time," said Mette.

"That's exactly what I was thinking," I said, experiencing a profound sense of joy for how natural it was that things would be this way.

We sat there for a few seconds, looking each other in the eye, vibrating with other possible words. Then the space between us broke and we pressed against one another, forehead to forehead, breathing all over each other, turning our heads in order to find a point of contact between our mouths. I caught my breath, and Mette let herself fall backward. I fell down on top of her. We kissed and embraced and pulled each other close again, anxious to follow pathways that could only be partially retraced within our ultra-recent memory. We wanted to confirm both their existence and the concatenated dimensions they led to. We were lost in the taste of our kisses and the smell of our skins and the shapes of our bodies, falling deeper than ever before into the electric, flashing interplay of rediscovery and recognition and chase and slowing down and extension and localization and extension again; the sudden simultaneities in our breathing stopping time, dilating it to the point where it disintegrated, shaking the minute fragments like drops of salt water over our palpitating, extenuated bodies.

I LOOKED AT THE WATCH
ON THE NIGHTSTAND

I looked at the watch on the nightstand. It read seven; only the light between the curtains and the window told me it was morning. Mette was beside me, deep asleep. She lay on her back with her hands underneath the pillow. I would have liked to lie there for a long time without moving, looking at her and listening to her breathe, but I was so saturated with sleep in every fiber of my body that I had to get out of bed and go wash under a cold shower. My reflection in the bathroom mirror was that of a shipwrecked sailor, my hair disheveled and my beard prickly. I brushed my teeth with Mette's toothbrush and toothpaste. It tasted like lemon peel essence, and felt like kissing her all over again. Then my beard started itching and I had a burning desire to shave and I realized that in addition to my razor, my passport was also in the backpack I'd left on the boat. It was time to go back and get it.

I got dressed as silently as possible and wrote *I'm going to the boat to get my knapsack and I'll be back* on hotel letterhead. I put the note on the nightstand, resisting the impulse to lean over and kiss her hair or even embrace her and wake her up. Then I went out.

There was nobody at the reception desk, and the street outside was almost empty. The sky was covered with great gray clouds like it had been the day before. The wind blew from inland. I walked quickly along the large street that flanked the port, following the sidewalk for a few hundred yards, crossing the street once I'd reached the marina. There were a few people at the beginning of the dock some thirty yards to my left, but they seemed entirely caught up in discussion around a little truck. I worked my way around the gate that blocked access to the piers just like Mette and I had done the day before, then slipped down behind a few boats in dry-dock and made my way to the pier.

The *Aqualuna* was where we'd left her, a little wet and salty but otherwise in good shape. I climbed on board and went down below. My backpack was on the couch in the dinette. I gathered up the oilskins we'd used on the way over, still wet with seawater, and rinsed them off underneath a thread of fresh water in the shower. I certainly didn't have time to hang dry them, so I dried them off with towels. I handled them carefully: the shells Mette and I had worn for a length of time that subsequent events had moved beyond, now left as part of the past. I thought about all that had changed between the two of us since we'd worn these things, still full of defenses that kept us from opening up and moving closer as we'd wanted to. And yet we had already been much closer than we were during the day before, and the day before more so than the day before that. If I turned all the way back to our encounter at the cemetery as perfect strangers, I couldn't bring myself to believe the cautious care we'd employed, the resistances we'd had to overcome in order to translate sensations and thoughts into words and gestures. I couldn't believe the gulf of the unknown and unsaid that had divided us, the effort we had to go through in order to embrace that which was waiting inside of both of us.

I rinsed off and towel-dried the boots too, sticking them into the bags I'd taken them out of together with the oilskins, then putting the bags in the bow peak. I was frightened at the thought of that which could have failed to happen between Mette and me, if it hadn't been for our ability to accept chance and apparent coincidences and act before it became too late. I dried the sink and faucets with a rag. I imagined my brother's reaction when he found out that his boat was in Corsica, but only for an instant. My brain was too occupied with thoughts of Mette: her standing at the center of the hotel room, a few feet away, then up close; an ankle, a breast, an eye, a tuft of hair, her smile, her way of sleeping with her face buried in the pillow and one knee up as if she were halfway through a suspended leap.

I folded the nautical maps I'd opened for the crossing and never used. I was about to put them back into the cupboard above the map table when I heard a dull thud on the hull and a hoarse voice shout out, "*Vous, là-dedans! Sortez! Vite!*"

I grabbed my backpack and made a dash for the hatchway, but when I stuck my head out I saw there was a blue-uniformed gendarme in the cockpit and another one on the pier, both sporting pistols on their belts and both extremely tense.

The man on the cockpit was frightened by my sudden appearance. He put one hand on his holster and backed up, saying "*Arrêtez-vous!*"

"Okay, okay," I said, raising my hands up, palms out to show them that I didn't have any weapons.

"*Vos documents!*" said the gendarme in the cockpit.

"*Sortez, d'abord!*" shouted the other gendarme from the jetty. A little way behind him stood a white-uniformed official from the harbor office.

I tried to stay calm, though my first impulse was to jump onto the next boat over and from there onto the pier and from there run like a madman across the marina. I pointed out my backpack to the gendarmes before opening it, assuming that they wouldn't react well to me sticking an arm into it without warning them first.

They reacted badly all the same: the one on the pier shouted "*Laissez-le, conard!*" while the gendarme onboard yelled "*Hé!*" and ripped the bag out of my hands. He laid the knapsack in a corner of the stern as if he were afraid it might explode from one moment to the next. He had a nervous boy's face with a pointy nose and blondish hair underneath his sharp cap.

I explained to them that my passport was in the backpack, using the most relaxed tone of voice and expression I could muster under the circumstances.

He started gesticulating and shouting, "*Vos documents, vos documents!*" without listening to me. He was obviously the underling of the older gendarme standing on the jetty, who continued to exhort him "*Faites attention!*"

I reached for my backpack to get my passport. He took his pistol out of its holster and shouted at me to stop. The one on the jetty had his pistol out too, and the white-uniformed official was gesticulating. It was such an absurd scene that I started to laugh, despite the trapped feeling that was starting to tighten up around my heart and legs.

Rather than relax a little, the two gendarmes and the port official got even more irritated: the man on the jetty started waving his pistol around and shouting at me to get immediately off the boat, the other one pushed me out onto the jetty with his free hand. I tried to make eye contact with the older gendarme, but he had a shifty, watery gaze. I tried to explain to the younger one that I was neither a terrorist nor an arms dealer and that the boat belonged to my brother, but he wasn't listening, either. He was entirely concentrated on patting me down with trembling hands to make sure I didn't have a pistol or hand grenade or who-knows-what-else on me. He pulled my wallet, a few coins, and the photo of my father out of my jacket as if they were fundamental proof of the crimes I would be charged with at some future date. The port official jumped aboard the *Aqualuna* and went down below to check things out.

A few shipyard workers had gathered further on down the dock. They laughed and pointed, shouting something. The fact that they had an audience excited the gendarmes even further, pushing their performances as the capturers of international maritime criminals to inspired heights. The younger gendarme opened my backpack as if he were defusing a bomb, pulling out my t-shirts and underpants and dirty socks and toothbrush and the little pocketknife as if they were burning hot. The little knife in particular must have struck him as a decisive discovery, even though it had a barely four-inch blade and could be purchased in any household goods store. He showed it to the other; both nodded with grave faces.

The only thought running through my mind was that I absolutely had to get back to the hotel and Mette before she woke up. It was such a dominating urgency that it erased any other considerations of time and method and opportunity and linguistic nuance: I shouted at the two gendarmes to let me go, I was in a hurry and I didn't have time for the ridiculous, pathetic little sideshow they were engaged in.

Once again, they reacted badly: the older one grabbed me by the arm and shoved me forward; the younger one followed with my backpack, which he'd haphazardly stuffed my things back into. The port official was still checking who-knows-what inside the boat, and stuck his head out to motion us onward. I looked out to the end of the pier, the dock further on, and the fence and the street beyond that. My heart was racing, all muscles tensed in anticipation of a wild dash.

I made another, calmer attempt to explain my position and where the boat came from and the fact that I didn't have time to counter accusations and alleviate suspicions and facilitate verifications, but I couldn't manage to maintain the necessary tone of voice. On the contrary: the deaf obtuseness in the eyes of the two gendarmes made me raise my voice again. The older one tightened his grip on my arm, the younger one grabbed my other arm. We walked past the little group of curious shipyard workers on the dock, a prisoner and his captors.

The police car was parked a little beyond that. The older gendarme left me with the younger while he opened the rear door. I realized I could probably free myself from the younger one with a head butt or a low kick and hit the street running, but it was clear that they would have followed me by car and maybe even shot me in the back, and even if I managed to distance myself from them and reach Mette at the hotel I would almost certainly have gotten her into trouble with even graver consequences.

I let myself be pushed into the backseat of the car. The two gendarmes jumped into the front, turned the car on, and hit the siren and flashing lights. We left the port at full speed, tires squealing.

At the station the situation got even worse than I could have imagined. The two uniformed gendarmes' plainclothes colleagues had the same blend of obtuseness and diffidence in their eyes, the same inability to utilize the information I offered them in order to resolve everything in the simplest manner possible. Standing or sitting down behind a desk, they repeated the same questions a hundred times with only the slightest variations, interrogating me about my itinerary and the ownership of the boat and the lack of documents and the reasons why I'd crossed over to Corsica and landed in French territory without notifying the port authorities. Seated in a chair, I repeated the same answers with the slightest variations: that I'd sailed out of Tuscany and that the boat belonged to my brother and that I didn't bring any documents because I was just planning to sail along the coast and then I'd lost my way, and that I hadn't had time to notify the port authorities but that I undoubtedly would have this morning if the two gendarmes hadn't showed up in search of the thrill of capture.

They seemed irritated by my tone of voice and by what I was saying, by the fact that I claimed I'd arrived alone and that I'd spent the night sleeping on a park bench. They asked, "Who did you leave Italy with?" I answered, "Alone." They asked, "Who was with you out on the open sea?" I answered, "I was alone." They asked, "What did you have on board? What were you bringing? What did you toss overboard?" I answered, "Nothing. Nothing. Nothing." Undoubtedly their technique of obsessive repetition was part an interrogation skill they'd learned at police school, but this bland, half-distracted version, devoid of bright lights or physical threats or overturned chairs proved totally ineffective.

They must have realized this too, because they moved on to making me to reconstruct my route from the Tuscan coast to Bastia as meticulously as possible, hour by hour and mile by mile. If I'd remembered it I would have been happy to answer them, but my memories were entirely filled with Mette's proximity and feelings of pure sea and wind. I didn't have a single bit of information from the wind gauge or compass to provide them with.

They busied themselves with asking other useless questions and checking other useless lists. They drank coffee or ate cookies and snacks they got from a vending machine out in the hallway. Sometimes they made calls connected with other affairs or went out to talk to their colleagues. They seemed unaware of the fact that the only real torture they were inflicting on me was the constant increase in the amount of time that had passed since I'd left the hotel where Mette lay alone and asleep. But then perhaps this was part of their technique, too.

I continued to look at the clock on the wall. Every click of the clock hands sent an acute jolt of apprehension through me. I imagined Mette waking up and looking around the hotel room, extending her hand to pick up my note, reading it sitting up in bed, standing naked and uncertain at the center of the room, in the bathroom, peering out the window. I imagined her thoughts and her mood: waiting turning into impatience, turning into perplexity, turning into worry that finally turns into fear. I wondered at what point worry or fear would drive her to go down into the lobby, out into the street, to the marina, to do who-knows-what risky or mistaken act. I looked at the doors and windows with a recurrent urge to jump up, knock over furniture and people and dash down the stairs. Every time I did, it took all my self-control to keep from acting on the urge.

I explained to the police that they could verify the boat's ownership with a couple of phone calls to Italy, but it was clear they weren't interested in such a direct route. They preferred to keep circling the issue, artificially extending the gray areas so that they could feel like they were grappling with an important case. On the other hand, I had no idea what my case really was. For example, I didn't know whether or not my name had been included on a wanted list after the explosion in Rome, as Nicoletta led me to believe, or whether such a list was solely for Italian police or had been sent all over Europe. I didn't know whether or not the police officers' fumbling questions would take a much more direct and dangerous tack once they associated my name with Mette's, or if I should try to clarify my position as soon as possible; whether I should hope Mette stayed in the hotel room, or that she should run off anywhere else as long as there was still time. I debated opposing positions, my nerves frayed and my heart racing and slowing down again, my lungs unable to take in enough oxygen.

At this point it was a little after one in the afternoon, and the police officers went out to eat. They left me alone in the room without even locking the door. I continued to imagine Mette, completely in the dark, time stretching out, wondering how I might get in touch with her. I thought of her cell phone, but it was turned off. My cell phone had fallen into the sea during our voyage. I looked at the gray telephone on the table, entertaining the absurd idea of lifting up the receiver and asking information for the phone number of the La Petite Ourse hotel.

At a certain point I got up and opened the door. I went out into the hallway, a desire to make a break for it coursing through my body. A uniformed gendarme came over immediately, saying "What are you doing?"

"Everybody left," I said. "I can't wait around here all day. I have urgent things to do."

"They'll be back soon," he said. "You wait right here."

"I have to go to the bathroom."

Unwillingly, he escorted me to a bathroom at the end of the hallway, waiting outside while I peed. I looked at the little window above the toilet, but it was too narrow to slip through, and in any case I didn't have the faintest idea what I would find once I was outside, whether I would be able to climb down into the street or end up in a courtyard.

The uniformed gendarme brought me back to the room I was in before, leaving the door open. I walked back and forth in the room until a quarter after two, glancing at the clock on the wall each time I walked one way, and at my wristwatch on each return trip as if there was some advantage to be gained from the three-minute discrepancy between the two. I looked at the gray telephone, considering its dormant ability to establish contact, the calendar hanging on the wall with its ordered rows of numbers indicating days that were anything but. I tried not to think about Mette and failed. I was increasingly overcome by a growing sense of separation. It now seemed incredibly stupid to have gone back to the boat, even more so to have forgotten my backpack there, and even more so to have failed to think things through more calmly and lucidly. I kept going back to seven in the morning, when I was still in bed next to Mette and she was sleeping tranquilly, but doing so only made things worse.

At a quarter after two the two policemen returned from their lunch break, but they gave me no more than a passing glance as they continued down the hallway. I stuck my head out the door and said, "What's going on?"

One of the two turned around and said, "Stay calm and take it easy."

"The hell with staying calm!" I said. "I've been here since this morning!"

He went into another room without answering. The uniformed gendarme waved energetically at me to tell me I couldn't stay there in the hallway.

Then it was thirteen minutes after three on the clock and ten minutes after three on my wristwatch when one of the two policemen came back into the room with my passport and some paperwork. In a tone of deep disappointment he said, "The boat has been seized. You have to pay an administrative fine due to its lack of documentation and your failure to contact the port authorities."

"Of course," I said, experiencing a sense of surprise that turned into relief and then a crazy sense of urgency to run out and leave.

The policeman put a piece of paper and a pen in front of me, saying, "Sign here. Pay the fine and bring a copy of the receipts and documents back to us. Until then, neither you nor your brother can use the vessel."

"Okay, okay." I signed the document and stood up, my hand held out for my passport.

The policeman said, "Wait," and turned toward the door. His colleague stood there, an equally disappointed look on his face. He motioned for me to follow him.

I wondered if by chance they were trying to lure me into a trap, and tried to figure out what kind of trap it might be. I followed the second officer into a room further down the hall and to a table where a superior officer (or perhaps just an older policeman) was talking on the phone. The older officer looked at me and said, "Here he is now." He passed me the phone.

On the other end of the line I heard the voice of a woman I didn't recognize. "*Allo? Allo?*" she repeated in a quiet, annoyed voice.

"Yes? Who's this?" I said, looking at the officers, who were looking at me.

"Ah, hello. Giulia Cerlato," said the woman's voice. "Hold on, I'll pass you your brother."

There was some interference, then I heard Fabio's extremely irritated voice say, "I'm absolutely dumbfounded by the unbeliev-able irresponsibility of your actions."

"Listen to me," I said.

"No, *you* listen to me," said Fabio. "You've exercised the most complete and total lack of common sense concerning an affair that we obviously can't talk about right now, you've thrown in with a person who doesn't deserve a red cent of credit, you've risked seriously damaging a direct relative, and now you've stolen my boat without saying a word and gone and gotten it impounded in Corsica!"

"I would have explained."

"There's nothing to explain, Lorenzo! But there's plenty of reason to be very seriously worried about your mental health!"

"Okay," I said. I had neither the time nor the desire to stand around and listen to his recriminations. I just wanted to leave.

"Fuck okay!" he replied. "Don't try to avoid your responsibility!"

"I'm not trying to avoid anything. But we'll talk about it some other time, okay? And it seems to me that there are some other, more serious responsibilities in this affair!"

"I said this isn't the right time to talk about it! But in any case, you've managed to create a completely groundless opinion of your own!"

"What's that supposed to mean?"

"Porziani and Ticonetti are not on our side!" he said, in what I believed was a parallel conversation he was holding with his assistant. "They're Oleander from head to toe! At this point, there's no use in them trying to play a shell game with the highways!"

"Are you talking to me or someone else?" I said.

Without skipping a beat Fabio said, "The fact that the explosion was accidental doesn't change the opinion of your Stopwatch buddies one little bit!"

"What do you mean, an accident?" I was looking at the two officers, who were listening to the conversation but pretending they weren't.

"After six in the evening, not at six!" said my brother. "If Manfroto wants to get together, Manfroto can reschedule his own life and wait, is that clear?"

"Hello?"

"The fact that the gas water heater wasn't up to code doesn't change a thing!" said Fabio.

"What heater wasn't up to code?"

"And the autopsy confirmed that poor Dante's cause of death was carbon monoxide poisoning from his own car exhaust, just in case you're wondering! Your absurd conspiracy theories be damned!"

"You weren't like this when you were eight years old," I said.

"I'd advise you to come back to Rome immediately!" said my brother.

"Sometimes you were a bit of a know-it-all and too indirect, but that was just because you were insecure. You didn't have to become what you are now."

"Don't you ever dare tarnish or damage my name in any way with unacceptable associations!" said Fabio. "And keep your hands off my boat! I'll send someone else to get it!"

"Bye, Fabio," I said. I hung up the receiver.

The officers gave me back my passport and the backpack containing my toothbrush and razor and dirty laundry. They slipped the keys to the *Aqualuna* into an envelope together with some paperwork and put it in a drawer, then one of the two accompanied me to the end of the hallway.

I went quickly down the stairs, and as soon as I was out in the street I started running.

Ten minutes later I was at the hotel. I looked up into the windows of the rooms on the second floor, but I couldn't see any signs of Mette. It was five minutes after four in the afternoon. Looking at my wristwatch made me short of breath and increased my heart rate much more than the run had.

I ran up the steps to the entryway in three bounds and was headed straight for the stairs to the second floor when the man at the reception cut me off, saying, "*Oui, monsieur?*"

"I'm going up to my room," I said. "On the second floor." I tried to move around him.

"There's no one there," said the man.

"What do you mean, there's no one there? Where?"

"On the second floor." His expression was hostile, as if he'd never seen me before in his life.

"When did she leave?" I asked, dozens of nerve-wracking thoughts sailing through the greenish lobby in all directions.

"Who?"

"The girl who was here with me!" I said. I felt like I'd fallen straight into a nightmare. "On the second floor!"

The man shrugged and said, "I didn't see any girls."

"What the hell are you talking about? Have you completely lost your mind?" It wasn't until that moment that I realized he wasn't the same bristly-haired man Mette and I had encountered when we'd arrived and when I'd left that morning. This man might have been a relative, or someone who simply looked like him (though not that much, to be honest).

The man went behind the counter to check the register. He shook his head and said, "There's nobody written down here for the second floor."

"That's because we didn't have any I.D.," I said. "We paid your colleague in advance."

"He's the owner."

"Okay, the owner. When did you get here?"

"I've been here since two. I cover the second half of the week."

I leaned over to look behind the counter, asking, "Are there any messages for me?"

The man shook his head.

"How can you be so sure? At least check!"

He made a sweeping gesture that included the counter and the space below. "You're free to look yourself, if you want," he said.

I went around to look, but between the register and the telephone number list and the glass full of Biro pens and cigarettes and snack packs there was no note with my name written in Mette's handwriting, which I had never seen before. I said to the man, "Please let me go up to the room to check. Please give me the key."

He didn't give in at first, but in the end he came upstairs with me, opening the door to the room on the second floor. It had already been made up: the bedcovers were taut and smooth, the bureau and mirror had been dusted off, the towels in the bathroom had been changed. There was no visual or olfactory trace of my or Mette's presence left, nor anything of that which had taken place between us. Our gazes, gestures, movements, words, breath, heat, body fluids, crumbs: everything had dissolved as if it had never existed, substituted by the faint odor of detergent and starch and smoke and synthetic wax and soap, the smell of a vacuum cleaner engine.

"We were right here," I said, more to myself than to him. I couldn't bring myself to believe that a room that could host such intense and prolonged sensations could return to its status as a perfectly neutral container in the space of just a couple of hours, one that could be occupied by any other traveler who happened to stop at this hotel. I walked around from one point to the next, searching for some small sign, but there was nothing there. I tried to imagine the reasons why Mette would have left without leaving any messages: prudence or lack of time or mistrust of the bristly-haired guy, or lack of faith in me. This last hypothesis was the one that turned my blood particularly cold; I wondered if she could have really believed I'd disappeared because I didn't care about her, or for who-knows-what other stupid, insignificant reason.

I looked in the drawers of the nightstand and underneath the bed, in the room's wastebasket and in the one in the bathroom, behind the curtains, on the windowsill, underneath the rug: nothing. The hotel manager watched me, displaying a sort of reserved perplexity. He walked toward the door once I'd finished searching all the same places a second time.

"Who cleans the rooms?" I asked.

"The cleaning lady," he said. By now he was probably convinced I had serious mental problems.

"I have to talk to her. Right away." I was imagining notes found and wadded up in one hand and tossed aside with the most complete insouciance. I couldn't bring myself to stand still.

"She's at home. She only comes when she's needed during the winter season."

"Then let's call her. Please. It's a question of life or death."

Together, we went down into the lobby, where he very reluctantly called the cleaning lady. He asked her if she'd found anything in the room, but his tone of voice foretold the disappointment I'd receive from her answers. "Uh-huh, uh-huh," he said, looking at me and shaking his head.

I grabbed the receiver out of his hand, interrogating the lady in a more demanding manner. The results were the same: she swore she hadn't found anything or thrown anything away that looked even vaguely like a written message. I thanked her and hung up, an unfathomably empty feeling in my heart.

The hotel manager looked at me through half-closed lids, his patience probably a result of the fact that we really were in full off-season.

"I'll stay in the room tonight," I said. "The one on the second floor."

He seemed about to object to something, but I pulled cash out of my pocket and put it in his hand.

I took a sheaf of hotel letterhead and wrote *This morning I couldn't come back to the hotel because they stopped me at the marina, but everything's okay now. I heard that in Rome they're talking about accidental causes for what happened. Go up to our room and wait for me, I'll be back after I finish going around looking for you.* I got an envelope from the manager and put the note in it, writing *For M* on the front. I underlined the initial as if this might reinforce the possibility that she would come into the lobby, go up to the counter, and ask if by any chance there was a message for her.

I gave the envelope to the manager and gave him a brief, I believe accurate description of Mette, going on to emphasize three times in a row that he should take the initiative and give her the message if she didn't ask anything but simply looked around uncertainly. I took the envelope back and reread what I'd written to make sure it was clear enough. Then I gave it back to him, running off outside before I could start trying to calculate the chances that Mette would really go back there looking for me.

I walked along the street all the way to the marina, staring at the *Aqualuna* through the fence. There was white and red tape in front of the boat, and an officer with the port authority talking to a dockworker some twenty yards off. I walked quickly to the commercial port further north, looking at the people waiting on the dock and inside the shipping company offices: nothing. I walked along the boardwalk and through the city streets, speeding up and slowing down along sidewalks and squares. When there was no one, I ran quickly, burning through empty sections. Where there were people, I stopped and looked around with a superselective eye that registered and discarded faces in a fraction of a second. I stuck my head in bars and bakeries and bookshops, I gazed through the windows of stores selling food or clothing or art supplies. I went into two or three travel agencies, asking if a girl with honey-red hair had come in to buy a ship or plane ticket, but apparently no one had seen her. I kept running and walking and turning around until it got dark and my legs started to hurt, in continuous alternation between burning hope and disillusionment that froze my heart and thoughts.

I went back to the hotel, asking the man behind the counter if anyone had come, but even from a distance his expression was a perfect prediction of the shaking head I'd receive up close. In the room I walked back and forth, barefooted. I looked outside the window every few minutes, trying to imagine Mette's possible movements. I still couldn't think about her. Once again I grew terribly hungry; despite all the bars and food shops I'd passed it had never occurred to me to eat or buy something to eat. There was just a small packet of salted nuts in the tiny hotel room refrigerator; I devoured them in three minutes, but still felt as ravenous as before.

Little by little the loss of my cell phone in the sea took on its most terribly definitive aspect: I couldn't believe I'd blindly put my faith in an electronic chip's memory rather than my own; that I hadn't even thought to write down Mette's number on a piece of paper or cardboard or piece of cloth or any other tangible surface. I thought back on all my reflections on the invasiveness of cell phones into people's daily lives, at the irritation I'd felt at Fabio and Nicoletta's obsessive use of them, at the stupid sense of liberation I'd felt as mine sank down beneath the waves, convinced I would never again need its system of invisible threads strung out through space. Now that I no longer had it, I realized I no longer possessed any one of the instruments with which human beings had maintained contact for millennia before the advent of the portable telephone. We had exchanged no street names or house numbers or geographical coordinates or calendar dates so that we could find one another again in an emergency. We had no routes to backtrack, no meeting points or shared places.

I kept mentally reviewing every minute of the days she and I had spent together; all I could think of was the brief mention of a Stopwatch headquarters in Lyon, and a hometown the name of which I'd either forgotten, or had never registered in the first place. That was it. It struck me as a landscape extraordinarily devoid of personality or recognizable points, created specifically to get lost in.

I stayed awake until late that night, tormented by the empty feeling in my heart and stomach. I got up periodically and looked out into the street, calling the hotel manager to see if there were any new developments. There were none. In the end, I fell asleep on the bed that had been ours, and which now belonged to no one at all.

Early in the Morning
I went back to the port

Early in the morning I went back to the port, once again searching through the group of travelers, but Mette wasn't there. I went to check the timetables posted by various companies, unable to decide whether I should leave or stay. My head was full of contradictory intuitions, each with its own set of images: Mette hiding out in some bar or corner of the city, waiting to see me walk by; Mette on a bus headed for the French coast; Mette already in Lyon or some other city somewhere in the world.

In the end, I decided I couldn't keep torturing myself with parallel possibilities forever. I bought a ticket for Marseilles, checking the departure hall and the entrances to the dock until the ship arrived. Once I was on board I went up and down the stairs inside and out and along the corridors and through the rooms and along the bridge with the meticulousness of a ship inspector: nothing, nothing, nothing.

I stayed outside in the cold wind on the stern deck for the first part of the trip, watching the foam trails between the waves and asking myself over and over again whether Mette was behind me or somewhere ahead; if there was any possible way for me to reestablish contact with her.

I thought of the photograph of my father that we'd studied together for such a long time. I looked for it in my jacket pockets, but it wasn't there. Then I remembered I'd put it in the backpack when the policemen had given it back to me. After all the shuttling about it had endured it was even more tattered, and yet it still struck me as conserving some magical powers thanks to the fact that Mette had held it for so long in her hands. I was just sorry the police had touched it after her. I held it up in the wind for a few minutes to blow away the patina of fingers put there after hers.

I went back inside for fear the photo would wind up in the water. I sat down on a fake leather couch in a lounge bar that was almost completely empty. A few television screens were broadcasting a scene set in Saint-Tropez starring protagonists as inexpressive as robots. A fat woman sat with her thin husband and two toy poodles, eating brioches at one table. I went to get one too, along with a cappuccino. I devoured the pastry on the trip back to my seat.

I studied the front and back of the photograph just as intently as Mette had. I realized just how distracted I'd been by her gestures and looks and simple vicinity while she was trying to decipher my father's handwriting. By contrast, my perceptive capabilities now seemed heightened by her absence. I could focus on every square inch of the glossy paper with all the mental energy I had available. The photo now seemed like the only connection we had left, and I had nothing else to concentrate on.

I reread my father's painful verse, which led to the keyword "bass," and the address in Rua do Sol. I read left to right, feeling like I could hear Mette read and interpret the same words, her voice vibrating in my internal ear. I tried to keep my thoughts out of rational channels, leaving them free to react to the associations that the written words and images might suggest.

I reread the sign behind my father that displayed the words *Cão que ladra não morde*, and suddenly I realized it was a perfectly clear reference to Oraf, the dog we'd had when I was a child. Contrary to that proverb, he had been a dog that never barked, but bit for any reason and every chance he got. In addition to the three lambs he'd torn apart in Tuscany, he had also managed to bite my parents' cleaning lady, the doorman, at least two of my father's colleagues, the woman who'd been his assistant before Nadine, even my brother Fabio one time when he was trying to take a ball away. Suddenly it was clear that if our dog was the opposite of the proverbial dog, the name of the city where the third copy of the memorial was located had to be the opposite of the dog's name.

I went to the onboard shop, where in addition to soft drinks and booze and candies and chocolates and toy mules and crude cloth dolls and all the other fake locally handmade products there was a rotating stand containing maps of Mediterranean countries. I took out a map of Portugal and opened it. I ran my eyes along the southern coast, and found Faro.

I bought the map and went back to the lounge bar. Now I had the name of the street, the name of the city, and the keyword I needed: the riddle didn't seem complex, now that it was resolved. I found its familial simplicity sweet. It reflected our father's spirit. I had a flash of regret for the things that I'd never known about him, for the way our shared communication had never evolved beyond the roles of a stylized game.

I wished I could share this regret and the euphoria I felt at having solved the mystery of the photograph, but the only person in the world I could have done this with was Mette, and this made me miss her all the more.

I kept making mental modifications of the past two days. I was struck by how it would have been enough to have moved just one of the infinite ifs and whens and hows that crowded every single minute of each day in order to make a decisive difference in the course of events. For example, if I had guessed the name of the city while I was sitting in the bar with Mette, or if I hadn't forgotten my backpack on the boat, or if I had gone back to get Mette after having checked the marina when I went back to get the backpack. It struck me as absurd that two people could find themselves irremediably separated because of a stupid distraction, a missed connection. I was overwhelmed by the disproportion between the two things, by the unacceptable implacableness of the facts at hand. I thought about all the accelerations and slowdowns Mette and I had been through together since that morning we'd met in the cemetery, all the sensations that had been transformed into feelings that had in turn been transformed into tangible data, only to get lost in the emptiness rippling around me now along with the ship's movements.

I went back out on the stern bridge to breathe in the cold, salty air, watching the trails of white foam run between gray waves.

IN MARSEILLES I TOOK A
TRAIN HEADED FOR LYON

In Marseilles I took a train headed for Lyon. I arrived late, and found a room in a small, sad hotel near the station. There was nothing but a narrow, desolate single bed. Before falling asleep I watched a television program about fake couples who pretended to get jealous or break up in the most traumatic and definitive ways possible, only to get back together before the fake benevolent gaze of a pretend participatory television host.

In the morning I went to an Internet spot and connected to the Stopwatch website. I vaguely hoped I'd find a coded message for me, but there hadn't been any changes since I'd looked at the website while in Rome. I wrote down the address of the group's headquarters in Lyon, then got a taxi and headed straight there.

The offices were as run-down as the ones in Rome had been, located in the courtyard of an equally dilapidated building. There was a girl and two young men inside. All three proved relatively diffident when they saw me at the door. I told them that I was a friend of Mette and Jorge's, not mentioning anything about the memorial. All three knew what had happened to Jorge, but only one of them—his name was Raimond—had met him personally, and knew Mette. This bit of information made him instantly interesting to me. I asked him when he'd seen her last. He said a year and a half ago, at a meeting with other environmentalist groups in Brighton, England. I asked him if they had written each other or spoken on the phone recently. He said they'd exchanged emails three, maybe four months ago. Discovering the rarity of his interactions with Mette dissolved my interest in him the same way exposure to the air takes the color out of a fish. But he still represented one of the extremely few possibilities I had for connecting with her, so I wrote *The place is in Europe, its name that of our dog spelled backward* on a piece of paper, as well as my name and address and the phone number of my house in the hills, and told him at least ten different times to make sure she got the note if he saw or heard from her again.

Then I took a taxi to the airport, where I bought a ticket on the first flight to Lisbon.

FROM LISBON, I TOOK A FLIGHT TO FARO

From Lisbon, I took a flight to Faro, arriving that evening.
A Christmas tree created by the local tourist bureau had been
installed in the arrivals hall. Its branches were decorated with
colored glass balls and fake snow, creating a strange contrast to
the pleasant weather in the little square outside. I took a bus into
the city and went to look for a hotel where I could spend the
night. I left my backpack in my room and went out to eat fish stew
with coconut milk and shrimp and dry bread in a half-deserted
restaurant. I did all of these things effortlessly, based on the logic
of images passing through my mind. The emotional void created
by Mette's absence made each step almost automatic. My intentions
were translated into decisions, and decisions into movement
without the least bit of resistance. I passed from one gesture
to the next and one place to the next without stopping to consider

or enjoy any of them. I was aware that I didn't have an unlimited amount of time available, and yet I didn't feel rushed. I lived both inside and outside the moment: above and beyond moving around and eating and sleeping; above and beyond the reasons for doing so.

The next morning I went down and had breakfast in a little room with only one other guest, a corpulent Englishman who worked in real estate investment. I went back up to my room and washed my teeth, and as sometimes happens I found myself enchanted by the toothbrush's tiny rhythm. It occurred to me that almost everything of significance that had happened to me up until that point in my life wasn't really the result of actual choices, but rather the consequence of a concatenation of events and circumstances dictated in part by chance and in part by my character and personal instinct, by the opportunities that the places in which I found myself had presented. None of my movements had been linear. On the contrary, I had followed a series of curves that formed waves and semicircles and sometimes turned right back on themselves. I didn't know if this meant that I was a fatalist, but I didn't feel like I'd ever desired or looked hard enough for that which I'd sometimes ended up finding. I had passed through moments and periods and entire phases experiencing a sort of fundamental reserve or distraction, never investing all the energy I had available in who I was or what I was doing. I realized I'd never felt like the undeniable boss of my own life, a hunter-gatherer chasing his prey with perfect determination through the jungle of life. I felt I had mostly gone with the flow, and little by little had learned to swim and row and sail a sailboat, while at the same time never really following the route I'd had in mind in the beginning.

I thought all of this from the point of view of a person who has reached a place without having chosen to go there, his brain and blood full of unfulfilled need for another person who is absent. I kept brushing my teeth for a good ten minutes, experiencing a strange blend of mental clarity, perplexity, and detachment. Then I dried off the toothbrush with the hotel's wall-mounted hairdryer, put it back in my backpack, and went down to ask the man at the reception desk to call me a taxi.

Rua do Sol is a short street just south of a square. Number 53/b corresponds to a building with a mustard-colored façade. I studied the names and numbers on the intercom for a long time, but none of them suggested any possible connection. In the end I pressed all the buttons together: a couple of residents protested, one opened the main door for me.

I walked up the stairs, reading the signs on people's doors and above people's bells, once again without the faintest idea which one was the right door, assuming that there was one. I decided that the most rational approach would be to start from the top, so I went up to the third floor and pressed the ringer at the last door down the hallway. After a long pause the door opened just a crack. I glimpsed the eye and nose and a portion of the mouth of an elderly woman.

"*Peço-lhe desculpa, senhora. Não sabe onde posso encontrar um documento que estou procurando?*"

The eye and nose and portion of mouth drew back and the door closed with a dry thud.

I went on to the next door, ringing several times, but nobody answered. At the third door a scene very similar to the first took place. A man who must have been a tailor answered the fourth door. He had a measuring tape hanging around his neck. I reformulated my question, even though I realized it sounded both absurdly generic and specific at the same time. He thought about it for a second, then pointed to the stairs and said, *"O advogado, rés-do-chão."*

I thanked him and went back down to the ground floor, locating the brass plaque that read *Sérgio Gomes, Avogado*. I rang the bell. A few seconds later the door buzzed open.

Inside there was a fat woman seated at a computer. She said, *"Faça favor"* without looking up or interrupting the clatter of her fingers on the keyboard.

I went over to her desk and said, *"Bom dia, chamo-me* Lorenzo Telmari." All of a sudden the odds of finding myself in the wrong office in the wrong city on the wrong continent seemed infinitely higher than the contrary. I glanced at the door with the intent of making a rapid exit.

The fat woman at the computer lifted her head, looking at me over the half-lenses of her glasses. She said, *"O senhor é de onde?"*

"De Italy," I said. "Rome."

She turned toward the hallway on her right and called in a penetrating voice, *"Avogado?"*

A door opened and an extremely short and solidly built man with a tuft of grayish-silver hair on his forehead came out. He walked toward me with his head slightly tilted to one side and his eyes half-squinting as if he had to make me out against a bright light, even though the lights in the office were relatively dim.

The woman at the computer pointed to me with a wave of one open hand and said, *"O senhor* Telmari."

The short man with the silvery tuft changed expressions instantly, taking my hand into both of his and shaking it energetically. "Sérgio Gomes," he said. "I heard about your father. I'm terribly sorry."

"Thank you," I said, struck as much by his transformation as by mine in his eyes: the total stranger miraculously recognized.

Senhor Gomes exchanged glances with the lady behind the computer and then took me by the arm, saying, "Let's go in here."

I followed him into a room as dimly lit as the rest of the office. I sat down on the armchair he pointed out to me. I wondered if he suffered from a form of photophobia, because the roll-down shutters outside the windows were down, and the light from the lamp on the desk was even weaker than that in the entryway. The room smelled of dust and paper, old wood and coffee.

Senhor Gomes sat down behind the desk in an armchair that had probably been artificially raised up, his gaze at the same level as my own. "Can I offer you some coffee?" he asked.

I said, "Thank you very much, but I already drank too much at the hotel."

He squinted a little again as if he were trying to figure out whether my words carried hidden implications. He emptied the little cup of coffee sitting on a small tray to his left in a single gulp.

I took the photograph of my father out of my backpack and laid it on the table. "It took me a little while to decipher the message," I said. I would have liked to add that without Mette I would probably never even have realized that there was a message to decipher, but I knew that thinking about her for more than an instant, or even pronouncing her name, would leave me entirely useless for conversation.

Senhor Gomes picked up the photo, turning it over in his hands. With breezy naturalness he said, "And do you know the password?" He had small, quick blue eyes and a short nose that continued an uninterrupted line from his forehead.

"*Spigola*," I said. "The password is *spigola*."

He nodded his head without changing expression, as if the word didn't mean much to him. He reached out to an index file on his right, rifling through the cards. He took one out, running his finger over it with meticulous slowness. He took a key out of a drawer and went to open a compartment in a dark wooden bureau, taking out a light leather pouch with a thin shoulder strap. He brought it to me and said, "Please check it carefully."

I unzipped the leather pouch, my heart racing because suddenly it seemed as if my father himself had handed it to me, and we hadn't shared many gestures like this while he was still alive. Inside there was a document roughly ninety pages long. The pages were thick with blue typewritten words, marked with black ink on each page. The name Évêque Jean-Léon Ndionge was written on the first page, and *La mer de la vérité* written immediately below it. I ran my finger extremely delicately over the faint carbon copy powder of this third copy. I read the first lines of the first page: "*Ce berger d'âmes ravagé par le monde, au monde ravagé s'adresse.*" I put the document back in its leather pouch and zipped the pouch back up. "This is it," I said.

Senhor Gomes said, "Good. Your father was a very courteous person."

"Really?" I said, because it certainly wasn't the first adjective that came to mind.

He smiled at me. "Is there anything else I can do for you?"

"No, thank you. I have to go now." I got up, following him as he led me back down the hallway.

We shook hands at the door. I nodded to the woman behind the computer. "*Até a próxima*," she said, and immediately went back to typing.

I went down the stairs with my backpack over my left shoulder and the leather pouch with the memorial over my right. It seemed much heavier than what it could realistically weigh.

I WALKED ALONG THE STREETS
OF THE LITTLE VACATION TOWN

I walked along the streets of the little vacation town. There were no tourists save a few old English couples who might have been fulltime residents. The sun was behind the clouds and there was a gusty wind from the southeast. I kept one hand on the leather pouch with the memorial, looking around very carefully. But I didn't see anyone following me or any suspicious faces. I walked along Rua Comandante F. Manuel, hugging the old bishop's palazzo until I got to the sea, where the wind became much stronger. I tried to think of what I would do, but I couldn't work out the practical details. After all the convulsed movements of the preceding days it seemed like I'd reached a strange point in which the reasons for action blended in with a sense of loss, universal stupor, questions without answers, and formless waiting.

I was neither tired nor uncertain; I was suspended between infinite simultaneous possibilities that had been reduced to just a few, well aware of their unpredictable nature.

I opened the zipper on the leather bag halfway, thinking I'd read the memorial immediately, but then I stopped. It felt like there was no room for the immediate in the almost motionless time I was currently experiencing.

I got up and walked very slowly along the ocean boardwalk. There were low-flying seagulls and a fishing boat bobbing up and down on the medium-sized waves. I walked past a maritime museum, watched a man pedal past on his bicycle. I thought about how I could follow the coast on foot indefinitely, working my way all the way up the Spanish peninsula without ever risking losing my way.

I reached the train station without having thought in the least that it would be there. I went inside to take a look at the train schedule. There was a boy scout group with hats and backpacks and shorts, a few travelers leaving or arriving, their suitcases in hand, a couple of American tourists. I gazed at the train timetables for a long time, but I tended to be enchanted by the names of the station stops along the way, and couldn't manage to decide on a departure time or destination. I was hungry again, too. With all that I'd eaten, it seemed incredible that I could still be hungry.

I left the station and went back out onto the boardwalk. I thought I might look for a little restaurant in one of the city streets, maybe even a hotel where I could spend the night. Some twenty paces ahead of me there was a couple walking arm in arm. He was carrying a suitcase in his left hand. They constantly turned toward each other, looking into each other's eyes, laughing. At a certain point he set down his suitcase and they kissed. I walked past them, experiencing a heartrending feeling that was a blend of participation and alienation.

I tried to concentrate on the sparkling sea on my right, breathing in its smells. Then I looked away, and perhaps one hundred yards ahead I saw a girl dressed in black, walking quickly and carrying a backpack over one shoulder. I thought that one part of my brain was arbitrarily elaborating the information my eyes were registering with the pathetic and dangerous intent of bringing them in line with my desires. I turned back to look at the sea, but a few seconds later I turned back to look at the girl again, walking more quickly without realizing it.

When I was roughly fifty yards off the girl stopped, taking a piece of paper out of one pocket and removing her black wool beret. She shook out a crest of honey-red curls, a flash of color in the gray light.

I froze, my feet glued to the pavement and my breathing suspended. My heart had practically stopped. Then it started beating again and I started running toward her, faster than I could ever remember having run before.

On September 6, 2006, when the first edition of this book was printed in Italy, the world population stood at 6,648,386,537 people.

On September 6, 2011, just five years later, it will reach 7,143,813,888 people.

On September 6, 2016, it will reach 7,679,196,663 people. In other words, one billion more people on our planet in just ten years.